Joanne Fedler
UNBECOMING

Lusaris

A Serenity Press Literary Imprint

Joanne Fedler/Lusaris
A Serenity Press Division in partnership with Joanne Fedler Media

Perth/Western Australia
www.serenitypress.org

Publisher's Note: This is a work of fiction. Names, characters, places, and incidents are a product of the author's imagination. Locales and public names are sometimes used for atmospheric purposes. Any resemblance to actual people, living or dead, or to businesses, companies, events, institutions, or locales are completely coincidental.

C.I.P data: National Library of Australia
Unbecoming/Joanne Fedler
Fiction/Literary
ISBN 978-0-6489376-5-4 (sc)

WHAT WOMEN ARE SAYING
ABOUT UNBECOMING

'Joanne Fedler's wild words always make me see the ordinary with fresh eyes. *Unbecoming* is no different. If I didn't already realise that time is running out, then this book has made it achingly clear. Yet Joanne's supreme gift is to reveal this with humour and compassion, fury and grace. Her characters are so real they have become part of me. Her insightful prose burrows deep into the heart of issues we all grapple with. *Unbecoming* is the book about women, men, friendship, love, lust, death and menopause — and so much else — that you have been waiting for.'

Katerina Cosgrove, author of *Bone Ash Sky* **and** *Zorba the Buddha*

'Fedler has that quality that is required to write with bracing authenticity: fearlessness. A refusal to look away, to make nice, to talk nice. The world needs these writers, the one who will look into the shadows for us. *Unbecoming* gives all the women who were teenagers in the '80's pause to consider our contributions, value our achievements, face what we've failed to do, and draw the breath we need to breathe into our children, who will carry the tools for making the world better, into the future for us. She does this lightly and with lyricism. *Unbecoming* is an intimate conversation on the edge of the burning world.'

Karin Schimke, award-winning poet and translator, essayist and editor.

'Breathtaking, magical and raw in its honesty, *Unbecoming* exposes the extent of women's sacrifices as wives and mothers, and questions whether a woman's body or heart is ever truly her own. This book is a celebration of the natural world, the magic of storytelling and the healing power of mutual witnessing. It is an important rite of passage for women in midlife, and a torchlight for younger women to follow.'

Faith Agugu, psychotherapist, visionary founder of Silver Sirens and sister mermaid

'Joanne Fedler is a perceptive and provocative writer who, with kindness, tenderness and generosity, explores the pain and liberation of leaving youth behind, the confusion and exhilaration of mothering adult children and the yearning for self after a lifetime of nurturing others. Passionate, moving and breathtakingly honest.'

Suzanne Leal, bestselling author of *The Teacher's Secret* and *The Deceptions*

'Insightful, tender, warm, and fierce, *Unbecoming* captures the fire and the pain of women in a time of transition. Wisdom and sisterhood and gratitude to the great Earth Mother mark every page of this delicious book.'

Lavanya Sankaran, author of *The Red Carpet* and *The Hope Factory*, winner of Barnes and Noble's Discover New Writers and Poets and Writers' Best First Fiction Award

'*Unbecoming* delves into one woman's psyche as she questions her marriage, changing body, friendships and what it means to live a full, rich life. Joanne Fedler plunges the reader deeply into characters who are wonderfully flawed, deeply emotional and entirely relatable.'

Abigail Carter, author of *The Alchemy of Loss: A Young Widow's Transformation*

'Watch out, I laughed so loudly I loosened up something I didn't know was buried there. *Unbecoming* is a book of comic, startling wisdom that raises up a mixture of mirth and melancholy from neglected places in your belly. I found myself deliberately stalling to catch every inward giggle and every bare truth for the sake of my own healing. While the character, Jo is throwing up her hands in the middle of her life, we feel the beautiful agony of her rebirth, not only for Jo, but for our earth. In its thoughtful, hilarious way, *Unbecoming* gives certainty and shape to a tide that has the power to save the planet in its very last minute - the rise of the feminine.'

Tracey Farren, author of novels and screenplays about people with their backs against the wall including *Whiplash*, shortlisted for the Sunday Times Fiction Award and the multiple award winning movie, *Tess*.

'*Unbecoming* is an absolute triumph of women's truth telling. Fedler has woven a tale of the heart's raw journey as mother, wife, friend. It is so very funny, so very devastating, so poignant, and so real that we never want to leave. In this brave circle of women, living through enough crumbled dreams that the only landing is far from domesticated clichés, the veil is pulled back so we can see ourselves clearly and begin to approach the reality of climate catastrophe. The sensuality of foods, spices, sexuality, sun, sand, water, sea, skin, and light-hearted banter juxtaposes the looming shadows of our apocalyptic times and 'the war' that our children and beloved grandchildren - our innocents - will be forced to fight. In this masterfully written tale, we somehow know it is only in a circle of women like these that we will be able to hold steady through whatever comes next.'

Thanissara, Dharma teacher, poet, co-founder of not-for-profits in South Africa and the US, author of *Time To Stand Up, A Buddhist Manifesto for Earth*

'Fedler writes about relationships between women and the sacred, wild circles we create with each other; places of cardamom and orange blossoms, leeks and paradox, secrets and embarrassments that contain an honest sisterhood that just may save our souls, if not the planet. I savored every word.'

Tanya Taylor Rubinstein, Mother, Founder of Somatic Writing, StoryWorker

Other Titles by Joanne Fedler

Ideological Virgins and Other Myths: six principles for legal revisioning, co-authored with Ilze Olckers (Justice College, 2001)

25 Essential Things You Should Do Before Getting Married (sixtyminutebooks, 2003)

The Dreamcloth (Jacana Media, 2005)

Secret Mothers' Business (Allen & Unwin, 2006)

Things Without A Name (Allen & Unwin, 2008)

When Hungry, Eat (Allen & Unwin, 2010)

The Reunion (Allen & Unwin, 2012)

It Doesn't Have to Be So Hard: the secrets to finding and keeping intimacy, co-authored with Graeme Friedman (Random House, 2012)

Love in the Time of Contempt: consolations for parents of teenagers (Hardie Grant, 2015)

Your Story: how to write it so others will want to read it (Hay House, 2017)

The Turning: poems from my life on my 50th birthday (Joanne Fedler Media, 2017)

Meditations and Visualizations for writers and aspiring authors (Joanne Fedler Media, 2019)

Lusaris acknowledges and honours that this book was written, published and printed on the land of the indigenous people of Australia.

Go to the Limits of Your Longing

Listen
God speaks to each of us as he makes us,
then walks with us silently out of the night.

These are the words we dimly hear:

You, sent out beyond your recall,
go to the limits of your longing.
Embody me.

Flare up like a flame
and make big shadows I can move in.

Let everything happen to you: beauty and terror.
Just keep going. No feeling is final.
Don't let yourself lose me.

Nearby is the country they call life.
You will know it by its seriousness.

Give me your hand.

Book of Hours, I 59

Rainer Maria Rilke

CONTENTS

Author's Warning

We have two lives
and the second one begins when you realise you only have one.
Mario de Andrade

You're about to enter perilous terrain.

Relax, there's nothing you can do to avoid it.

You'll stumble into it no matter which route you choose, the furious, fearsome knowledge: *Shit, I'm running out of time.* Blame it on menopause, but a sudden empty nest, or the slamming shock of losing a parent, spouse, friend, or your health, will deliver you here just the same.

You may wander the paths of anxiety, burn-out, depression, joylessness, infidelity (yours or your spouse's), resentment at events long past, heterosexuality-remorse, irrational rage, disappointment and emptiness (and those are just the over-crowded ones).

You'll have some questions, alright. Like whether your spouse is more of a habit than a soulmate, a barrier to something more, even if you have no idea yet what that is. You'll be itching to peel off the one-size-fits-all life you were certain fit perfectly when you made those in-sickness-and-in-health vows. It's a seismic jolt between 'I do' and 'fuck you'.

You'll be perplexed by the way the young adult kids have turned out, and wonder whether your time might have been better spent on _____ (fill in the passion you never pursued for the sake of the darlings).

You'll declare that what you used to want isn't doing it for you anymore; that you have changed your mind. The urge to empty your pockets of friendships, sexual orientations, expectations and life goals will make you feel like a nutcase. In the tussle, you'll regret the half century you've spent being polite, responsible and dutiful (as a daughter, wife, partner, mother, caretaker) and realise that, frankly, you're fucking over it all.

This is it.

This is where your second life begins and where *Unbecoming* kicks off. It is entirely a work of fiction. But as in *Secret Mothers' Business* and *The Reunion*, the two books that precede it, I've drawn on real encounters, personalities and experiences to populate it. I spent several nights in the wild (including the Australian outback and a cave in the Blue Mountains) and immersed myself in a sacred healing circle, writers' group and a dancing and new moon ritual with different women. We spoke long and deep and generously into the furies, wildness and broken-heartedness of being alive at this age in this era.

It's been impossible to write this book without being affected by the tectonic breakdown of our natural environment. Many of us have long intuited the troubling times that lie ahead, and the hard work of being a wise adult has never been more necessary.

The trek to my fiftieth birthday was shaped by the work of some of the greatest thinkers on ageing, midlife, dying and elderhood including Carl Jung, James Hollis, Joanna Macy, Dawna Markova, James Hillman, Adam Phillips, Leonard Cohen, Mary Oliver, Maya Angelou, John O'Donohue, Ram Dass and Stephen Jenkinson. I hope I've managed to speckle flecks of their wisdom through the characters in this book.

This story takes place in a world just before the devastating Australian bushfires (over the summer of 2019–2020) and the subsequent coronavirus pandemic when our worst fears were nothing but forecasts, a deep-felt dread one might mistake for a symptom of menopausal anxiety.

We know better now.

It is my prayer that we each make our way consciously and courageously into the uncertain tomorrows, wise, fierce protectors of the only mother who has yet to fail us - the earth.

Go, dear ones, claim your second life.

JOANNE FEDLER

'What have you packed? It's so heavy,' Frank grunted as he lifted my white and blue wheeled bag from the boot of the car.

Believe me, I had tried to take an Uber. But he'd insisted on driving me to the airport. We hugged urgently in the drop-off zone.

I pressed the knob on my bag's handle to release it, but the mechanism was jammed.

'Here, let me,' Frank offered.

'I can do it,' I said, frantically pushing the button.

'You'll break it…'

'I've got it.'

The handle suddenly thwoinged up.

'See?' I bent forward to kiss Frank on the cheek, just as he stepped backwards to make space for a woman with a pram.

'Call…text me when you arrive…will you? Or…just… I'll…we'll…'

'I'll let you know when I land.'

'See you on the other side,' he said, hugging me. 'I love you. I hope you find what you need.'

I squeezed his hand and tilted my bag onto its wheels in the direction of the Jetstar self-check-in.

'Jo…'

I turned around. Something in his face read differently, even though I had not been gone more than a few seconds.

'I don't want you to ever not feel…'

I waited.

'...free.'

I couldn't meet his eyes.

'I may not know what fatherhood has taught me, but I know what I've learned from being married.'

I looked down at my unpainted toenails in the only pair of sandals I was taking with me.

'I don't want you to feel like you're in captivity.'

When I looked up, his eyes were brimming. My heart bounced.

How long had he known my secret?

1

Two Reasons I Didn't Say No

I should probably have texted Frank this morning to let him know I'm spending the night out in the wild. And that, despite everything, you know, I love him. You never can tell when the last time will be that you'll get to say the things you need to say to the people you have to say them to.

I know Frank. He would respond immediately, 'R U sure? Remember what happened last time?' I'm not the outdoorsy type – that's the version of me he's familiar with, anyway. But that's so last-century me, because here I am, strapped to a way-heavier-than-it-looked backpack, bringing up the rear of this procession and clueless about what I've signed up for, except there is talk of a 'ritual' when we get there, wherever 'there' is.

Come to think of it, he'd probably have taken my text as a cue and called me. He'd want more details. 'So, who are these women again?'

And what would I say? That I knew two of them when the kids were little, but that the rest are strangers? He'd be silent, analysing whether I've done my due diligence. Was the threat of bushfires real, what with the drought and all? Or had I finally gone full tilt screaming mad and made off into the wilderness to die or something? Which is not a bad way to go, all things considered.

He'd want to know if I've packed cortisone ointment for my itch. What he'd really be asking is, 'Has it gone? Is it worse?'

Three months of country air hasn't been a miracle cure, not for the skin irritation that's likely just another unglamorous and insoluble symptom of menopause. I'd bend the truth and tell him, 'Haven't had to scratch myself til I bleed – not even once,' just to put his mind at ease.

One of the reasons people lie to their loved ones is to spare them anxiety, though that, I have come to learn, is the slipperiest of slopes, and the makings of a hideously unsatisfactory sex life.

Then he'd enquire, 'How's the eye?' and there it would be, in his voice – relief that my visual migraines which shatter vision in my left eye for a few panic-inducing minutes, seem to have stopped (so we know it's not brain cancer). 'See, I make you sick,' he'd joke, and I'd have to laugh, *don't be silly.*

Then he'd slip in the probe, the one he'd been patiently holding back on, like that detective Colombo with his killer question, 'So where exactly are you walking? Is it a recognised trail? Does it have a name?' and have Google-mapped it by the time we said goodbye.

There'd be too many 'I don't know's' for his liking.

And weirdness – like the fact that we're walking in silence. But that's Fiona's call, not mine, and why I agreed to be here in the first place. You can go your whole life trying to be seen by others, *talking the hindlegs off a donkey*, as my mother often says of the needlessly garrulous, but finally, it's just the quiet that lets you be yourself.

I take the silence as a sign that I'm meant to be here, since I cannot siphon another ounce of myself to anyone. I've barely scraped what's left, in the wake of two decades of motherhood, into a neat little pile by the door and I'm shielding it like I've seen mother elephants do with their calves.

Twenty-four hours of no-talking would just freak Frank out.

Yes, it's better that he knows less.

I'm not thinking as much about snakes as I usually would out in the bush. Fact is, I haven't seen one since that weekend with Helen out in the country seven years ago. Maybe I've outgrown pointless and improbable anxieties given all the real ones that have taken their place. This trekking pole leads the way, announcing my arrival before my feet hit the ground. It's the most unconditional support I've had in a while, bras and backrests included; a sincere and sturdy friend. It's lightweight and fits my hand as if it was made for it, the way a stiff cock can fit inside you with homecoming snugness.

Not that you're asking, but I also haven't thought about cocks much in the past months. Fondness isn't invariably tethered to absence, though I'd never verbalise this to Frank. I'm not a complete cow and it would just come out as another Hurtful Thing.

Around us, the wizened trees loom, majestic, mythic titans, Nature's paparazzi- free celebrities. Without any force, they shut you up. They don't pull rank, but it's best that you know your place here, as an underling. As the morning sturdies herself, the trees become entangled with sunlight ribboning through their branches. I keep halting to watch the light shimmy and change. It entwines itself around the trunks like a dirty dancer. You have to stop. Often and completely. It should be a rule in life.

Now that the silent walking has begun, I'm relieved I didn't send that cold-feet text to Fiona that I typed this morning: *Woke with headache.* I had moved the cursor to the front of 'headache' and added 'crippling'. Deleted both words and typed 'migraine'. Deleted everything. Bullshit always has a smell about it and Fiona deserves more on her first birthday all on her own.

I slow my footfall down so that the treading sounds of the others ahead don't intrude on mine.

The distance deepens so I now have perspective on my five companions as they walk ahead of me in single file.

I used to think I could read people. It was my superpower, like a sniffer dog's nose for smuggled contraband, no matter how devious the hiding. I could tell by the way you dished up food on your plate if you were a generous or stingy lover; a rule follower or a renegade; a Tiger or Jewish mother.

I was quick to work you out and extrapolate from how you dressed (with or without earrings – the studded or dangly kind), the silences you guarded, the comments that earned your laughter, whether I wanted you as a confidante, acquaintance, or Facebook friend.

An hour into this hike, I'd have worked everyone out – the state of their marriages, relationships with their mothers and whether they resort to Kentucky Fried Chicken, vodka or prayer in times of trouble. Based on Cate's free pass to carry nothing but a little daypack and a ukulele (how that will aid us in an emergency is still unclear to me), Kiri's bossy rebuke before we took off and Yasmin's brightly coloured lips, I'd have filled in the blanks, labelled and pigeon-holed the lot of them. I'd have an angle on everyone's story.

But I'd be wrong. As I have been so often in my life. I have blundered my way through my fifty-two years, lurching from one certainty to another. And there comes a point – like that seemingly never-ending supply of toilet-paper at the back of the linen closet – when you simply run out. Let me tell you, it's bloody splendid to be so bereft of conclusions. It's almost as liberating as running out of periods.

Not so long ago, I'd have weighed in on the plans and certainly, the food. But today, I'm the straggler. Don't ask me where we're sleeping and what we're going to eat. I couldn't tell you. It's a shuddering relief to be this useless and bereft of authority. You'd think by now the message would have struck home, what with the way things have worked out with the kids.

I play a game now. The silence allows it. How many choices and decisions does it take? A hundred? A thousand? Tens of thousands? How many for each child? First name (shout outs on the primary school playground are life-defining). Surname (Frank and I married post-kids, it had to be nutted out). Breast or bottle? When to immunise. Introduce solids. Circumcise? Grommets? Operate? Antibiotics or flower remedies? Is yoghurt/carob/Nutella/Fruit Loops a 'treat'? Yes or no to fizzy drinks? What time is bedtime? Which school? Tennis or karate? Violin or drums? Sleepovers? Birthday parties? Violent video games? Makeup? How many driving lessons?

Close to a hundred thousand, I conclude.

No wonder I am shredded and shrivelled from decision-fatigue. Seriously, I do not want to be asked my opinion about anything. Ever again.

The backpack will get lighter. It's just heft and gravity. The fire-making will be someone else's problem. I did netball at school, not Girl Scouts. Outdoor Survival Skills is on the list of Things I've Missed Out On, like learning to ride a bike, change a tyre, perform CPR, and the one I regret the most, have multiple orgasms (though the last time I saw her, CJ assured me, 'It *is* teachable').

I should get a tattoo somewhere conspicuous: *Hopeless in the Wild.* We could all very well starve or die of hypothermia if things were left to me.

Fiona's planned the logistics for this overnight ritual under the stars with a few special friends. It was generous of her to give me a free pass into this coven as I sure haven't earned it. The last time we spent time together our kids were in the same playschool. I was still reading bedtime stories. Aaron would cry if I left without him. Jamie would ask when I was coming back, even if I was ducking out for milk and bread.

I used to be the centre of a small universe.

A sun.

But becoming a black hole isn't as ghastly as you might imagine.

I could have made an excuse when Fiona invited me.

There are two reasons I didn't say no.

The first is semantic. The second, because despite everything you might come to think of me after what I've done to Frank, I'm still a half-decent person.

'My goodness, Jo, is that you?'

It had taken a moment to register someone was talking to me. I was shopping for groceries amidst the stands of soy candles and handmade dreamcatchers at the weekly farmer's market. I hadn't heard my name spoken out loud for more than seventy-eight days and nights. That's how long I'd been on my own. Housesitting, a thousand kilometres from home in the Sunshine Coast hinterland.

'It *is* you.'

I didn't have time to hide my disappointment that my anonymity-fast had been broken. It's an assault to be indiscriminately recognised, like a mole in witness protection whose cover has been blown. But it was *Fiona* – and as soon as I turned, warmth flooded me. We did share something of a history, and this was serendipity, no matter which way it headbutted you.

It had been, *What? Fifteen years!*, we both chimed in unison, since we'd last seen each other at the mothers-only-no-spouses-no-kids sleepover our friend Helen had organised. '*What a night, right? All that food. That bucket of strawberry daiquiris.*'

An orgy of feasting and libation we'd all thrown ourselves

into with the impudence of the temporarily reprieved. It had been nothing but a window of time, but enough to crack us open, one by one, as we'd spilled our darkest thoughts and others murmured, '*Yes, yes, same here.*' After that night, I understood motherhood was an ancient #MeToo Movement and each one of us, an undercover agent.

Under the shade of red gum trees, in the heat of the morning rising, surrounded by farmers with broad-brimmed hats, rough hands and earthy smells, I saw something new had dropped into Fiona's face. Age, yes, but more ruinous than years. Her once auburn hair had ceded most of its copper, but it caught the sunlight here and there, like a red-gold disco ball.

The first thing she told me was that eight months ago her husband Ben had died. It had been a long, protracted battle with heart disease. 'We waited for a heart transplant. Never found a donor. He died gasping for breath, slack jawed and terrified.'

She lay each concentric ring of his dying down between us.

'His medical care consumed all our life savings. All it gave him was more time to die.'

'I lost my business, earthtouch. It was impossible to keep it up and be Ben's full-time carer at the same time.'

Jesus. I'm so very sorry.

'After he died, I had to sell our home in Byron Bay and move in with a friend. I'm helping her with her hives. She's an apiarist. You know the Earthwatch Institute has declared bees the most important living creature on the planet?'

I didn't know, but bees would get my vote any day.

I scooped her into a hug. She softened and rested her head on my shoulder. She smelled just as delicious as she had fifteen years ago, of vanilla and ylang-ylang and a hint of dewberry. It was a mysterious commitment, her dedication to those aromatherapy oils, but a favour to those she hugged.

When she pulled away, her eyes were moist.

'I'm…a widow now.'

I'd reached for her hand and squeezed it.

A *widow*. The shadow identity that lurks in every 'I-do' and flower-laden anniversary. When we pair up for life, we know someone will go first. It's implied – our consent to being unpaired. Split. But when does *knowing* ever prepare us for the real thing? Frank and I play the 'who will die first?' game all the time, to inoculate the unthinkable with humour. As if a half-million-dollar life-insurance payout would palliate the grief. Frank assures me it would. If I go first, he'll inherit my Moroccan lantern collection which we both know is destined for landfill. He's not the sentimental type.

'And are you in complete remission?'

'More than ten years now. I'm an official breast cancer survivor.' Fiona made a fist and pumped the air. Now she was Fiona After Cancer. I'd only ever known her Before. A continent of all we'd missed of each other's lives lay uncrossed before us. I didn't offer any excuses for why we'd drifted apart. I had looked for her on Facebook every now and then, with no luck, and that's where my imagination for how to get in touch with someone who wasn't on social media had failed.

The second thing she told me was, 'I'm not much one for celebrations, but it's my birthday next week. I'm going on a silent walk through a rainforest to a little cove. I want to do a sacred ritual under the stars with a handful of special friends. It's called a *yatra*, it's a Hindu word. Any chance you'd want to join us?'

Some people use words as spells, to inflate and overdraw. This is how marketers have wrecked intimacy. But when Fiona said 'sacred,' there it was – a simple line drawing of a word, that meant nothing but itself, not a term in drag to charm your eyes. It landed, soft as a moth on my palm like that one in a rainforest in Tasmania years ago, its wings ahum.

Suddenly I was famished for what was missing in my life.

We'd have to carry all our own water, food, lighting, first aid, ablution-paraphernalia and sleeping bags. It was an anti-advertisement: *comfort and luxury not included.*

My excuses tussled like Powerballs in a lottery barrel: *Lower back isn't great; been a bit anti-social of late; not really in the right headspace for meeting new people; is it safe, you know, to just wander off into the bush?*

Fiona's lovely green eyes stared back at me, without expectation or judgement. It was an invitation. To be discomforted.

I'd inhaled, ready to thank her for including me, but I wasn't up for it, when she said, 'It's my first birthday... without Ben.'

Leaves waft, soothing shrapnel. Something bops me on the head as I pass. I pull my ponytail out and shake my hair loose. I know for a fact that there are jumping spiders. I learned about them on *Planet Earth*. The males get caught up in an elaborate song and dance to attract a mate. The stakes for the talentless are more than merely dashed hopes - if he doesn't turn her on, she might just gobble him up. It's one of Nature's few feminist statements.

Our footfall makes crunching sounds. The land is parched, a woman unloved, her body brittle with longing. An absence of wetness is always a warning of what is about to vanish.

A ladybug lands on the back of my left hand. It crawls from the crease of my wrist up towards my ringless fourth finger. For safekeeping – that's why I left my wedding band in my dresser at home. If Frank has rifled through my drawers and come to any premature conclusions, well, that's on him. I can't monitor his curiosity.

But Fiona had noticed it was missing.

'So tell me, how's Frank?' she'd smiled. 'You are still

married to Frank?'

'Yes, yes, of course. He's…great,' I'd managed.

I couldn't help feeling like a spoilt brat, taking off without my husband by choice, while he was still alive and well. 'And Gabriel? What's he up to?' I asked.

'He's in Alice Springs. With his boyfriend. They're LGBTQ activists there, working in mental health, HIV prevention and safety. You wouldn't believe the number of suicides and self-harm attempts in the gay and transgender community. It's heartbreaking. They're actually saving lives.'

'Wow, he's really adding value to the world.'

'I'm proud of him and Mark,' she smiled. She'd asked after my kids. Had Jamie done anything with her artistic talents? Was Aaron still such a fussy eater?

How she remembered these details only made me feel less of a friend. It had been a long while since I'd spoken about my children as if I had anything to do with them. For years I'd been forbidden from posting anything about them on Facebook. It was a *violation of their privacy* to be photographed, lauded over and, godforbid, tagged. Young adults have a way of using your own language against you in the same way carrying a gun is a serious threat to your own safety in a tussle.

'I've been preparing for the empty nest for two years, waiting for the big departure, the quiet after the noise of family life. So far, none of this has happened,' I told her. 'They both still live with us.'

Our home which was big enough for two adults and two

kids was now occupied by four grownups. You had to wait in line for a shower. Hold in an urgent bowel movement. Make a reservation in the loungeroom to watch your show on TV. Book the dining room to have your friends over.

'Jamie won first prize in an international short story competition last year,' I said. 'She's been awarded a scholarship to do a master's in creative writing at California State. She leaves in a few months.'

'She takes after you, clearly.' Fiona seemed genuinely delighted.

'She's...very much her own person,' I bandaged. 'And Aaron's...going through the rigours of applying for...the military.' I didn't add, 'or the police-force, if he doesn't get in.' I didn't offer further explanation. The truth is, I had none.

It must have showed on my face – that neither of my adult children is comprehensible to me. I would never use the word 'disappointment' because that would shame them, as well as me, and is clearly unfair. Of course, there's no mothering recipe or simple correlative between what you put in and what you get out. This isn't cheesecake we're talking about where you add sugar and you're guaranteed sweetness. But I swear at times it seemed as if we'd raised them entirely in English and one day, they broke into fluent Mandarin.

Fiona had ooh-ed and aah-ed over Jamie, but what choice did she have? I'd set her up, by colluding in the ritual of rolling out the trophies, medals and six-figure salaries of our offspring; tale-telling of how this one was headhunted; that one landed the executive position; the wedding was *gorgeous*; the baby is *perfect* and what more could a parent ask for? I'd done it again, defaulted into the palatable mothering story like a smoker who lights up after weeks of abstinence. The alcoholic who succumbs to 'just one drink,' only to have to start all over. It's all so Sisyphus-ian.

Fiona hadn't flinched at the mention of the army and I'd remembered with a gush, under the lavish shade of those trees, how much I'd liked her. She had always been the least judgemental of mothers, unblemished by bitchiness or the need to compare.

Right there, she'd put a hand on my arm and said, 'My father was in the military. It teaches all kinds of great life skills.'

'I didn't mean to be insulting.'

'Trust me, it wasn't easy for any of us. Besides, I wouldn't want Gabriel going into the army given who he is and what's going on in the world.'

'I've no idea how I raised a son who has chosen that route – of all the ways there are to be a man these days...'

'Natural pushback. He's experimenting with who he wants to become...'

'When did Gabriel find his way into social activism?'

'He went up to Alice Springs for his field placement during his social work degree and fell in love with the place. He met Mark and seems to have found where he belongs in the world. I've never seen him happier.'

'What luck.'

She nodded. 'He did have an emotional breakdown after Ben died. They were …estranged.'

She'd strained for a smile with her sad eyes, and in that failure, it showed – grief's double shift, for both her husband and her son's father. We'd bear our own sorrows a thousand times over rather than see our children suffer. This vicarious business, it belts us.

'And how's…your stepdaughter… I forget her name. Are you still so close?'

Fiona groaned. 'Kirsty. Things have changed since those glory days.' Defeat crawled into her voice.

I waited. The first gush of words is a reflex. If we leave an empty space, sometimes people venture deeper with what they say next.

'She's contesting the will. Ben left everything to me, until I die, and only then to the kids. She's convinced that I've stolen her inheritance. So now, we only communicate through our lawyers.'

'Grief does strange things, especially where money's involved. Maybe she just needs some time.'

'I don't know. She detests me.' She pushed the d-word out, hard against her teeth.

It was a strange telling. I'd never found Fiona remotely dislikeable, never mind detestable.

'You did so well for so long, overturning that stereotype,' I offered.

She gave a weak laugh. 'It finally caught up with me. I am the wicked stepmother after all.'

'Daughters can be…vicious,' I said, though I hoped she wouldn't press me for details. She didn't. See, she was anything but unlikable.

Then the inquiry I had dreaded.

'What are you doing so far from home without Frank?'

2

Bagless

My eyes were bigger than my shoulders.

An hour into the walk, I cannot escape this miscalculation. My backpack should be getting lighter as I sip on my water unless there's some quantum physical explanation that eludes me.

I blow onto my chest to relieve the heat.

The sandstone cliffs vibrate with orange, aglow in the morning's light. Without human jibber jabber, you can hear every waft, rumble, skitter and shriek. The trees are bearded Vikings in need of a haircut. Bark peels off them like massive scabs, leaving white flesh, bright raw and fresh. One tree leans as if on an elbow, eaten out at the base, eroded by ants or wombats. I stop and stare at her hollowed innards. It's ridiculous to take it as metaphor for my own life, but that's how an author's brain is wired. Even in the thick of writer's block.

'Just bring a toothbrush,' Fiona had said.

Only Helen would have known what a useless instruction that was to me.

A backpack was packed and ready and waiting for me when I arrived this morning at her friend Cate's place.

'Everything's in there,' she'd smiled. 'Sleeping bag, sleeping mat, cup, plate, cutlery, windbreaker, beanie, gloves and three litres of water.'

I had to reshuffle a few things to make space for my toiletries, snacks and a large Tupperware. I hadn't forgotten the 'leek' – in response to Fiona's cryptic text request from yesterday, which I hoped wasn't autocorrect for something more survival-oriented. It's wrapped in its own plastic bag, to stop it getting funky or making me smell like I haven't showered in a week.

Today I'm wearing the few items of clothing I removed for the first time from my suitcase this morning. The airline traced my lost bag after three days. But by then, I'd gotten used to less. It's chilling, really how rapidly you stop needing the things you imagined you couldn't do without.

I had been the last schmuck at carousel three when it whined to a halt. My blue and white suitcase on wheels had not nudged its way through the floppy plastic teeth of the baggage aperture.

I had stomped my way to the unstaffed airline counter. 'Hello, anyone here?'

Eventually a man, nametagged Brad, came through the Staff Only door, chewing something.

'Yeah, it happens all the time,' Brad said when I explained my bag was missing. I surveyed him for an apology, but found no evidence of one. 'Just fill in this form and the airline will try to locate it.'

'You have got to be kidding.' I wasn't trying to be princessy. Everyone as far as I know, prefers their bag to be waiting when they arrive at their destination.

Still, I was conscious of the pitch of my voice rising. If only Brad had known my irritation was a veneer for what Frank had come to call my 'murderous rage'.

'Seriously, Mam, I'm going to have to ask you to calm

down,' Frank had taken to tutting whenever I exploded. Even I'd stopped being able to predict what might provoke my own eruptions.

'I'M CALMER THAN YOU ARE!'

'Not going to argue, but I'm removing all the knives and sharp objects from the kitchen.'

Frank always deflected with humour. Until his humour became what enraged me.

Brad, with his Jetstar uniform, had no idea who he was toying with.

But look, I'm not a barbarian. I was mindful that I was in public. And that Brad was just a poorly paid clerk simply doing his job and probably had the shits that he was working Sundays when he'd much rather be at home barbequing.

'What am I supposed to do now?' That may have slipped out as a whine.

Brad might have tried harder not to look bored. He likely had his own issues and was not a life coach. I felt somehow that he ought to know that I was not just visiting Queensland to have a good time while he was working a weekend shift. I was here on deep secret personal business. I was here to… what? Grieve? Reset? Re-align myself? I had made my way here to work out what I wanted to do with the life I had left behind in Sydney, apparently with my luggage. I was a woman at a crossroads in her life; couldn't he see that? I was on my own personal *Eat, Pray, Love* quest.

But one look at Brad and I realised I should not mistake

him for someone who cared. Like Frank, for example.

'I'll enter your details into the system. Read this form, it explains everything,' he finalised in case I got the impression he was up for explaining it himself.

He'd exited through the Staff Only door, leaving me standing alone at the counter, bereft of my bag containing everything I had so tenderly and studiously packed, filled with all my special comforts, the stuff you might take if your house was burning down, or say, you might not return at all.

Whoever had misappropriated it, was welcome to enjoy my brand-new purchase, still in the box. I'd only bought The Womanizer because CJ had said it *takes orgasms to a whole new level.* I mean, who could resist a clitoral stimulator designed by women for women? The bright purple had been a personal preference. I'd figured three months on my own was the perfect opportunity to determine if there was a whole new level for orgasms to get to.

I was also, mind you, following Alyssa's recommendations as she sat opposite me at her desk and drew my internal organs upside down so they were right side up for me. It takes no more than a few lamentable incidents of urinary incontinence to admit you need a pelvic floor physiotherapist. Vaginal atrophy in menopause – it's a thing. Regular orgasms act as pussy push-ups. What I'm getting at is that it had also been a functional purchase.

Frank had seen me packing it. 'What is that?'

'A friendly machine specifically designed to cause suction

on the clitoris in exactly the right spot with eight different strengths.' I was just repeating what was on the box.

'I've been replaced by a robot.'

'No machine can replace you.' I'd reached out to touch his face, to reassure him. 'Are you going to miss me?' I don't know why I'd asked.

'Of course.'

'What are you going to do for sex while I'm away?'

'I'm going to wait til you get back, store up all my horniness. One thing you can count on when you get back is a good fucking. It won't be an ordinary or sub-par fucking. Jeez, I'm getting turned on just thinking about the sex we're going to have when you get back.'

'That sounds nice,' I said, avoiding Frank's gaze. 'But I won't be offended if you masturbate yourself silly while I'm gone.'

Bagless, my instinct was to text Frank. 'They lost my fucking bag. Can you believe it?' Frank would know what to do. He would send a lawyer's letter. He'd take up the cudgels on my behalf as he has done for the past twenty-two years. But as I reached for my phone, I remembered I was Frank-less by choice. I had no right to rope him into my distress. He was, after all, part of the reason I was here.

'Landed safely,' is all I sent.

'Sometimes I don't know what I see in you.' This had streamed from my mouth before I'd stopped to think how unkind these words would sound if Frank had said them to me. More and more, I was becoming capable of saying The Hurtful Thing, the sort of remark that would fail the 'is it true, is it kind and is it necessary?' test I was always going on about to the kids. For someone who claims to be mindful and aspirationally spiritual, it was a terrible new talent I had become unable to control.

It had begun as all calamities do, quite innocently.

We were sitting on the beach under an umbrella, he with his radio, me with a book.

'What has being a father taught you about yourself?'

He'd sighed. 'Jesus Christ. I don't know, I never think about it. Can't we just sit here and enjoy the moment? Does everything always have to be so meaningful?'

My eyes burned under my sunglasses. It had been an invitation, a diving board for a conversation that wasn't about logistics and chores, a place to begin to sift through what we'd just been through with Jamie. Questions had been tumbling through me, the wet laundry of discontent. I wanted to unpack it, lay it out, separate the whites from the colours and hang it all up in the revelations of sunlight. Where had we failed? Had we, in fact, failed? Was this all normal? Why hadn't she just told us?

But it was a Sunday morning. The sea was blinking silver sequins. The cricket was on the radio. Time and place. I could have picked them better. All the self-help books on relationships advise as much. But if sex should be spontaneous, why not a thoughtful discussion? When were we supposed to have our D&Ms in between his work and TV-watching? I couldn't outsource all our intimacy to the conversational equivalent of The Womanizer. Unlike sexual pleasure, which can be delegated to equipment, this was one area of the relationship Frank had to participate in, in person.

Forget infidelities, boredom and incompatibilities. This interaction was where my tolerance for what it meant to be a married couple was running aground. It made me question whether I was being too lenient with our marriage; if I had settled, and in settling, lost a certain personal horizon.

That's when I'd said The Hurtful Thing.

Seeing my crestfallen face, he tried again.

'What you see in me is a mystery,' he said, adjusting the volume on his radio. 'It's probably my undeniable charm and wit. And then of course, my considerable girth in the penile department.'

That day I was immune to his cuteness. I shut my book with a clap. I pinched the bridge of my nose. *Settle, just settle.*

'Do you think we'll ever get beyond the usual banter? Beyond this…' I gestured lamely at the space between us.

Frank had removed one earphone, reluctantly. 'I don't know what's bugging you.'

I'd inhaled. Where would I start? With Frank, there couldn't be too much of a preamble before his attention strayed. 'For starters, you're emotionally dense and repressed.'

'I've always been like that, ever since we met – nothing's changed.'

'Exactly.'

'And even if that's true, I'm happy, so what's the problem?'

I had wanted to strangle that permissive word 'happy'. People bandy it about to describe miniscule contentment.

'It's such a thin happiness. Football. Golf. Beer. Cricket. Sex. Netflix. Don't you want a deeper, richer happiness? Something a bit more…soulful?'

'Don't judge my happiness. I'm a simple guy. You know my shallowness runs deep.'

Frank always goes for the one-liner. The joke. He uses laughter to fix everything. It had worked for twenty-four years. But it had stopped working on me.

'That's laziness talking. You just don't want to do any personal growth.' I became lonely when he spoke like that.

'But that's your thing. I don't force you to do the stuff I

46

like. We've always given each other freedom to be ourselves. It's a strength of our relationship, not a weakness.'

This had been true. But couldn't he see? Our work as a team was done. The kids had sputtered into adulthood. We'd gotten them over the line. After war, battalions disband, soldiers go home to their wives and kids, bonded forever by what they survived, but unlikely to ever see one another again.

'Right now, it's breaking us down the middle.'

'Nah,' he said, plugging his ear with his earphone again. 'We'll be fine, you'll see.'

It had all happened suddenly and was easier than you imagine.

A random Facebook feed. 'Looking for a house-sitter for three months.' Penny was a friend of a Facebook friend. The photos showed wallabies and guinea fowl in her backyard. I sent Penny a private message and within fifteen minutes I'd promised to water the vegetable patch and not wear shoes indoors. By lunchtime I'd booked an airline ticket and a rental car. Frank was surprisingly supportive when I told him I'd be leaving in two days' time. *If nothing else, it'll be good for your writing.*

I sent a family WhatsApp, *Jamie and Aaron, Housesitting in*

Queensland for 3 months. Leaving day after tomorrow. Call dad if you need anything (car, money, advice). See you in a while. Love you, mum.

I took my time with Archie. I scratched his nose and pressed the cool, mossy pockets of his ears between my fingers until he got skinny eyes and the pink slip of his tongue showed. His trunk pulsed like a fuzzy heart. 'You're on a watch list for Native Wildlife Terrorism, buddy. They know all about the rats, lizards and birds that go missing. Lay off Game-of-Throning it in the backyard, will you?'

I farewelled my pot plants, with special affection for the basil I'd grown from seed, because we both knew that Frank's track record with plants was abysmal and that this was goodbye for good.

Penny's cottage was remote enough that I was sure no-one I knew would find or spot me there. I stood at the cherry coloured front door for a full five minutes, catching my breath. Inside, the hallway swallowed me in its buttery yellow embrace, the kitchen sang to me in ocean blues and forest greens, and the pink peony-coloured bathroom hugged me in its bosom. There were seven towels in the linen closet, stacked in their rainbow line-up. It would have all given Frank a blistering headache. Out on the deck, I had a vast outlook into a valley towards a fringe of trees and, beyond that, water twinkled.

That night, I slept like I meant it, far from the clumsy slumber I'd become used to; the partial eye-closed, waiting-to-hear-kids-come-home, teeth-grinding straining for respite from consciousness. The air streamed through the open doors filtered by the screens, and I woke purified, air-ed out, as washing left to be combed by wind all day on washing lines must feel.

For the first fortnight, it took huge willpower to break the tic of calling Frank every afternoon to find out how his day was. It was odd not to hear him natter on about the tram works jamming the traffic all the way back to Alison Road, a co-worker's body odour, and how many questions he'd gotten right on *Who Wants to Be A Millionaire?*

But without these daily touchstones of our enmeshment, the lily pads of our banter, I sank deep down into myself. After weeks without a screen in my face, a fury sprang out of me as clear as an artery erupting – against reality TV which has gnawed away at my life, one elimination and rose ceremony at a time. I was relieved to discover that I did not give even a miniscule fuck whether Airlie, the Bachelorette, ended up with Sam with the cheekbones, or Matt with the personality.

It took two weeks for the confetti of my emotions and the fireworks of my nervous system to settle. I began to remember my dreams on waking. I went bra-less, then panty-less, and pretty soon I was walking around naked. I didn't cross my legs or suck my tummy in, not even when passing a mirror. I ate my dinner bare. I soaked in lavender baths. I cranked up Leonard Cohen and Joni Mitchell. I sang brazenly and danced ugly, as no-one watched.

I owned the wide field of the king-sized bed with my legs spread wide. I hogged the duvet. I wondered whose idea it was – Frida's or Diego's – the separate homes joined by a bridge. Frank and I can barely afford a single joint home, but still, once the kids move out, technically there will be spare bedrooms. It would be a hard sell to Frank. 'What's the point of being married then?' he'd say, as if a shared bed in a room in which two people are compromising, unlike a spontaneous conversation, was the final frontier of togetherness.

I thought of Laura Brown, pregnant with her second child, who leaves her three-year-old with a neighbor and books herself into a hotel room for the day to read Virginia Woolf's *Mrs Dalloway*. She's just a fictional character in *The Hours*, by Michael Cunningham, but every now and then you identify with a protagonist as if she's you and that book tells you exactly where you are in your life.

Every Sunday, I took the longer scenic route to the local organic market to get weekly supplies, fresh vegetables and fruit, cheese and breads harvested by neighbouring farmers and made or baked by the locals. I'd return to my one-bedroomed cottage, queenly with my basket of asparagus stalks, fronds of rosemary and basil, mushrooms moist and fleshy, tomatoes plump and cheerful, and eggplant, in their tight indigo skins. I'd sometimes eat straight from the basket, breaking off the corner of my sourdough wrapped in brown paper, freed of the manners sharing food imposes on us. I was un-protocoled, untied to schedules of breakfast, lunch or dinner. I woke at the first wisp of daybreak and curled into my pillows when the sun went down. I waited for birdsong like army wives wait for news of their spouses. I feted each nightfall and sweet soft dawn. One by one, they threaded me back like a fine filament into the needle eye of myself.

I only used my iPhone for my weekly WhatsApp call, across time zones to find out how my dad's pacemaker was settling and whether my mother had booked her knee replacement. It had and she hadn't. My mother was struggling to stand at the stove while cooking. The stairs were getting harder for both of them. They had doctor's check-ups booked. Of course, they'd let me know as soon as they got the results.

They always asked, 'How are Frank and the kids?'

And I always said, 'They're fine, nothing to report,' which if you think about it, was not technically a lie. Frank knew to call me in the event of an emergency.

My parents never asked where I was, and I didn't tell them. They would only have worried.

Halfway through week four, Jamie sent her first text. 'Where do we keep the cake tins?'

Under the sink.

I received a thank-you emoji.

Aaron made it to week six. Then I got a, 'Sorry, broke a teapot. It fell out of the cupboard while I was getting a glass.'

I didn't know how to respond.

He followed it up with, 'Hope you're having fun.'

I sent back a smiley face.

I started to feel less crazy. The pain over my left eye lifted and I found I had gone weeks without one of those dreaded visual migraines that cracked my vision as if I were looking through broken glass.

As the haze cleared, I thought about my friend Helen and everything that had been lost since she'd moved to the US. I stopped pretending that I didn't miss her. No-one had ever replaced her. I allowed myself to know that perhaps no-one ever would. As that sorrow peeled back, it exposed all the other leavings Helen's departure had overlaid, like a cover-up paint job that time has finally defeated.

I cried and cried and cried.

And in that open rawness, I found myself making notes for what could be a new book.

It was about the end of a happy marriage.

3

Fiona's Friends

Up ahead, Cate is neck and shoulders above everyone else. It's a wonder to behold, really, a woman over six foot. I'm a fan of Nature, almost devotionally, but why human females aren't routinely larger than our male counterparts like the spotted hyenas and blue whales, can only be a design flaw. It's not that men over six foot don't do it for me. Menopause doesn't immunize you against wanton hunkiness or fossilize your vagina. Mothers of teenage daughters would sleep unmedicated is all I'm saying.

This morning, in Cate's kitchen, Fiona introduced me to the others as 'a friend from our early mummy days'.

'These are my soul sisters,' she'd gestured at Kiri, Cate and Yasmin, though this could be how Fiona refers to all womenfolk, her equivalent of 'darling' or 'honey'.

They divided the essentials (kettle, stove, gas canisters, sleeping bags and mats, mosquito repellent) amongst the backpacks that were lined up in Cate's kitchen. I stood lamely to the side and watched the four of them attend to the details of preparation: the sorting, counting, list-ticking, double-checking, mental calculations which became adjustments, little labours of folding and fetching, organising, waterproofing and assembly.

Each object had a purpose; nothing extra. We would take just enough, only what we needed for sustenance and safety (three litres of water per person, a tarp, a gas stove). We would carry items in case things didn't go according to plan (water-purifying tablets, torches, a flare, a snakebite kit).

As a gatecrasher to this sisterhood, I could not rationally be relied on for anything. My ignorance gave me immunity. Like people who find themselves stuck in a lift or on an airplane together, we were coincidental companions for the next twenty-four hours. Cordial strangers. They were Fiona's friends.

I owed these women nothing.

Kiri, a wide, big-bellied mountain of Pacific Islander woman, was clearly the leader, the matriarchal elephant in charge of the herd. All muscled and meaty, she looked like she could march the Israelites through the desert on the non-circuitous route and get them there early. Her shorts, serious hiking boots and a man's waterproof jacket were offset by the long and dark but greying braid of hair down her back.

She approached me, took both my hands in hers in a gesture of such familiarity that I was completely blindsided, and then leant forward so her sweaty forehead and nose touched mine. It was a little early for this. I instinctively recoiled, but she pulled me from the arms towards her in a tug that brooked no resistance.

'It's our hongi, a Maori greeting. To share the breath of life. You can't excuse yourself.'

Right there, my boundaries were hopelessly breached. But it was too late. She'd breathed me right in, and well, I did the same. I hadn't counted on wearing someone else's perspiration – but it would have been rude to wipe it off. Would I ever be satisfied with a mere hug again?

Yasmin's dark eyes were fringed with Nike swoosh eyelashes. Her thick calves were trussed in tight navy leggings, and her bright floral dress of red poppies strained over her enormous breasts. Around her head was a plume-like yellow and purple headscarf. A small nose ring nestled between her nostrils, and her lips were ablaze with a deep plum lipstick. I had to stop myself from staring at her. Up close, I could see a scar under her right eye, a white vein of tissue her beauty arranged itself around. She kissed me on the left cheek, the right cheek and again on the left, in a trifecta of affection. She was boss of the food, a role Helen and I used to share. I watched on as she brought out containers and tin-foiled items for packing that radiated fabulous smells.

Cate was seated at the kitchen table with her hiking pants rolled up, fixing knee-guards on both knees. She was tall, rakish, hunched over as if to avoid hitting her head on an invisible doorframe. Her grey hair was tamed into a parting down the centre and her light-blue eyes were set in an olive-complexion. She had a tough Patti Smith air about her, a once-was-rock-chick aura as if she'd done her share of smoking, swearing and shagging but she sure as hell wasn't going to brag about it.

After the first two greetings, I braced myself, but she laughed in her gravelly voice and in a pucker English accent said, 'Where I'm from, luv, you're goddamned lucky if you get a handshake.'

'Here you go,' Fiona had said, handing me a pole.

'Do I need a walking stick? I'm hardly that old.'

'You're gonna be happy for it, specially if you walking in

those shoes, eh,' Kiri had said pointedly.

I looked down at my trainers. Was I already error-riddled before we'd even set off?

'Those shoes are fine,' Fiona said. 'Don't listen to Kiri. She's hardcore, very precious about the equipment.' But that seemed easy from one wearing hard-core hiking boots.

'You one of those women who can't accept help?' Cate asked, her head tilted to the side like she was assessing the kind of woman I was.

'The pole is your friend,' Yasmin said, placing her hand on my arm. She flapped those great wings of her eyelashes, and godhelpme if she couldn't convince someone to give up their only child.

I took the stick. As soon as I gripped it, there was no doubt about it. It felt intentional and fortifying. It meant trekking business.

When we pulled up along a dirt track in the early morning, a car was already parked there, idling in the semi-dark.

'Ah, good on you, Liz,' Fiona had exhaled.

'Liz?' I gulped. 'I didn't know she was coming.'

'I wasn't sure she was going to make it,' Fiona said. 'Didn't want to get your hopes up.'

My pulse clattered. I wish Fiona had mentioned she'd invited Liz.

They're old friends and go back all the way to first periods and crushes in a line of historical longitude. For those who share it, the past is a country you can safely cross. You know all its dangerous borders and hidden ravines.

Fiona had brought Liz to our first sleepover. Back then, she was the only mother with a career, style and unflappable calmness about her. When she'd divorced Carl and left the children with him to run a multi-million-dollar advertising empire in London, I wasn't surprised, though it hurt to imagine the kind of breaking-it-to-the-kids conversation that would involve. I'd never say Liz was selfish. She knew what she wanted. You had to envy that, whatever else you might whisper behind her back.

'Liz is back from Europe,' Fiona had disclosed, as we'd sat at the market and sipped our liquorice tea. 'She's been gone twelve years. Can you believe it?'

When I'd last googled Liz, she only had a public figure Facebook profile – someone you couldn't befriend, only follow.

'She had to come back, after Brandon's accident...'

When people leave a dot dot dot after the word 'accident', it is your cue - to inhale and prepare yourself. There will be no talk of prizes and trophies.

'What happened to Brandon?' I clenched my belly and squeezed my pelvic floor.

'Oh Jo, he was in a terrible skiing accident five months ago. He lost a leg. They had to amputate above the knee. He's in rehab with a prosthetic now.'

I swallowed hard. As a mother, sometimes you can forget. You go for a time not fretting about your kids being led astray, making poor life choices and being struck down by misfortune. And then you hear. A friend's child with leukemia. A kid at the school committed suicide. An overdose. Meningitis. We all only signed on the dotted line for the kind of motherhood that tapers and morphs gently into a rapport with our adult kids we can relish now and then. Not the version of palliative care with no end in sight. No, we never signed that. That is not our signature.

'How terrible,' I whispered, 'just when you think you've got safe passage.'

'Brandon was an outstanding athlete, an up and coming Australian Football League player. He had a huge career in front of him,' Fiona had continued.

My heart tilted in coronary vertigo. Why do we do this? Put ourselves in the shoes of those with whom we never want to swap footwear? I immediately imagined Aaron in Brandon's place. For one thing, the army wouldn't take him. He'd have to readjust his life goals and settle for optometry or physiotherapy where his safety could be secured with a pair of plastic gloves and a surgical mask. I was grateful Fiona couldn't read my thoughts. Seriously, there are moments when your own lunacy is a shock even to you.

'Brandon's whole life has been turned upside down. Liz's too - she had to come back because he can't live on his own, not yet. He's got such a difficult road ahead of him.'

My basket had slipped from my hands and landed with a small thud as if an anvil had found its way in there. A memory of Liz surfaced from that long-ago sleepover as she'd sipped her expensive red wine. *Control is an illusion,* she'd scoffed.

'You need such grace, such luck in this life… It could happen to any of us, to any of our kids,' I whispered to Fiona. I had closed my eyes and tried to feel what it must be like for Liz to be nursing her grown son, just as some of us were verging on becoming empty nesters. But my brain tugged me away from the edge, a hardwired mothering instinct.

In the early morning light, Liz emerged from a rental car, dressed in obvious brand-new hiking gear. Liz bore Fiona's hug as they murmured things into each other's hair, inaudible to all of us, in a lukewarm display of affection. Helen and I used to fling arms, bump boobs and slap backs, but why make it a hugging competition?

When Liz finally fixed on me, she dropped her mouth

in genuine surprise. I wasn't sure whether to go in for a hug. She'd be mortified to think Fiona and I had been talking about her. But then again, perhaps she and Fiona had talked about me, and who knows how Fiona had relayed our chance encounter at the market. *She's left Frank. She's leaving Frank. She's thinking of leaving Frank. She's aged horribly. She's lost the plot.*

I went for a hug. Liz was as lean as she'd been a decade and a half ago and could likely fit into the same chiffon blouse and pencil skirt she'd worn back then. But what had passed for slim and trim in our forties had calcified into gauntness, bereft of any glow. The skin under her eyes was puckered and the colour of a two-day old bruise. It told the story of a brutal insomnia. Her hair was completely grey, but the way age had settled onto and into her was, to my eye, endearing. If she had been intimidating in the past, it had lost its edge. Glamour had evacuated, but a gritty elegance was still there, revealing an essence, the way something that's been threshed to its limit becomes the truest version of itself.

'Fiona didn't tell me you were coming,' she'd said, pulling away to look at me.

I shrugged. That made two of us.

'I thought it would be a nice surprise,' Fiona said, 'like a mini reunion.'

'You look really well, Jo.' With Liz, you could count on straight talk.

Eleven weeks alone in the country, I had wanted to say, grateful it showed.

'Thank you… It's fantastic to see you again.' I paused. 'I'm so sorry…'

She had positioned her hands up like a stop sign. '…it's okay. We're okay. No need to talk about it.'

And just like that, she shut me down and let me off the hook in one deft gesture.

Fiona had gathered us together in a circle, as our backpacks rested at our feet. The North Face price tag was still on Liz's bag. I pretended not to see what the backpack alone had cost her.

'Thank you all for coming,' Fiona had smiled.

'Hold the thanks for when we get back in one piece tomorrow,' Liz suggested.

'Guarantee you'll be smiling – Yasmin's cooking for us,' Kiri said.

'Just simple food,' Yasmin cautioned, '…not a usual feast…'

'I didn't come all this way for the food,' Liz pronounced. And there it was. The scab of cynicism, clotted over, a telltale of the tragedies she's bled through. I hoped she was not beyond joy; that somewhere tucked inside her, there was still a pocket of spontaneous delight.

Yasmin, Kiri and Cate linked arms. Yasmin threaded hers through mine, and so I reached for Liz. But she didn't want to be hooked into this circle.

'I'm so grateful to have the chance to walk in noble silence with the women I love,' Fiona smiled.

This made me awkward, because in my case, love was a strong word.

'Quick clarification for the unspiritual among us. What exactly is *noble* silence?' Liz asked.

'It's a mindful state of quiet so we can remain completely present,' Fiona explained. 'It frees us from socialising. In that space, we find opportunities to connect deeply with ourselves, rise above ego and feel at one with the earth and Spirit.'

Liz's eyes narrowed. 'Does that exclude me listening to a podcast?'

There was a discomfited momentary pause. A small glance passed from face to face.

'I'll use my ear pods. I won't disturb anyone.'

'Yeah, sure… Whatever works for you,' Fiona faltered.

That was love right there. I'm pretty sure electronics were not part of the noble silence treaty.

'I won't do it, if it's like against the *rules*.'

'Okay, thank you,' Fiona smiled, clearly relieved though Liz didn't look very thanked.

Cate made a gesture that looked like she was holding a penis, but surely, I had got that wrong.

'Ah, yes, thanks for reminding me, Catey. I have a little gift for each of you,' Fiona smiled.

She pulled out a paper bag from the boot of the car and handed each of us a plastic tube.

I opened mine and out popped a squishy lavender object.

'They're urination funnels. No crouching to pee, for those of us with dodgy knees and backs. You just have to rinse it and you can use it over and over.'

'I love it,' Yasmin chuckled.

'This'll stop backsplash on the socks and undies, then?' Kiri asked.

'I won't need one,' Liz said, examining hers.

'Just hang on to it, in case,' Fiona suggested.

'I'm holding everything in until we get back,' she decreed.

'…said someone who thought she was the boss of her bladder,' Kiri clucked. 'It's gotta come out somehow.'

I hoped Fiona had briefed everyone, *Be kind, Liz is going through hell.*

'Anyone menstruating?' Fiona asked.

We all snorted. *Fuck no. Thank god that's over. Best break-up ever.* The air was vivid with shared relief.

Though I hadn't had a period in eight months, I still carry spare tampons and sanitary pads in my Menopausal Survival Kit, in case it decides, like a teenager with a giant appetite, to come home for dinner out of the blue. It's not an invitation, mind you. Unlike the poet Lucille Clifton, who wrote the poem *to my last period*, I do not mourn mine's extinction.

Some things should be over, once and for all. Why a woman has to hold out for menopause to finally be free in her own skin is an injustice swaddled in a mystery. For forty years, I've had to manage my female parts with padding or a proximate vessel to catch bodily fluids. It's a long wait to be in a body that does not ooze, seep or betray you at any moment. A body asking for trouble. Calling for help, attention. A body in need.

'What about a number two?' I asked, even though like Liz, I was relying on constipation to get me through the next twenty-four hours.

Fiona held up a spade, toilet paper and bottle of antiseptic gel.

'Nothing like taking a shit in the bush,' Kiri said, making it sound like a bucket-list item, which it surely cannot be.

In this crowd of strange, strong women, everything was clearly under control. Fiona knew where we were going, Kiri was in charge of logistics, Yasmin had the food sorted. Cate, Liz and I could just follow blindly.

Nothing *going right* depended on me. I was deliriously free.

'You've all agreed to come with me without actually knowing where we're going. Thanks for your trust in me,' Fiona smiled as we adjusted the buckles on our bulky backpacks. Cate was the only one with a small daypack, which for a big, tall woman, seemed, well, a tad unfair.

'Exactly where are we going?' Liz asked, affixing her sunglasses to a strap around her neck.

'If all goes according to plan, we're headed for a cove my dad once took me to on the one and only bushwalk we ever did together.'

'Your dad?' Liz seemed surprised.

'Before his breakdown.'

'What kinda breakdown?' Kiri asked.

'He was a Vietnam vet and…'

Kiri nodded, 'Say no more.'

'He planned a hike on my seventh birthday – he'd been wanting to show me the Australian bush for years. I think we took a wrong turn, maybe he devised it, but we ended up overlooking a cove where the sand was unbroken by human footprint. It was something out of a dreamscape. Idyllic, sheltered, wild. We made our way down, even though there wasn't a proper path. And when we got there, we swam in the clearest water, built a fire on the sand, and ate oysters off the rocks. Neither of us wanted to leave. We stayed overnight and all through the next day.'

'Such a delicious memory,' Yasmin said.

'Except he'd promised to bring me back before sundown.

When we wandered in late the following afternoon, the police and bush rangers had been out looking for us for twenty-four hours. My mother had been through hell.'

'If you don't come home when you say you're going to, what must people think?' Kiri asked. 'Rule number one, you gotta stay in contact.'

'She never forgave him. And he never took me hiking or bushwalking again. He started drinking again…' Fiona trails off. 'But today is fifty years since that day, and we're going back to that cove. I want to retrace my steps and find my way to that place where I felt at one with all of creation for the first time.'

'Now I got goosebumps,' Kiri said, 'genuinely, feel here,' taking my hand and placing it on her prickly arm. Kiri clearly had a thing about public participation in her metabolic symptoms.

'This is an important pilgrimage,' Yasmin smiled.

'It is. But a lot has changed in fifty years. I've done my research and we have to cut across private property for the first kilometre or two. But there is no other way to get to the path.' Her tone was bashful. 'Then it's pretty easy going to the top of the cove. The only tricky bit is getting down, so we'll take it slow. The best part is that there's a cave where we can sleep…'

'Hold on,‘ Liz said, her hands doing the time out gesture.

'A cave?' I interposed. There had been no mention of a cave.

'Don't worry. These mats we've got will make it super comfortable.'

'Easy for someone who sleeps on the floor,' Liz said.

Fiona sleeps on the floor? By choice?

'Firstly, we can't just walk through someone's property, that's trespassing,' Liz continued. 'And what if something goes wrong? Someone twists an ankle, gets bitten by a snake, we get caught in a bushfire? Who's going to pay the fine if we're caught trespassing? We can't just ignore the legalities.'

'Nothing is going to happen. We'll be protected and guided all the way,' Fiona said brightly.

'Really? Did you consult your crystals? Your astrology chart? Did the tarot say so?' Liz's tone was a reminder that she ran a huge advertising empire. My god, I wouldn't want to bring her a skinny flat white if she'd ordered a double shot latte.

Fiona looked mildly strained but steadfast. 'Kiri is a nurse and a seasoned hiker. Cate is a biologist. Yasmin has a wealth of herbal knowledge. I've done some geomancy, which may be a little esoteric for you, but I trust its wisdom. And we're carrying emergency medical supplies.'

'But we're heading off on unmarked paths?' Liz pushed. 'A secret cove? A cave? We're not troglodytes.'

Before Fiona could respond, Cate stepped forward like a bouncer, interposing herself between Liz and Fiona. 'Ownership of land is nothing but a colonial fiction isn't that so? Bloody Brits didn't give a fowl's fanny about who or what was already here when they gouged their greedy fingers in the cookie jar of land title and grabbed what wasn't theirs. Not to mention all the plundering and raping they did while they were at it. We're not taking anything but a walk, peaceful and harmonious as fuck, leaving nothing but footsteps on the land those goddamned pillaging cunts stole.'

Her swearing caught me like a mad kiss. I couldn't help the giggle that escaped. *Let anyone stop us. Just let them try. Goddamned pillaging cunts.*

'Whoa, language, girl,' Kiri said.

'Liz, you got children, yes?' Yasmin asked.

'What has that got to do...'

'We've given birth. To overnight in a cave is easy,' Yasmin smiled. 'Or we can sleep under the stars, on the beach, with the sky above us.'

'You're welcome to my mat and sleeping bag,' Fiona offered.

'I've got my own brand-new bag and mat. It's not about...' Liz exhaled. She turned away from us and walked away to look out over the hills with her hands on her hips. Her shoulders rose and fell as she breathed.

Kiri, Yasmin and Cate huddled around Fiona as we waited to see what Liz would do. Cate rested her hand on Fiona's shoulder.

This had nothing to do with me – I was an innocent bystander. Still, I found myself walking over to Liz.

'If it makes you feel any better, I'm also shitting myself.

A mysterious cove. Caves…and all that.'

Liz gave no indication that she'd heard me.

'You're a good friend,' I said. 'For coming all this way. Getting all geared up.'

I could smell her exhaustion. She was disfiguringly stress-indented, as if this was the last damn thing she needed right now. My heart opened wide to her.

'Ha, is this what you call being a good friend? Whining and moaning and spoiling the mood before we've even begun? I'm behaving like a bloody adolescent.' Her voice was taut with exertion.

'You're here.'

'Under false pretences. Being a widow doesn't give her the right to be manipulative,' Liz said turning to me in a harsh whisper. 'But that's Fiona for you…*be at one with Spirit*… I mean, really?'

This was inside information, a keep-to-yourself-summation of the faults of a loved one. I was not meant to hear this. She'd regret this indiscretion later. I wanted Liz to know I would forget this slip, that I too knew how to say Hurtful Things.

'Maybe it's her way of reclaiming something that's been lost, with Ben gone and Gabe far away. It can't be easy being on her own for the first time…'

Liz lowered her chin. Our eyes locked. I detected the channels changing. She sighed a long and overdue exhalation. 'I heard about CJ.'

My heart folded like a cheap beach chair.

Being reminded was like having to learn the news all over again. I grimaced.

'I was going to tell you…at an appropriate time.' I shrugged. I was relieved Fiona had gotten there first.

'Quite a way to make an exit,' Liz sighed.

'It was quick, she didn't suffer.'

Liz turned a cocktail ring with a sapphire stone around and around on the third finger of her right hand. Her nails were perfectly manicured and painted in a dark maroon.

'You understand there will be no sleep tonight. Not in a cave. Not on a beach. That's if we even find the bloody place.'

'No-one ever died from missing a night's sleep.' And then, 'I have a stash of tranquilisers. And whiskey,' I whispered. 'Japanese.'

Liz apprised me with a gaze I couldn't quite make out. 'Now those are the kind of spirits I'm interested in.'

'Right, so now that's all sorted, let's begin our journey,' Kiri said. She corralled us all into a circle. 'Fiona, you wanna talk us into silence?'

Fiona gazed from face to face. She clasped her hands at her chest, closed her eyes and began to breathe in and out. I shut my eyes as Fiona began to speak.

'We are gathered here today on the land of the Nalbo and the Dallambara – of the Gubbi Gubbi tribes, the Traditional Owners of the land. We pay our respects to the spirits, ancestors and elders. We ask for permission to walk the land, for safe passage and a safe return. We agree to honour and take care of the land as we pass through.'

'God, it's all so earnest,' Liz muttered under her breath so only I could hear. 'Let's just get on with it already.'

But Kiri was not done. 'Where I come from, the land of the long white cloud, we have a saying, "*He kotuku rerenga tahi*," a white heron flies once. We use it when something special happens, a moment that won't come around again. We have been called here, each one of us from all different places, to perform one job.' She held up the sentinel of her forefinger. 'To walk together in our grief.'

'No-one said anything about grief,' Liz said.

Kiri continued, undeterred.

'This summer, we had the kind of heat we never seen before, and the land burned. So we gonna be walking on earth that's sacrificed its trees and creatures who belong to it, like a mother who's lost her children. All the tracks of those who came before us are gone, gutted by the fires. And they predicting the same or worse come next summer. We been called to witness these tragedies, past and future, even if we didn't know it, but it's why we're here. You can call it Shiva like the Jews or Shraddha like the Hindus, or Sorry Business like the first nations of this country – it's all the same thing. We've been summoned to do the mourning, even for those that haven't yet died.'

Kiri seemed to know a lot about grieving rituals. *Summoned.* I felt its gravity.

Liz pursed her lips with the finesse of a woman who knows how and when to pick her battles. 'Let's hope we don't end up sorry this turned out like *Picnic at Hanging Rock.*'

4

A Bit of Ubuntu

Leaves and twigs crack and pop underfoot, nature's bubble-wrap. We stride through the striations of sunlight impressed through the stencil of trunks along our path. I pause at the sculptures of tangled roots, the radiating sinew of each tree. It's sentimentality that brings you to read longing in these patterns. In the silence, you feel it – small, intrusive, a visitor. We are being granted passage as we watch our footfall and bow to the hidden hierarchies of the land as it lives.

If a tree fell here, it would make a racket, with or without our presence. Wildlife have far superior hearing to humans and why should they not count? I guess the point of that koan is our need for alibis. If someone's life collapses in on itself, and no-one notices, did it really happen?

It's peaceful at the rear, a little-known ambient fact anuses and tails keep to themselves. Besides, someone always has to be last. Spider webs, brambles and fallen branches will be dealt with long before me. I'm not trying to be Cheryl Strayed like every other woman my age determined to walk the Camino or the Pacific Crest trail before she dies. I know my strengths and leading the way through the wilderness is not one of them.

Liz walks ahead of me. Something crouches at the back of my skull; it trails her. I want a chance to acknowledge what she's been through. But she wants no witnesses. *Run along, nothing to see here.* She couldn't have been clearer. We're not here to swap war stories or catch up.

The silence is a shield. We can skip the performance of feigning curiosity about how our kids turned out given the divergent mothering strategies we chose. It's obvious now. I feel she ought to know – she was right. I have come to feel sheepish and profligate about the time and energy I shovelled into my kids. I could have been trilingual (with Italian and French to my repertoire), learned to play the Spanish guitar or penned a literary *Fifty Shades of Grey* had I only channelled those ten thousand hours more shrewdly.

I let the space between me and Liz grow as we march single file, a bobbing of greying hair, swishing plaits like horse's tails, sensible hats, bright turbans and backpacks. We are a posse of matriarchs, two-thirds strangers – though the head-rub with Kiri and three-cheeked kiss with Yasmin may have altered our relationship status. I can still feel a slight warmth on my forehead from this morning's 'hongi.'

The trees reach into their sky-yearning and I find myself copying them, unfolding the tendrils of my tendons, swinging my arms, looking up. Life contracts us. We prune ourselves, fold in, shrink, desiccate. Around us, I hear chattering. This is Nature's jargon, from the startling of wallabies that skitter into the brush, to the smaller rat-like bandicoots, the tussling in the leaves, the flicker of Birdwing butterflies, the 'chew-chew' of the Eastern whipbird.

My ear has changed. Eleven weeks without the constant pings of Facebook notifications, buzz of text messages and ringtone on my iPhone, and I am hearing differently. In Penny's place, I have tuned into the screeching of crickets at dusk, the hum of afternoon air, a skittering of insects as markers of time and the bleating call of the kookaburra. At first it tricked me – the lyrebird, that avian-imitating savant. I listened out for it, willing its impersonations of fire alarms, chain saws, camera shutters and mobile phone rings. I wondered what its own pure song sounded like and why it chose to spend its life mimicking other noises.

'When you get lonely, just call me,' Frank had said before I left. People who care about you extend lifejackets, check airbags, install safety nets. It was the 'when' in his kindness that niggled. He didn't trust me with an 'if'.

I wasn't sure which way solitude would spin me – into isolated terror or unfettered vastness, and there was only one way to find out. I'd never contemplated 'hermit' or 'recluse' as a life goal. Like everyone else ushered by the signposts of civility, I'd been indoctrinated into family-making as the natural project of my adult life. Wasn't that normal?

Ants, bees, penguins, buffalo and flamingos may be the darlings of the animal kingdom because they're good sharers and collaborators in their smug little herds and colonies. But there are loners who only seek companionship in mating season and for the rest, face the world alone. Admittedly they might rip the throats of their extended family if forced to stay together, never mind engage in unmentionable incest. Take the snow leopard – once she's satisfied her cub can hunt and survive, she walks away without a backwards glance. They may never cross paths again. That's natural too.

'I don't think you're somebody who can be alone for too long.' Frank hadn't intended to undermine me.

But he was wrong. I know his eyes and how he looks at me. I've been trying to tell him, but he's blinded by the same kind of loyalty we display to a pair of trousers that stopped fitting us five years ago. At some point, as Marie Kondo tells us, it's time to thank it and let it go.

I've been weaning myself off being somebody for years now.

The nobody-er, the better.

I'd painted a monobrow with eyeliner to join my eyebrows, pulled my hair into a bun, and laced a lei through it. Frank declined to dress up with the obstinate refusal I've reserved for certain types of sexual experimentation, even though it was his colleague Bettina's sixtieth birthday party and the invitation specified, 'Come dressed as your alter ego.' Frank's excuse was that he didn't understand the instruction.

'What are you dressed as?' Bettina asked as she air-kissed his cheek, a garrulous dominatrix in a black leather lace-up bodice and stilettos.

'My wife dressed up for both of us,' he said, gesturing to my outstanding rendition of Frida Kahlo. Frank left me to get drinks as I roiled over how my labour in the eyeliner department exonerated him from all effort.

I made my way around the room, refilling my glass with sparkling wine only to get me through the next round of, 'So what do you do?' and 'How are your kids doing?'

'What's gotten into you?' Frank had asked, puzzled, when I'd tapped my nose after an hour, which in our shared body language means, *I'm ready to go.* 'We can't leave yet. It's rude.'

'I'm sorry, I just can't… I've had enough. I'm not feeling great.'

Of course, when Helen was available, I had a partner. Between us, we could rouse a group to hilarity, the Macarena and even, on occasion, full-blown nudity. We were always performing. I could do it when it wasn't a solo show. Around her, I knew how to be that person. Alone, I tanked.

After she left, I began to loathe parties. I'd try to wriggle out of as many as I could, and those I couldn't, I'd attend, sulking, not that Frank noticed. I'd flit from person to person, offering the same frayed narratives, listening to theirs with a look that did not betray how little I cared about their renovations, children's accomplishments or engagements, while nodding keenly at images on their iPhones and politely watching videos of babies' crawling and graduation ceremonies.

It was a jolt to realise I was not the caring, generous, open-hearted extrovert I thought I was. I was a jaded, judgemental introvert, counting down the clock until it was acceptable to leave. What had made do for 'friendship' no longer did, as if I'd woken one day to find that I'd developed an allergy to, say, pineapples when just yesterday I could eat an entire one without my tongue blazing.

In the car on the way home, I'd coiled into a shell of silence.

'You okay?' Frank asked.

I didn't know how to knit these emotions into words that made sense.

'That was quite fun, wasn't it?' he pursued. 'Those

sausage rolls were excellent, I think they had cheese in them.'

'If it was a chapter in a book, I'd skip it.'

'You looked like you were having fun.

That was just it. I knew how to look like I was having fun. I could masquerade these interactions, by the same distorting treachery that might propel you into faking an orgasm, while never letting on that you'd rather be reading a book, or even, dare one admit, tidying the kitchen.

'It's the same old, same old. Why do we keep having the same conversations? They don't take us anywhere.'

'Where do you want to be taken?'

'To a conversation that hasn't happened yet. It's not like we have all the time in the world. Why do we keep rinsing and repeating? I'm tired of nice, polite exchanges.'

'We're supposed to enjoy hanging out in packs and doing what social beings do – share food and stock market tips. Talk about how to survive the next winter.' He was mimicking David Attenborough's idiolect. 'Unless we cut ourselves off from society, become loners, we're caught in the vicious cycle of human interaction. Friendship is relentless. Relationships are inexorable. But *ubuntu*, baby, don't forget *ubuntu*.'

This was his move – to invoke Africa, the country we'd left behind eighteen years ago as wide-eyed immigrants. Did I really need to be reminded that we'd lost everything, including the radical hospitality of *ubuntu*, that soulful connection to others which holds us to our shared humanity? In Australia, I'd never felt that measure of belonging. I would always be an add-on, a latecomer, someone who'd missed the crucial introduction and would have to deduce what things mean without having the full story. I'd forever be flailing in the gap.

We'd left *ubuntu* behind, like a lost bag, when we landed on these shores. In our new home girt by sea, we were adrift, a small raft of a family, history-less, harbour-less. But when I'd met Helen, sixteen years ago, she'd pulled me in to her ample bosom and insisted on being our surrogate family. We were never left to fend for ourselves. We always had an invitation, a place to go, a table around which to share food and celebrate. In some moments, I forgot we were newcomers. I felt familied.

'Maybe I'm more of a snow leopard than a penguin.'

'A snow leopard?' Frank had scoffed. 'You're the biggest penguin of all. You're the one who brings everyone together. It's why everyone loves you.'

I'd turned and looked out the window at the passing lights of the city, wondering who might I be when I wasn't trying all the time to be so terribly likeable, someone people would want as a mother, a wife, a friend. Everything became a blur as I vaguely heard Frank say, 'You really should have tried the sausage rolls.'

I'm disappointed we weren't caught trespassing. Not to wish a tantrum on anyone, but I was holding out on witnessing Cate in action. She has secret bandwidth, a strength belied by her slow progress – a reservoir of operatic curses I may yet get to hear if someone pisses her off in just the right way. Every now and then we concertina as the front of this procession slows down. Cate seems to be the cause. She stops regularly. She bends forwards, her hands on her thighs. Fiona checks on her wordlessly, tiny gestures that speak of the distance and durability of their friendship.

It's hard work, resisting envy.

'Promise me, you will never have a best friend like me again,' Helen had shouted drunkenly in my ear, above the sounds of Michael Jackson's *Man in the Mirror*.

Maybe it was the foam-filled jumping castle. The little shot glasses with plastic penises she found hilarious. But her fiftieth birthday was the last party I genuinely enjoyed.

'Who the hell could ever replace you?' I'd swooned, hugging her to me, boobs and all. Then we danced and danced in bare feet until they were black and sore.

Then she was gone. My world got quieter and Santa Monica, wherever the hell that is, got their cheerleader.

I circled the black hole of her absence with a dizzying loneliness. I tried to keep in touch. The one left behind always does. I called twice a week at first, but the phone went to voicemail. I wrote emails. She seldom replied. I knew she was busy. Four kids in a new country. It couldn't have been easy.

She set up a Facebook account she never learned how to use. We said we'd Skype. We managed once or twice. She didn't have the right internet connection. She'd forgotten her login details. I promised her we'd visit. We never did. All our spare cash went towards renovating our bathroom and fixing the leak in our ceiling.

At times it felt as if she'd died. Though it's obscene to think such glib thoughts given everything that's happened.

I deep dived into writing a new book. But something had flittered out of me. I panicked. I tried to resist superstition. The harder I tried, the more my writing eluded me. Writing, like all terrible loves, is filled with both longing and terror of how you would cope if you lost it. If you have ever loved someone or something this much, you will know then, the arrangements and bargains you will make to ensure its safety. You will understand that if you feel it is disappearing, you will imagine that you are dying.

I read that getting a dog would help with anxiety and grief. We chose a Labrador pup the kids named Stewie, after a character in the TV series, *Family Guy*. Dogs are an excellent enterprise for lonely people – all that toilet and behavioural training substitutes for social arrangements. I went for weeks at a time without thinking about Helen.

Aaron broke his leg playing soccer. The following year he shattered his collarbone jumping off a second-floor balcony because his friends dared him to. Frank needed surgery to remove a mole. We had an anxious week waiting for test results. They came back negative, and I sobbed like I'd just received bad news.

Helen missed out on all of it. Who knows what I was missing out on in her life?

She started a business, *Dinner's On Me*, a rotating list of a hundred easy recipes and shopping lists for busy mothers so they don't have to think about the last big task at the end of the day – which was just genius. She'd always been the better cook.

When our kids were little, Helen and I had shared an almost spiritual love for food. We shopped, cooked and ate together, inventing new tastes and recipes. But when I went on a strict new eating plan in my forties, our friendship took strain. I lost weight, but I lost something else too – our connection. Without her to share it with, what was so special about food?

Last year I called a family meeting to let Frank and the kids know that I wasn't cooking anymore. If anyone wanted dinner, they could bloody well cook it themselves. I'd done my time in the kitchen. I vaguely daydreamed that someone might offer to cook me a meal now and then. No-one did. For the past year we've all been helping ourselves to Weetbix and toast. When Frank said he'd cook, he meant he'd order

UberEats. The fridge remained threadbare, barely covering the milk-eggs-cheese bases. Every time I opened it, I'd envisage Helen's reaction. That fridge became a reminder that she was gone.

I imagined we'd be side by side through the thicks and thins of life – BFFs and all that. I guess I didn't expect to be so survivable. It hit me that no-one would collapse if I died. Not that I want the world to stop spinning when I do. But a decent amount of bereaved struggle would be respectful.

I had voiced this to Frank, and he'd said kindly, 'I'd fall apart.'

'Don't you dare. You'd have to be strong for the kids.'

'I'd be strong on the outside and fall apart on the inside.'

I was okay with that.

Helen promised she'd come back to Australia for my fiftieth birthday. A week before, she called to say she couldn't make it because Cameron's American football team made it to the finals. Kids should take preference over friends, I understand how things work. I turned fifty without her. Frank knew better than to suggest a party. He took me away to the Hunter Valley for a weekend where he played golf and I had three overpriced spa sessions.

Then Stewie got run over. I found him on the side of the road. I cannot, really, no, I cannot talk about this. No-one warned me I'd spend three months crying over a pet.

It's a mistake we make all the time – thinking we can ever replace what we have loved.

I'm looking at the treetops above us, and so I almost bump into Liz.

'Sorry,' I murmur before I remember. She turns and puts her fingers to her lips in an exaggerated hush. Is she *mocking* noble silence?

We have come to a standstill again. Everyone huddles as Yasmin points through the foliage. A snake? A bird? A mammal? I smile at Yasmin and shrug.

She points again through the trees.

'What is it?' I mouth silently. She brings her forefingers to her ears and then mimics dinosaur arms. I look again. And suddenly there it is – a mother wallaby with a joey in her pouch, though it's more of an adolescent than a baby. It looks odd, like a five-year-old still breastfeeding. That would always get a reaction out of Helen. She was a 'breast is best' mother but had a snarky thing to say about mothers who just couldn't let go.

I had timed my call to Santa Monica when it was late afternoon there and I knew Helen would be home making dinner. As soon as I heard her voice on the other side of the line, my heart twanged for the times when she lived just up the road and we'd talk daily.

'Hey,' my voice trembled. 'What are you cooking tonight?'

'Beef Rendang.'

'Never heard of it.'

'It's Indonesian. Slow simmered beef in coconut milk, with lemongrass, galangal, garlic, turmeric, ginger and chilies. The secret is to stew it for four hours. Wanna come over for supper?'

'Sounds...divine.'

'You think you've tasted heaven, but this is a whole new experience. I'll send you the recipe.'

'Thanks.' I let myself have this soft moment of imaginary dinner plans and easy-to-follow recipes.

'Helen, I've got some really bad news.'

'Menopause has finally arrived?'

'...seriously...'

'What?'

'...CJ...our friend CJ?'

'Yeah...CJ...'

I'd paused. '...she was killed last week in a motorbike accident.'

Verbalisation and repetition are necessary for the brain to start stitching a story together. We have to announce a fact to start believing it.

'Fuck no, that's horrible.' We breathed together without speaking for some moments. 'Her poor kids. Jesus. A motorbike, hey?'

'It was her boyfriend's. Remember, Kito?'

'Her toy boy.'

I'd flinched at the belittling label. Kito was now a young man in anguish. He would never be the same again.

'What about her kids?'

'They're with Tom, her ex.'

'TFB?'

'Actually, she'd stopped calling him That Fucking Bastard. They'd reconciled.'

In old times, I'd have spilled it all, itemised the intimate details CJ had confided to me. But on this day, vying allegiances tugged at me.

'So did you keep in touch with her after our last reunion?'

I'd swallowed. 'We saw each other a few times. She had a spare ticket for a Robbie Williams concert. We went together.'

'Never understood what you saw in him.'

'We both adore Robbie Williams.' I stumbled over the words, the present tense now grammatically incorrect when speaking about CJ.

'Didn't she get on your nerves, I remember you saying…?'

'She'd changed. She was going to stop practicing law to start a charity. For pregnant girls in Rwanda.'

'That does not sound like the CJ I remember,' Helen said. 'Sad for her kids and Kito. But way to go, CJ.'

'It was a horrible, violent death.'

'But it was quick.'

'It's too sudden. She didn't get a chance to wrap things up.'

'Of course, you'd choose the protracted, agonising, burden-on-everyone-around-you way to go.'

'Just time to say proper goodbyes. And burn my diaries. If I go out with a bang, you'll have to come back and get to them before Frank and the kids do.'

'Yeah, I'm onto it. As for me, I want a chocolate-binge induced aneurysm, but it must be fatal. None of this 'lose half your brain, speech and movement and hang around for ages' shit. Alternatively, a knife to the heart in a crime of passion.'

'In what scenario in your life would there be a crime of passion, Helen?'

'I have a bout of late onset lesbianism and David walks in on us...'

'You're being irreverent – CJ is dead.'

'At least she really lived her life. She probably had more fun in those last few years with Kito than you and I've had since we were single. She knew how to be spontaneous and impulsive.'

'She was funny. Smart.'

'She was the best looking of all of us – a MILF with all that sex appeal,' Helen said.

This had landed with a thud against my chest.

She was sexy. That I would never forget.

5

Flamingo Juice

'It works if you get the angle right,' I whisper to Yasmin.

We are facing each other with our pants at our knees while the others are taking a snack break up ahead. It's only because leakage is at stake that I've ruptured the silence.

She and I fiddle with our pee funnels. I hesitate having my dripping bits so far from the ground. Urination, like defecation, menstruation, childbirth is surely a more intimate experience, between you and the earth, not a flamboyant, swashbuckling gesture from up high. Perhaps pissing on two feet is what drives men to fencing and paragliding.

I can see that Yasmin does not have an airtight lock

between the funnel and her girlbits. I can't possibly offer to position hers. We only just met this morning and I am not an ablution doula.

'Look,' I say, pressing the funnel tight up against my vulva.

'You have no hair on your foofy,' she exclaims as we conspire in harsh whispers.

I glance down. 'Oh yes, I know. I had it all lasered off a few years ago.' Did she just refer to my vagina as a 'foofy'?

'Why?'

I shrug.

See, this would be the value of noble silence. It would free one from explanations. Instead, I now have to justify using those laser treatments I'd bought as a gift for Jamie on a Groupon special. I'd had my underarm hairs lasered a few years back and what a liberation from razors and hot wax that had been. But Jamie was insulted in having depilatory expectations thrust upon her, by her own mother of all people. It was *anti-feminist. Undermining. Unwoke.* And, fair enough.

But there they were – three treatments, no refunds. Someone had to use them. I went for my bikini line. I'm at a bit of a loss to clarify how I then allowed myself to be persuaded by Sally-Anne, who preferred the term 'cosmetologist,' rather than 'beautician,' to go *all the way,* though she did mention that *everyone was doing it* and it *enhanced intercourse.* I was excited to show Frank.

But it freaked him out. He was just as astounded as me to discover he was a pubic hair guy. Who knew? So no, laser-down-there had not changed my life, as advertised. Nor did it ramp up my libido – Sally-Anne had clearly not factored menopause into the equation. It was like renovating the house just as all the kids move out. Now every time I catch a glimpse of myself in the bathroom mirror, I can almost hear my vagina laughing: *Haha, all this and for nothing!*

'Everyone's doing it,' I whisper. 'And it enhances intercourse.'

Yasmin nods, wide-eyed, impressed. 'Easier to squat like a duck.' She abandons the funnel.

I am not specifically looking but I notice she has a large pantyliner in her undies.

'Four kids, natural birth,' she says. 'My pelvic floor is ground zero. I wee when I sneeze, cough or laugh. So please, no jokes.'

'I see a pelvic floor physiotherapist,' I commiserate. 'I go through pantyliners like…pantyliners. See,' I say pointing to my panty-lined undies.

'We must do exercises. Fiona, she can squeeze ping-pongs balls from hers…'

I am mystified by the alliance between table tennis and vaginas. Whose idea was it to push a ball up there without a means of extraction? Have we learned nothing from tampon strings? It's only because it's attached to the rest of him that Frank can count on his penis' safe withdrawal. In there is a deep dark forest. Enter at your own risk.

'How does Fiona do that?' I ask, though I'm more curious as to why.

Yasmin laughs and shrugs. 'Tantric exercises. But that's playschool. Her teacher is a foofy-guru and can lift a surfboard with hers.'

This leaves me with more questions, maybe even the start of a story. Yasmin lets out a long pee. It splashes all over her shoes and pools around her feet. A trail makes its way to me. As I step aside, I land in the puddle I've let out through my pee funnel, goddammit.

The side of the mountain we have been skirting for hours becomes visible, though it's been there all along, veiled by the trees.

We lose the shade just as we start to climb. My calves grumble. We move sluggishly. Cate stops every hundred metres or so. We all stop. We wait. Her breathing is hurting. I can almost hear her alveoli hissing and grasping. There is a slight hushed skirmish as Kiri wrestles the small backpack from her and swaddles it to her chest, the straps over her shoulders, a beast with a front and back hump. Fiona takes the ukulele case off Cate. Even denuded of loadbearing, she moves at a shuffle – as ungenerous a thought as it is, she is a liability out here. I don't know if Liz and Fiona's friendship will survive if Liz's pessimistic projections come to pass. *What if this, what if that?* Some of us dance at the edge of faith, others at the bridge of consequence.

The sun scalds through my long-sleeved shirt. My neck is wet, my eyes burn as sweat finds them under my sunglasses. The heat niggles in my throat. Autumn is addled, a season with dementia, all its cues forgotten. Summer is dallying, extending herself, lounging and settling, as if she has no intention of moving on, so just get used to her, like adult children prolonging their leave-taking; goodbye-almost-but-not-yet.

My shoulders complain. My backpack feels heavier though I'm down two apples and half a litre of water. I'm aware that weight-bearing is good for the bones *'what with osteoporosis beckoning',* which is the kind of thing you pay doctors to say to you. I'd made the appointment so my GP could check out the darkening spot on my thigh. 'Not a melanoma, just a *senile wart,*' she'd said, taking out the liquid nitrogen. I'm relieved it was nothing more than an ageist verruca, but why use a medical term to add to the torments of approaching senescence? I left stunned by the outbreak of referrals for a colonoscopy, mammogram, pelvic ultrasound, bone density and blood cholesterol tests. When was one supposed to merely enjoy life?

I take my iPhone out of my pocket. SOS only.

Undetectable. I am officially off the grid. Both Jamie and Aaron know my one rule – stay connected. I don't expect them to answer my WhatsApp messages; I simply need to see that they've read them.

Frank has tried to get my buy-in to upgrade from 4G to 5G because faster, quicker mobile network technology allows us to stay in touch with the people who worry about us faster and more quickly. But I can't lose the anxiety that these upgrades might be scrambling the migratory instincts of birds and bees and upending Nature's air traffic control. While Frank fears missing out on the special family early bird deal, I'm dreading the download speed of the approaching apocalypse.

Suddenly I am longing for the walking to be over, to arrive wherever it is we're headed. If only I knew how much longer we have to go. But I can't ask – the silence and all – and Liz has used up all the complaining and bitching in one go this morning.

I now feel it as a certainty, beyond my aching shoulders and my thirst. I should have texted Frank to let him know where I am. We watched that movie *127 Hours* together. We both promised we'd never *not let each other know*. It's rule number one when you head out into the wild. He's the first person someone would call if anything went wrong; he's the contact in my phone listed as ICE (in case of emergency). The one responsible for identifying the body. My next of kin. The surviving spouse.

But more than that, he is the person waiting for me. And when someone is waiting for you, you are not the sole shareholder of your own time. You are not free to do with it as you will. You have an investor. You are expected back. Your side of the bed will still be there, unslept in. Unless the cat has taken liberties. If you do not consult, at the very least, you are obliged to report and give notice of your movements. By all accounts this waiting doesn't end, even when your other half dies. Oscar has been gone for more than eight years, but my friend Shirley still sleeps on 'her side of the bed'. Books help. I came across it after CJ's death – Joan Didion's *The Year of Magical Thinking*, which tracks the year after her husband died. She imagined his disappearance was a mistake, an interruption and that he'd walk through the door at any minute.

Frank is waiting for me. It is a weight and a tether. He's the shore I swim back to when the waters get dark and murky and I need to step back into my life on land.

The morning after I heard about CJ, I went down to the beach for my morning swim. I pulled my pink cap over the bob of my ponytail, fixed my goggles and dived into the water, heading straight for the island.

I'd been staring out at that little piece of earth they call Wedding Cake Island for years, wondering what was there, on that rocky outcrop peeking up through the ocean, eight hundred metres from the shore. It reminded me of my favourite Enid Blyton book, *Five Run Away Together*. Some days it looked within easy reach, on others, as far away as never.

That day, I did not tell Frank where I was going. I did not consult the other swimmers on whether it was a good day to be swimming out so far and so deep. I propelled my body through the water, looking up every ten or twenty strokes to make sure I was heading in the right direction. I did not think about the sharks, or the stingers, or the dangers I couldn't see.

As I approached the island, I turned in the water and looked back at the beach. It was a miniature land, a shrunken picture of where I'd been staring at Wedding Cake Island all this time. But it had been gazing back at me. Right then, as thinking settled into me, as I came to know where I was, I began to panic, swallow saltwater, sense peril. I could drown right there, and no-one would know. I could be gone, just like CJ. Tears filled my goggles. I felt the swell and sway of the water beneath me, and I swam back to my life on the shore with a strength I'd never previously possessed.

Not then, but later, it shocked me. That I could be so disloyal to my personality: do things I've always told myself I couldn't because I was too startled, frail, needed if anything should teeter horribly wrong. But I had been there. Out in the darkest of blue waters, without thinking myself out of 'fuck-it-I'm-going'.

For that hour, as I'd alternated between freestyle and breaststroke, I wasn't me anymore. I was *her*. That other self I might have been if I hadn't been chastened into safety and proximity to the shore *just in case*. I was not the jittering 'what-if'-er, who stays between the flags, dons the life vest and never swims alone. I dropped the existential audit and grabbed the moment without double-checking to make sure it was sutured with sufficient guarantees and warranties.

When I stumbled out of that water, pickled with brine and studded with seaweed (nestled, I discovered hours later in the shower, even in my bellybutton), I was wild and wondrous with dehiscence from all I knew. Something was peeling back and I wanted to see what part of me I incarcerated every time I shrank. Who else was I besides the responsible, respectable mother of two who always put her children first?

Suddenly, I wanted to be unfastened, unaccountable, to anything or anyone – only to answer to the flicker in me pulsing, 'Go…go…go.'

'I swam to Wedding Cake Island.'

Frank had stopped cleaning his bike and turned to look at me.

'By yourself?'

I nodded.

'It's like a two-kilometre swim...'

'Bit less, I think.'

'But...but you've done no training... It's...'

'Dangerous?'

'It could be. You shouldn't have gone on your own. It's beyond the nets. What would've happened if you'd gotten a cramp, or you know, encountered a shark?'

'I wouldn't be standing here telling you I swam to Wedding Cake Island.'

'I don't know whether to be proud or cross.'

'You can be both.'

'You should at least have told me you were going to. It was irresponsible.'

'It was.'

He shook his head. 'Why did you do it?'

'I felt like it.'

Frank scrutinised me with wary eyes that weren't sure what they were looking at. 'That's so unlike you.'

And with that, he clinched me back. This temerarious tearaway was not the wife he recognised.

'Maybe not anymore.'

It pulls, has an energetic verve, the sound of the ocean. I hear and smell it long before I see it. The feet quicken, slant in its direction, a visceral heliotropism, like marigolds to the sun. Rock now gives way to view, and in front of us, in a sweep of glory, the sea rolls out. Fiona beckons us close to the headland and points below. There it is – the beach of her childhood, the recovered cove.

Cate collapses on a rock, exhausted. She drains the last dregs of her two-litre bottle of water. Fiona extends her hand to her, and Cate gets to her feet, steadies herself with her two trekking poles. Her blouse is soaked through.

Now all we have to do is make our way down. Kiri leads, clearing brush for us.

As we descend, the air is different. We are entering wetness, lichen-lush rockface where ferns unfurl their sweetness and trees sprout from rocks. My pole goes first. The gravel makes it tricky. We can see it; we can smell it. The beach beckons us. We should be watching our feet, but the cove, the cove.

Kiri and Fiona guide Cate. Kiri holds onto Cate's elbow. But she lets go, and I cannot help my shriek as Cate stumbles. She lands against Kiri, a sea lioness brace, and doesn't fall. My heart clatters like a flock of cockatoos behind my ribcage.

'Magical. Unparalleled. Inspiring.' The marketing brochures had hyped the hell out of Uluru, Ayers Rock in Australia's Red Centre. So when Frank and I took the kids there to celebrate our Australian citizenship, I was expecting enfeebled astonishment given that I'd seen Uluru by sunrise and sunset in a thousand online images already. But the radiance of that ancient rock hit by dawn's first light slipped through the knot of advertising copy, surprising me to tears. Perhaps that's what sacred places do. They wriggle free of incarceration, including our praise of them.

Fiona couldn't have done this place justice. You have to be here.

I am the last to make my way down through the scrub onto the beach. Fiona turns to us, euphoric with open palms. She drops her backpack, falls to her knees, lowers her head in child's pose, and lays her forehead on the sand.

Kiri heaves Cate's little pack from her front, then her heavy one with a huge sigh before pulling off her hiking boots and socks and making her way towards the water, rolling her pants up. Her entire back is stained with sweat. She has borne the heaviest load, without complaint or hesitation.

Yasmin twirls around with her arms outspread.

Liz removes her sunglasses and seems dazed by the intact splendour of this place.

Cate sinks onto the sand and sprawls out as if she's crossed a finish line. She is sopping with perspiration. She removes a small facecloth from her pants pocket and wipes her face down.

I make eye contact with her. I cock my head as if to say, 'Are you okay?'

She nods, squeezes out a smile and gives me two big thumbs up.

'Splendid, luv, never been better,' she croaks.

'Magnificent,' Yasmin says, unclicking the buckles on her backpack and lowering it to the ground. 'Now I must let out the biggest wee.'

'I'll come with ya,' Kiri says. 'Let's walk down to the end of this cove and see what's round that side.' She points right.

They head off in search of a toilet-able spot.

'Need to get these damn boots off. My right foot has been killing me for the past two hours,' Liz says, dumping her pack and collapsing on the sand.

'I need a stiff-as drink,' Cate says. 'Espresso martini, double shot.'

'You'll have to be happy with water. Here, have some of mine,' Fiona offers.

Leaks – they happen. I'm not beyond a white lie. I could pour my flask of Japanese whiskey out. Or I could chug it down when I next go pee. I think of Liz's dark-ringed eyes this morning. I mean, I technically promised it to her.

I am confused by the sudden hum of activity as a collective amnesia kicks in.

What has happened to the sacred silence?

'Where's the cave?' Kiri asks.

Fiona points to the right. 'Tucked in behind those trees, about a hundred metres up. Should we go find it?'

I follow Fiona and Kiri to investigate. We cross the beach and scramble up the rocks. It is a small climb and more of a discovery than an obvious sighting, but once we find it, it is not scary as scary goes. The chamber of rock is a full storey high, bitten by weather and wildlife. There is evidence that other campers have been here recently. Kiri hollers. Her voice echoes back. She goes as far in as she can with a trekking pole, checking for bats.

'Yeah, we'll be right, even if it rains,' Kiri says definitively. 'We should leave our backpacks here.'

Back at the beach, Kiri pronounces, 'First order of business is to make a fire. Anyone wanna volunteer to get us some good, solid fire-making wood?'

'You want to chance it?' Cate asks. 'It's a tinderbox out

here.'

'We'll keep her small, on the sand near the water,' Kiri says.

'We don't need it for cooking – we have a gas stove,' Yasmin says.

'Do we even need to cook?' Liz asks. She is stretched out on the sand, one boot short. Her right foot is extended as she airs out a nasty blister.

'Fire's to keep the animals away,' Kiri says.

'And for our ritual,' Fiona smiles.

'Animals?' I venture.

'Ritual?' Liz asks.

'There could be snakes, feral cassowaries…'

'Cassowaries?'

'World's most dangerous bird, big as an ostrich, claws like a velociraptor – can shred you to pieces,' Cate says, pinching her hands into Edward Scissorhands prongs.

'Old bloke almost bled himself to death in casualty after he was attacked by one,' Kiri adds. 'Messy business. And who do you think had to clean up while we're waiting for cleaning staff at 3am?'

Since Kiri is the one giving out instructions, Cate is not in favour, Liz all a-blister cannot budge, Yasmin is cooking, and Fiona is the birthday bride, just like that, the gathering of firewood falls to me.

'I'll go.'

'Legend, you are. Here, take this for small dry twigs,' Kiri says, handing me a hessian bag from her pack. 'And don't get yourself all splintered up. Do you think I want to spend all afternoon pulling them out?'

I nod but think technically, I should be shaking my head. I take the bag from her.

'Fiona,' Yasmin says seductively, 'why don't you keep her company?' I catch Yasmin's glance. My job is to keep Fiona busy for a while.

Fiona and I make our way along the beach, skirting the edge of the brush. It's generous with fallen detritus. Soon we cannot see the others. I trail behind, watching what she's aiming for. The rockface we've just scaled is striated with bright orange, washed with aubergine, like layers of a cake. Trees grow almost at right angles, squishing out between the rock, determined as leakage.

We collect twigs, snap off small branches with our hands and use our feet to break bigger ones.

'You must miss her,' Fiona says.

A splash of heat rises from my chest. 'We weren't that close. The last time I saw her was more than a year ago...'

'Helen?'

'Sorry, thought you meant CJ. Yes, I do. I miss her terribly.

It's not been the same…'

Fiona places her hand on my upper arm. She squeezes it slightly. It is the touch of a caregiver, a comforting, gentle reassurance, a gesture mothers know by instinct: *Never mind, you don't want friends like that; there's always next time; it's going to be okay; I wish I could make it better.*

'We have to learn to breathe again when the air changes.'

I nod. It is easy to be with others whose suffering is well-felt.

'Can I ask, what's up with Cate?'

Fiona chuckles. 'You get used to her foul mouth. It's just how she was brought up, four older brothers and all.'

'I mean, physically.'

'Oh, right,' Fiona pauses for a moment. 'We haven't got an official diagnosis yet, she's had lots of tests. Hoping it's multiple sclerosis.'

I wait.

'She didn't want to do any investigations, it's been going on for a while, this muscle atrophy. Anyway, I don't feed energy into worst case scenarios, but…'

Fiona picks up another branch.

'I mean, it could be ALS – Motor Neurone Disease.'

'Jesus.'

'She's going to be fine. I have faith.'

'Should she be out here on this long walk?' I seem incapable of minding my own business.

'You try tell Cate she can't do something. She's the most

106

stubbornly brave human being I've ever met. Tough as they come — been an environmental activist all her life. Nothing scares her.'

'Nothing?'

'Maybe one thing but she'll never...' She stops herself, aware she's just trespassed into a confidence. 'Can you hold this end?' she asks as she grabs a large branch and stands on it, pulling the branch towards herself. The branch creaks and cracks.

'Great teamwork,' Fiona says. 'Kiri will be impressed.' I help her tie a yoga strap around the branches so we can carry them easily between us and I can tell she's done talking about Cate.

As we lift the branches, she says, 'I have to thank you, Jo.'

'For?'

'...bringing Liz around this morning. I don't know what you said, but it worked. She really needs to be here, even though she doesn't know it.'

I open my mouth to confess.

I smile weakly. 'It was nothing, really.'

'Oh, bless them,' Fiona says. 'Look what they've done.'

We return after half an hour, jointly lugging the hessian bag which is now impossibly heavy with leaves and twigs, our spare arms laden with broken branches. It takes me a moment to catch up to what is in front of us.

A bright sari-cloth is laid out. Fairy lights, hooked over a piece of driftwood, flicker. A circle of rocks marks a firepit. And then this – a confetti of yellow rose petals.

It all snags Fiona. Her tears unsettle something in me.

Now as a witness to all that has been prepared, carried and laid out in her honour, I am happy for Fiona, I really am, that she has friends who know exactly the kind of woman she is.

'You gonna make the fire?' Kiri asks me, having returned from her own reconnaissance, dragging what looks like half a tree. 'Here's a mother-log, to burn, found her down the other end of the beach. Good spot for a crap.'

'I wouldn't know how to.'

'What's that now? C'mon, it's easy. Build a nest of leaves and twigs. Then we add the bigger logs. One at a time. I'll hand them to you.'

While the others scatter off, some to the cave, some to the water's edge, Kiri stands next to me as I fumble on my hands and knees to make a small pile of kindling. I would like to get it right, but the scrutiny might undo me.

'Pile 'em up, not like that, like this...' she interferes, taking over.

'Matches?' I ask.

Kiri exhales, 'Oh damn myself to hell. I meant to pack them – they were on the counter. I got distracted what with everything going on. You didn't think to bring any?'

'No, sorry.' I feel silly and amiss.

'Lemme go see if Catie's got a lighter on her. Nothing ex about a smoker. Even after they've given up, they always carry one, like they hoping for something else to set on fire. I should give her hell about the smoking, with her condition and all, but we all got our crutches. I shouldn't eat sugar with my diabetes. No-one's all clean, eh?'

'Kiri, what's Cate's...prognosis?'

'Do I look like God?'

'I mean, as a nurse, you probably have some idea...'

'Anything but Motor Neurone Disease is what we're hoping. That would be bad news – that'd give her two to five years max.'

'What causes it?'

'Bad luck? Genetics? Catey's got a bee in her bonnet that it's all the pesticides and plastics and pollution, all the endocrine disruptors in the food chain. Who knows? What difference does it make? Not that she's a whinger. Opposite, really, you never know if she's in grief, gotta be a bloomin' mind-reader with that one.'

She trundles off before I can ask another question. My heart staggers in my chest.

It's not long before Kiri comes back with a big smile, holding up a lighter. 'Sometimes a bad habit can save the day.'

'Bravo, Jo,' Yasmin smiles. 'You have fire-fingers.'

The fire has worked. The big logs have taken and everything is ablaze. This must be how people discover secret talents and desires late in life and wonder what else they don't know about themselves. It's quite disconcerting, really.

A feeling of arrival settles on us now that the fire is crackling. We are all seated in a circle around it – Fiona on the sari, the rest of us on tarpaulins.

'Mango, date, cashew and ginger energy balls,' Yasmin says, passing around a container. Out here, you can't be blasé about nutrition, but my teeth still feel furry after the coconut bark she silently dispensed on the walk. I can't do more sweetness.

'Not for me,' I say apologetically.

'What, you don't like ginger?' Yasmin asks, shocked.

'I need something salty.'

Helen used to give me hell, as if I was making her life a misery. But just like skinny, pale, and overly pretty men are not my flavour of sexy, you cannot bribe me with confectionary. A single scoop of ice cream (salted caramel) or a wedge of sticky date pudding if someone's go-on-have-a-taste-pushy is as much as I can take.

Now throw me a pickled onion or a stuffed olive and we can talk. A roasted artichoke with garlic and lemon dressing, and I'm all yours. Anchovy-anything. Teriyaki this or that.

I pull out a packet of Kettle Fried chips from my backpack. I don't care if it's tacky. These are my favourite. Comfort food was made for just such uncomfortable places. I salivate at the mere whiff of salt and vinegar, the way the body lubricates for pleasure.

Fiona laughs. 'Jo, I took you for a food connoisseur. I thought chips would be beneath you.'

'I am a complete chip slut,' I confess.

'Oi, over here,' Cate says, dipping her hand in and pulling out a bouquet of crispy petals. 'I frigging love these.' She dangles the packet at Liz.

Liz shakes her head. 'I'm still fasting.'

'Liz has that thing – you know, the thing I don't have,' Kiri says.

'Her own teeth, darlin'?' Cate cackles.

'Discipline, you gammy goose.' But then, to my shock, Kiri jiggles dentures for all of us to see.

'Yep, all my teeth fell out after Tiffany was born. If that weren't an omen, then I dunno, hey. Baby just sucks all the calcium out of your system.'

Of all the unkindnesses motherhood delivers, this surely has to rate as one of the most heinous. Birth exacts its toll; it always sneaks off with something – perfect bladder control, a vice-grip vagina, belly strength, un-stretchmarked skin. But in the end – aren't these all vanities?

I birthed both my children with conscious amnesia, purposely not remembering my friend Barry's mother in her wheelchair, the way her body slumped to the side, and how no-one spoke about the postpartum stroke she'd had after her labour with him. Or my mother's first cousin, Henrietta, who died in childbirth. It's an impulse that becomes a bad habit, to bemoan the physical humiliations of pregnancy and birth when tragedy hovers inches away. Still, am I ever grateful I survived childbirth with all my teeth.

'It's the flamingo effect,' Cate mutters. 'You know baby flamingos are born grey?'

'If I could be any animal, I would pick a flamingo, so radiant and so full of pinkness. Where does such beauty come from?' Yasmin asks.

'Flamingo juice. The mothers feed their babies bright pink juice which they gargle up in their throats and regurgitate into their babies' mouths.' I am astonished I remember that.

'Well, that's Nature for you,' Yasmin says brightly. 'We can't change what Nature intended. Mothers have to sacrifice for the sake of the children.'

'Now see, that actually makes me feel ill,' Liz says. 'Breastfeeding is gross enough.'

'It's a bird thing, luv,' Cate says. 'How else you going to get food and bring it back to the nest? Now Jo here seems to know quite a lot about the habits and habitat of flamingos. How's that?'

'An overdose of *Planet Earth*. My head is full of bizarre animal facts.'

I'm not trying to impress Cate. But she eyes me side-on, as if she's reassessing the kind of woman I am.

'By the end of breeding season, the females are bedraggled and bleached, sucked dry. Why motherhood has to be such a fuckery, is a mystery. You poor suckers, you should have thought about that before you bred.'

'You don't have kids?' I ask Cate.

'Not me,' she says.

Fiona turns to her. 'Really, Catey? Is that the truth?'

'Giving birth doesn't make you a mother. Be a love and pass those chips back here?'

I hand the packet over. She dives back in.

Miscarriage? Stillbirth? I can't picture her as a surrogate.

Finally, my precious salt and vinegar chips make their way back to me. I don't think too hard about the limitations of antiseptic gel. I finally dip my hand in.

Nothing but a few crumbs remain. I would lick my fingers but that seems kind of desperate. I just wipe them on my hiking pants.

'Ooh, sorry, Jo. We didn't leave you any.' Yasmin is mortified.

Cate cackles, 'Not much fun being the mother flamingo, eh?'

6

Vitamin P

'You said you're fasting or maybe I didn't hear right?' Yasmin turns to Liz, genuinely concerned.

'I only eat every few days.'

'Why?'

'Intermittent fasting.'

'Not my place to comment on another woman's body but you look like you could do with a few kilos making their way over to you,' Cate says.

Liz sighs, a woman beyond justifying her choices or her body.

'I'm hardly doing it for my weight. Fasting has health

benefits. It lowers blood pressure, cholesterol, even reverses diabetes.'

'Like in Ramadan,' Yasmin nods. 'Very good for you.'

'You gotta be careful with that. We get a run of folk in emergency with kidney stones during Ramadan,' Kiri says, shaking her head. 'Have to watch your fluids.'

'With intermittent fasting, you can drink – water, herbal tea, black coffee,' Liz says.

'First rule is stay hydrated,' Kiri nods.

'In the West, we all overeat to excess,' Liz continues. 'We could all survive on so much less.'

'Righty-oh and all that jazz, but can you suggest a single good reason to wake up if there isn't a custard slice to get you out of bed and some fried lamb chops at the end of the day with that delish piece of fat all crisped up on the barbie?' Kiri asks. 'Specially if Yasmin's on kitchen duty.'

'Or sour figs and pepper crusted goat's cheese on fresh bread,' Yasmin smiles, cradling her belly.

'Baked potatoes with butter,' Cate swoons. 'Garlic bread and mushroom risotto…'

Liz looks fatigued by these descriptions. 'I can take or leave food. Now a gin martini…that could swing things.' She swivels her head to give me a look-nudge. I don't know how much longer I can stall her.

'Never did learn to say no to food,' Kiri sighs. 'Growing up, if you got seconds, you knew you were in mum's good books. She always saved extras for her favourites.' Her chuckle peters out. 'You see, this,' she says, gesturing to her huge belly, 'is how you know your mother loved ya.'

Yasmin nods. 'Cooking is *I love you* and eating is *I love you too.*'

Helen would lap that up, Yasmin's pithy summation.

Regret is a midlife station. You need a gradient to look back from. From there, you notice moments you'd erase if you had a second chance at them. At our reunion seven years ago, I refused all of Helen's scrumptious offerings, in the spasms of my desperate age-phobic crisis when I imagined saying 'no' to everything delectable was a recipe for happiness. How many times did I say, *'Not for me,' 'Watching my figure,' 'Salad, not chips'*?

I see now where X marks the spot – precisely where to place the pin on the board. That's where my relationship with Helen started to fray, when we lost our language – because despite what Dr Gary Chapman claims in *The Five Love Languages*, the book Helen and I read together when we were trying to make sense of our husbands' failures in the gift-buying department, there are actually *six*. And with all due respect, what does a Baptist pastor know about the orgasmic properties of food?

Liz removes a flask from her backpack and pours herself a small mug of a steaming liquid. 'Anyone for some green tea?'

'All yours,' Kiri says. 'Knock yourself out.'

'Hey, Zilly, how about some honey with that?' Fiona asks.

Liz seems to wince at the nickname she probably last heard when she was in pigtails.

She shakes her head. Then, 'Actually…maybe just a spoon after that long walk…'

'Excuse me, everyone, this is a special moment. Let me savour it.' Fiona closes her eyes and takes it in before scrambling to find a plastic bottle with her honey.

'Let's see what all this fuss is about,' Liz says.

We all watch as Liz mixes a spoonful of honey into her tea. She sips it and then adds another spoon.

'Fiona and Cate's honey is the moon and the stars in your mouth, isn't that so?' Yasmin encourages.

'I wouldn't mind a taste,' I say. It would be rude not to and besides, my chips are all gone.

Fiona dishes up a spoon of clear amber goop onto a teaspoon. It is as Yasmin conjured – a carnival of wind and blossoms and nectar on the tongue.

'Can you taste the Grevillea? The spider flower?'

I close my eyes. Something tangier hangs in the undernotes.

'Eucalyptus?' I ask.

Fiona nods excitedly.

'Don't know how you can tell one honey from the next,' Liz says, bemused.

'It's like wine,' Yasmin explains. 'You can detect the hierarchy of flavours, the undernotes.'

'Are you still such a fabulous cook?' Fiona asks me. 'I've

never forgotten that incredible feast you and Helen made for us all those years ago. I still remember those butternut ricotta pancakes. Nutmeg was the secret ingredient, right?'

'How do you remember all that? I can't even remember where I parked my car when I go to the mall.'

'It was unforgettable, wasn't it, Liz?'

'There was an excess of food,' Liz concedes. 'And drinking. We had some good red wine that night, as I recall.'

'I don't spend much time in the kitchen anymore,' I venture.

'What a pity,' Fiona says. 'I thought you and Yasmin would hit it off. She's a goddess in the kitchen. So were you.'

'Aaai, Fiona, stop with all that applause,' Yasmin chides. 'You're setting the table so high. Food must take you by surprise.'

But Yasmin reaches out for my hand, like we're a team or something now.

As Fiona speaks, it is as if she's describing someone other than me. It's dislocating in the way of coming across an old photograph and thinking, 'Who is that?' before realising, 'Oh, that was me.' *Was*. Not *is*. Maybe this is what it means to lose yourself, to become bewildered by the way others understand who you are. To see a reflection in the mirror and to have questions, not answers, for the person you see there.

'Why don't you cook anymore?' Fiona asks me.

'It's too boring to discuss.'

Yasmin turns to me and says, 'I am interested to hear why someone would give up a God-given talent.'

'I don't know about that...'

'What made you stop?'

It's a story of loss, like any other, an ordinary everyday break-up. I opened my eyes one morning and felt it – the chronic fatigue, the depletion of my life force, which I'd diverted for decades into answering the question: 'What will I cook for dinner?' On that day, I couldn't pull myself out of bed. The apparently minor decision had sapped my desire for whatever lay ahead in the hours to come.

For sixteen years, I'd mentally calculate – even before my morning wee: *Can't rehash Wednesday's black bean Mexican. Do we have the right ingredients for gluten-free macaroni cheese? Can I fit a quick grocery shop in before my 4pm in the city? When will I have a free hour to cook?*

It was a ledger of Nothing to Be Proud Of, the inventory of hours I'd squandered into the grinding labour of discerning the filament of overlap amongst three diverse diets. No fish for Aaron, gluten-free vegetarian for Jamie and Frank's meat and potatoes. Don't even ask about my own preferences. I couldn't tell you what they were.

'Anything you have to do, day in, day out, relentlessly, without thanks for twenty years, can kill your passion,' I say.

'It is a life's job to feed a family,' Yasmin agrees.

'And you had four – plus Rajit to feed,' Fiona consoles.

'Four kids?' I don't imagine Liz means to clutch her arm

to her chest in dismay.

Yasmin smiles and nods slowly, as if she's not sure she indeed has all those offspring and is mentally counting them.

'Whose idea were all those kids?' Cate asks.

'Rajit wanted a big family.'

'And you, luv?' Cate asks.

Yasmin shrugs. 'I don't know. It is many mouths to feed, many bodies and hearts and souls to be a caretaker for. I am very tired now.' She wipes her forehead with the back of her hand.

'We had six for a time when we were fostering,' Kiri says. 'I'd cook up a one-pot-monster. Chuck it all in, the meat, the veggies, and you can feed as many mouths as turn up to the table.'

'You fostered three at once?' Fiona asks.

'However many needed it,' Kiri shrugs. 'It's as easy to feed six mouths as it is to feed three.'

'Yes, that I find is true,' Yasmin says. 'I'm not sorry for a big family. It has been my classroom since I never did get to go to university. I learned to cook for many people – it was good practice for my Welcome Feasts. If it's all gone, you know you made happiness on the table. If you have leftovers, that's tomorrow's good fortune.'

'What are your Welcome Feasts?' I ask.

'For new immigrants, Welcome to Australia.'

'Every month, Yasmin cooks a vegetarian banquet and opens her home to anyone who wants to come,' Fiona says.

'You're looking at the Mother Theresa of cuisine.'

'No,' Yasmin swats away the compliment, but the tremble of a smile teases her lips. 'Last month we had eleven countries in my house including Syria, Iran, Pakistan, Nepal, and for the first time, Mongolia. I had to look on the world map to find it.'

'You'd have to *tranquilise* me before I'd open my home to a troupe of strangers,' Liz says, looking in my direction again. I am starting to feel tormented by my own generosity.

'You're only strangers until you eat a meal together. Only one thing fixes homesickness, and that is food.'

Sunlight floods my chest. I want to reach out now for Yasmin's hand.

'What do you charge?' Liz asks.

'Charge for what?'

'For a ticket or an entry fee, or whatever you call it, to your feasts?'

'Nothing,' Yasmin seems confused by the question.

'So who funds these events?' Liz asks.

'I do. From my catering business, I use a percentage of my profits. I also know how and where to buy cheap and in bulk, and sometimes I get donations from grocery stores. I must find more sponsors. But that takes lots of time, and I am rich with everything except hours.'

'Why don't you charge people?' Liz is bewildered.

'It is a welcome party, not a business.' Something delightful happens to Yasmin's left eyebrow. It hikes up into an upside-down V, a quizzical what-don't-you-get-about-this stretch that draws my eye to the scar beneath her eye.

'You could easily monetise them,' Liz says.

'I will never charge for a welcome,' Yasmin laughs.

'You're one of those pay-it-forward types, then?'

Yasmin shrugs. 'I'm a love-to-cook type. What do you love to eat, Liz?'

'Love to eat?' It's almost like she doesn't understand the question.

'Yes, what arrives with great joy when you put it in your mouth? What makes you close your eyes, feel its music, taste its song?'

'Food is fuel, functional to me. I go for protein, fibre and greens. If I can put it in a smoothie and down it in one go, that's me sorted out for the day.'

'Protein, fibre and greens,' Yasmin repeats sadly. 'These are words with no food soul.' Yasmin's look is one of genuine pain. 'We must get you Vitamin P.'

'I didn't know there was a Vitamin P.' Liz sips her green tea.

'Pleasure. The body makes some special chemical – it's got a long name and I can't pronounce it – when we swallow protein and fat. Inside the brain, it causes pleasure, and the body sucks up more goodness from the food. This is true. Pleasure is good for digestion, isn't that right, Kiri?'

'Pleasure is good, full stop,' Kiri snorts.

'Food isn't what gives me pleasure,' Liz says.

'What then?' Kiri asks.

'A good night's sleep. A great haircut with a free manicure thrown in. *Japanese whiskey.*' Liz is starting to terrify me. It was just a casual murmured exchange. What kind of pressure would she exert if she had a signed contract?

'My problem is that all my pleasures are forbidden,' Kiri sighs.

'What is forbidden in pleasure?' Yasmin asks. 'It's not just what we eat – it's when, and most importantly, how. We can't eat like a thief, guilty, quickly, hiding. We must eat slowly so we can feel the crunch, taste the sticky, nutty, sweet, salty, sour, umami in our mouths. You must let your body relish everything, crispy wings of fried chicken, dark cherry chocolate, butter on fresh bread.'

I wipe my mouth. I hope I am not actually drooling. As she speaks, Yasmin is conjuring, turning over the soil of an untended garden inside me, a place where delight and food flower together. It's so rare – to meet a woman who has reached this place of body-friendship, intoxication with her own flesh, adoration of the skin she's draped in. Most of us are in an endless negotiated tolerance with our bodies, refusing to make eye contact in the mirror, grasping at a catch-me-if-you-can ghost of beauty, never embracing the beauty already here.

In the year before Helen left, I was slowly divorcing food, loving everything less, suspicious of taste-inspired joy. Throughout my forties, I treated food like a terrorist.

Incriminated deliciousness. Bought into abstention as a marker of maturity. I said 'no' to most things I wanted to guzzle. I criminalised the carb, demonised the dressing, banned the brioche. I became an expert at salivating silently as I watched Frank and the kids order whatever they felt like with *extra chips, creamy pasta, fried not grilled*. Every time someone used a flattering word like 'willpower' or 'self-control', I thought, that's me, a person who can say no. But one day I realised I'd been congratulating myself for not having, not celebrating, for my aptitude to abnegate desire.

Then, as soon as my periods stopped, without changing anything in my diet or lifestyle, five kilograms climbed on board like I was the last bus of the night. I cut more things out, all sugar (including, godforgiveme, fruit), alcohol (even the occasional glass of wine), carbs (as well as the high-fibre kind). I went vegan for a month. Paleo for a time. Keto. Low FODMAP. I abstained then binged. Each attempt just brought with it more frustration. Gas. Bloating. Clothes I couldn't wear anymore. I stopped thinking about my plate as a place of pleasure and wondered what havoc its contents would wreak with my hormones, gut and cholesterol, as if food was a horde of teenagers without parental supervision.

There were occasional moments when it slipped my mind, when I ate with gusto, deliriously undaunted by the consequences. The last time I did that...? Oh, yes. I remember now.

After Robbie Williams had sung his last song of the show, 'Angels', I was drenched from dancing, my heart skittering. CJ and I had gone to a bar where we'd ordered pink gin cocktails and shared the seafood platter with chips.

She doused the fried chips in salt, picked one up in each hand, dipped one in tomato sauce, one in garlic aioli. 'Last meal on earth. Which one do you go for?'

'No brainer.' I pointed at the garlic aioli. 'Garlic is one of the gifts of the gods.'

She brought it to my mouth as she ate the other chip.

'Tomato sauce all the way to the end for me,' she declared.

'Full of preservatives. And so tacky.'

'Well, you know me,' she laughed. 'I'm full of preservatives and nothing if not tacky. You know KFC is my favourite treat in the whole damn world. Would be my last meal. Besides, preservatives are good for the organs, keeps them in good nick for when I donate them all.'

'You're an organ donor?'

'Yep, want every bit of me to be repurposed and reused.'

I called the waitress over and asked her to bring us half a lemon. When it arrived, I squeezed it over the chips. 'Taste this.'

'Oh my god, yes,' she bellowed.

'Salt and lemon, just fancy salt and vinegar. My last meal on death row would be a huge plate of fries.'

'Do you reckon you could enjoy it if you knew it was your last meal?' she asked.

'I'd slow right down and appreciate every bite. I think there's something to be said for knowing,' I said.

'Fuck that. I'd rather not see it coming.'

Now Yasmin removes another small container from her bag and passes it straight to me.

'Olives stuffed with preserved lemon.'

I couldn't adore her more than I do in this moment. I put my grimy fingers in and try to grab one of the thick oily bulbs the size of small plums, but they dodge my grasp like fish underwater. Yasmin hands me a toothpick.

'You thought of everything,' I gush.

'Not too many, or you will be too thirsty.'

It could be that we're out in the middle of nowhere with limited food options, or that I haven't eaten anything salty all day, but this really may be one of the most ridiculously delicious combinations I've ever eaten. I close my eyes and chew slowly. The bite of the lemon peel inside the olive flesh is a match.

They are soulmates. I could make a dish with these olives, and I know just the ingredient I'd pair it with.

Eggplant. Chubby. Sleek. Silky. Moist. A perfect purple.

Frank can't eat it. It makes his tongue blister. I stopped buying or cooking it years ago. I'd never order it off a menu – that would be selfish. We select dishes we know the other one will eat. He orders lamb because I don't like beef. I always swap prawns with calamari – he finds the feelers creepy.

There's something to be said for always taking someone else's needs into account, but when our own desires blur, this couple thing has gone too far. In banishing our pleasures for the sake of another, we forget what we once loved. This unspoken rule of ongoing commitment means I've given up anchovies, oysters, cabbage, beetroot and mushrooms for as long as I've been married to Frank, unless I eat by myself.

Alone at Penny's place, eggplant resurfaced like a long-lost lust. On my next visit to the organic market, I'd stocked my basket full of them. Back at the stove, I cooked as if my time with eggplant was running out.

With toasted sesame oil. In a green curry. Deep fried with garlic and lemon. Braised alongside a salsa verde. Skewered and smoked. Doused in Tandoori paste. Sautéed in a spicy miso glaze. Snug and soft between mozzarella cheese and tomatoes in a *melanzana parmigiana*.

I gave myself to eggplant like a sub to a dominatrix. I was the prodigal daughter returned to the table. I binged. I feasted.

I slowly felt myself coming back to eating with elation.

In every celebratory dish, I rewrote the hieroglyphics of almost forty years of various versions of dieting. What did I have to show for it? Was I a better or happier person when I was a size 10? From when she was a little mite, I'd urged Jamie to eat whatever she felt like, whenever she wanted. But it had to be gross hypocrisy to pride myself on her absence of an eating disorder when I couldn't be sure that I, in fact, didn't have one.

Sienna, Aaron's girlfriend, is a sales rep for a meal replacement programme she's been trying to sell me for the past eight months. When I get back home, I'm going to take her aside and tell her, 'I'm happy with my body just as it is.' I will not take a nineteen-year-old's look of disbelief personally. I will look her in the eye and say, 'Sweetheart, someday, if you're lucky to still have both your boobs and your uterus, you won't want to waste another moment not loving whatever is left of your body. You'll stop with the, "Why can't you be more like Julia Roberts? You can't wear that. Cover up that cellulite." When you get to my age, you'll realise no-one is looking at you, except you. Just make sure that person is not a self-critical bitch.'

In Yasmin's presence, my body wants to eat and dance and jangle.

I turn to her and say, 'You remind me of my best friend, Helen. She would adore you.'

7

Old Enough to Die

I sigh and exhale, opening my arms wide to the sun; and as I do, I inadvertently snag Cate's jumper, draped over her shoulders, revealing a tattoo. I blink. I look again.

'What's that say?' I ask, leaning over to get a closer look.

'DNFR. Do Not Fucking Resuscitate.'

'That's a waste of a tattoo,' Liz says. 'You could wear a Medical ID Alert Bracelet. They make pretty stylish ones these days.' She dangles her arm to reveal a leather bracelet with a silver disc.

Cate arches her neck to look over her shoulder. 'Had that one done when I was in my twenties after my pop was resuscitated after a stroke. Took him five months to finally let go. That's how long he was brain dead and hooked to machines. It was a clusterfuck of everyone's time and money. And that's exactly what he'd have said. No way he'd have wanted to linger like that. He should have had a living will. This is mine. Can't mistake my dying wishes, can you?'

'The "F" in there might throw people off,' Kiri says. 'Folks might think it's Do Not *Forget* to Resuscitate and then you'll have served yourself a backhander. Why you gotta swear even on your tattoo, I'll never understand.'

'Profanity is our birthright, precisely because it's so fucking unladylike,' Cate chortles.

'I've just signed a living will,' I say.

I'd made sure to include one when Frank and I finally got our wills done last year, just before we headed overseas, leaving the kids alone for a month. I'd nagged for years, but he kept putting off the grisly task of putting in writing how our 'assets' and 'estate' should be dealt with and appointing an executor. As it turns out, Frank is the squeamish and superstitious of the two of us.

We even assembled a 'death file' with details of passwords, insurance, banking, and power of attorney for the kids. 'This feels eerie and ominous,' he'd shuddered.

I'd explained to Jamie that it was necessary, just in case both of us…

'What? Die in a car accident or an airplane crash? Why are you making me even think about these things?'

'It's in the top drawer in Dad's…' I tried, but Jamie plugged her fingers in her ears and said, 'You're being morbid. Nothing's going to happen to you and Dad.'

Aaron said, 'Just make sure Jamie knows what to do.'

Frank tried to talk me out of the living will.

'People recover from comas, years later. Did you hear of that case where…?' Frank had begun.

'Switch everything off. For goodness sake, I'm old enough to die.'

Yasmin offers me another olive. 'Me, I've stopped going for all those annual screenings: bowels, breasts, uterus, ovaries, cholesterol, skin, heart. Where does it end?' she sighs.

I too have routine-check-up-fatigue. All it's ever taken is one horror story recanted casually over dinner conversation about so-and-so, who 'if only she'd gone for her yearly mammogram' wouldn't be facing her final days, to instigate a flurry of personal investigations, tubes and radiation to see what's brewing silently inside. We all know what's cooking there. Finally, it's just our demise. Sooner or later.

I have always rationalized this hyper-vigilance as the responsible thing to do so I could extend any lease of time for the sake of my kids. But when I turned fifty, I felt reckless with relief that it could never be said of me, 'Poor thing, she died so young.' At worst, the mourners could sob, 'She died middle-aged.'

'Every single day is borrowed time. It's all bonus material,' Cate says.

'I reckon you got heaps more life left in ya,' Kiri says.

'Frida Kahlo died at forty-seven,' Cate says.

'Princess Diana was only thirty-six,' Fiona exhales.

'Don't myself get the obsession with living as long as you can. Some of us have outstayed our welcome,' Kiri says, 'and some of us under-stayed...'

'We have to live so that if we died right now, we would die happy,' Cate says.

'Right now?' Fiona asks.

'Now. I mean, that's the test, right?'

'No-one's going to die right now,' Fiona says.

'That's the fun part of being human – you just never know,' Cate winks.

'Let's wait for a proper diagnosis,' Fiona says. 'It could be nothing,' she says to the rest of us. 'Without a proper diagnosis, it's all speculative.' She is invested, managing the situation. This is what friendship is – a collusion with hope, a buttress against a tide that's coming for us, no matter what.

'Long as I'm not a millstone to anyone,' Cate says.

'You still have outstanding business...' Fiona says softly.

'Reckon I've ticked all the boxes, and then a few extras.'

'You have had a soap opera for a life,' Yasmin says.

'Trouble has had a longstanding crush on me.'

Fiona turns to me and says, 'Cate spearheaded an environmental activist group. They shut down a coalmine.'

'She spent four nights in jail,' Yasmin says.

'What about that pub fight?' Kiri adds. 'Some fella was sexually harassing a woman and she just had to stop him.'

'Then she spent a year in a Buddhist monastery in Tibet,' Fiona says.

'Fuck off, you lot. Speaking like I'm already dead. I'm in the room, you know.' But Cate is lapping it up, her living obituary.

I glance around at the faces of these women, and much as I've watched Yasmin pee, been perspired on by Kiri, collected firewood with Fiona, made false promises to Liz and had all my salt and vinegar chips scoffed by Cate, I would not die happy if I died now.

I've not done anything close to 'it all'.

While Cate was having that huge un-flamingo-like life, I was making emotional flamingo juice, in overcrowded auditoriums while Jamie performed in school soirees and in child psychologist's waiting rooms to get Aaron tested for ADHD.

I haven't tasted Helen's Rendang, seen Aurora Borealis or the Galapagos Islands, read all the classics or held a grandchild. I probably won't get to a swingers' party, dangle from a trapeze or walk the red carpet, but there is still so much I want to do with my life. I can learn to surf, get another dog, start a charity for pregnant girls in Rwanda. I could travel to southwest China like CJ had planned.

'This will surely be my last walk after taking it all for granted, hiking, sailing, paragliding…' Cate sniffs. 'Yeah, it's brill to be here with you all.'

'You don't know that, Catey,' Fiona soothes. 'Let's wait and see, and take it week by week, you know.'

Cate cocks her head and gives Fiona a look through half-closed eyes. It is the gaze a parent might give a child, as experience shields innocence, as knowing bows to naivete, a gentle, *have-it-your-way*. 'Just don't get too attached to the idea of me getting old.'

'You'll make an eccentric old woman,' Yasmin says.

'Like the ones in all the fairytales that scare the children?' Cate snorts.

'I am looking forward to being an elder with you, with our white hair and wrinkles, grandchildren and lots of knitting and baking.'

Liz grimaces. 'Spare me, please. I'll take a dignified exit long before decrepitude sets in. Geriatric diapers are not part of my fantasy.'

'I'm with you,' Cate says. 'And never did understand the obsession with living forever. At some point, you just want the exit.'

'Ever heard of the Greek myth of Tithonus, the immortal?' I ask. 'Tennyson wrote a poem about him.'

'Tell us,' Yasmin prods.

'When he realized his choices didn't matter – nothing he could do would have fatal consequence, he begged the gods to make him human. There's a line in Tennyson's poem, "happy men who have the power to die." What gives our lives meaning is knowing we don't have forever.'

We think we don't need death. But we do.

I'd arrived at the mall with my list of groceries on the back of an envelope. I checked Facebook as I made my way from the parking lot to the shopping level. There was a message request from Jorja.

The fact that I had to think, *Who?*, coupled with her words, 'I'm CJ's daughter, please call me urgently,' gave me a twitch in the gut. It had been just over a year since I'd last seen CJ. I hadn't responded to her last text, the one she'd sent the day after the concert. I hadn't known how to respond.

It seemed important for me to find somewhere to sit down. I made my way outside to a coffee shop and found a concrete bench. A small foot fountain splashed water on the black marble tiles. It was a decent people-watching spot. The square jostled with ordinary activity. Maybe Jorja was planning a birthday celebration for her mum. I was conscious that there was something frantic about my calm. That I was in the bargaining stage of grief before I even knew what I was mourning.

I sat and waited. I watched people go about their business. I breathed in the sweet ordinariness of this scene.

It was a two-minute phone call.

It doesn't take long to tell someone, 'My mum was killed in a motorbike accident last week.'

The information entered me through a synapse. I could feel my brain working, the fizz and sizzle of wires making connections in the squishy folds of my brain tissue.

I sat on that bench in the sun. My grocery list was still in my hand: *toilet paper carrots bread milk chicken breast green apples cat food*. The words I'd written with my purple pen bled from the clutch of my sweaty hand.

I felt something shaking in my ribcage, as if someone was rattling bars to loosen it from its hinges.

A small word fell out of me. 'No, no, no, no, no. Oh Jorja, what happened?'

Jorja seemed ready for this question. 'She was on Kito's motorbike. Just going out to get some beer and KFC. A car went through a red light.'

Her words were small blasts of detail, like subliminal frames on a reel of film. The motorbike. The light changing. A speeding car. CJ smacking the windscreen.

'She died instantly. She didn't suffer,' Jorja added.

'And Kito?'

'He was at home watching the footy when it happened.'

Her voice had sounded faraway, like she was rehearsing a script.

'Jorja…' A sob burst from my throat. 'I'm so sorry…I'm so very sorry…when's the funeral?'

'It was yesterday.'

'I missed it?'

'I'm sorry. I'm only going through her phone today…'

'That's okay. We hadn't been in contact for a while, your mum and I…'

CJ had texted me the day after Robbie Williams. *I'd do that again. Salt and lemon…mmm, can still taste it on my fingers.* I'd looked at that text for a long time. I hadn't been able to come up with the right words.

'If there's anyone else you think needs to know, could you contact them for me?' Jorja asked.

'Of course, I'll call Helen. She's in America,' I said numbly. 'And if there's anything, anything you need, please keep my number and reach out to me. How are…your brother and sister?'

'Liam flew back from London for the funeral, but he's going back tomorrow. And Scarlett…well, she's pretty cut up.'

'How old is she now?'

'Just turned fifteen last month. But…she's had a tough year, other issues going on…' She slid into a silence that had many secret doorways.

'I'm so sorry.' I wish I had left it at that, but somehow

it didn't seem right to end the conversation there without knowing anything more about this brave young woman going through her deceased mother's phone and making these impossible phone calls. And before I could stop myself, out tumbled, 'So are you at university? Are you taking a gap year?'

'Um…I'm studying to be a hairdresser. At a community college.'

'That's so sensible. People are always looking for a good hairdresser…' I clutched my hand over my mouth lest anything more ludicrous flop out of it.

'…anyway, I better go now.'

'Yes, of course. And…Jorja, were you able to donate any of her organs?'

There was silence on the other end of the phone.

'What do you mean? My mum wasn't an organ donor.'

After we'd said goodbye, I'd sat motionless as the idea of CJ dying tried to pry its way through the bottleneck of my throat. Disbelief rustled in my veins. Had CJ not told anyone but me about her organs? What about all the repurposing and reusing she had planned for her bits? Or was she just spinning me a line? I'd never know.

I could barely swallow. I'd called Frank just to have

someone to tell.

'That's terrible,' he'd consoled. He had hardly known CJ. It didn't feel enough.

I needed someone to wail up against. I checked the world clock on my iPhone. It was 2am in Santa Monica. I couldn't call Helen now.

And then I stood up and with tears spilling down my cheeks, I'd gone and done my grocery shopping.

I catch Cate's eye but can't read her expression.

'The end is coming alright, not just for each of us, but for the earth,' she says as she fumbles for her water bottle. She's down to the dregs and her hands tremble as she holds it. 'What the fuck difference does it make what each of us want individually?'

'It matters more than ever,' Fiona says, handing her water bottle to Cate.

'How we doing with the water situation? Let's see what's left so we don't run out,' Kiri says. 'I still got a litre and a bit.'

'I've finished mine, sorry. The heat's really hit me…' Cate says.

'I have finished half,' Yasmin says. 'We need a little for cooking, not much.'

I pull out my bottles. I've drunk more than I thought, I'm down to one litre.

'We'll have enough,' Fiona says. 'We just have to be careful.'

'See this,' Cate says, pointing to the water bottles in front of us. 'It's the fractal of the whole.'

'What do you mean, Catey?' Yasmin asks.

'Well, we got, what…five litres of water left among six adults. We're running out. It's a limited resource.'

'Only coz we couldn't carry more,' Kiri says.

'I'm talking about everything – phosphorus, oil, iron, even oxygen, the big picture. Never mind that we're losing species every day. If the bees and other pollinating insects get wiped out, how're we going to produce enough food to feed this fucking overpopulated planet? We're stumbling towards the sixth mass extinction. It's only a matter of time.'

The mood has darkened around us just as the afternoon sun starts to dwindle, the day's handover to the night shift. The day is a husk.

'Tell us the good news,' Liz says.

'There is good news,' Cate smiles. 'But I don't reckon you want to hear it.'

'I want to hear it,' Fiona says.

'Me too,' Yasmin says.

I nod. Who would say no to good news?

Cate gets a sly look on her face. 'Humans will be wiped out, sooner rather than later.'

'That's the good news?' Kiri says irritably.

'We won't survive, but the earth will. She doesn't need us. And once we're gone, some slimy little oceanic creature will evolve and mate with the last remaining cockroaches, and a new order will come to be. And they'll all live happily ever after, without us.'

'I don't think it will come to that,' Fiona sighs. 'We've got brilliant young minds working on solutions to all our problems. It's going to be okay.' She gets up to add another log to the fire, and the Jenga tower of kindling and branches I so carefully stacked tumbles, setting off a cascade of sparks.

'Remind me to call you when I'm having a bad day,' Kiri grumbles. 'Bloomin' doom and gloom, down the tubes we go. The only thing left to do is eat. Yasmin, make your magic, woman.'

8

Once a Food Witch

Yasmin asks if I brought the leek, as if it were the key to the kingdom.

'I brought *a* leek,' I say, unsure if there is a difference between 'a leek' and 'the leek.'

This news delights her. 'Good, good, Jo,' she smiles. 'The leek makes all the difference.'

I scramble in my backpack to find it. I have a fondness for leeks, the more graceful sister of the onion. For one thing, it doesn't make you cry when you handle it. It works the same bass note magic as an onion – for soups, stews, roasts and other dishes – but it oozes sweetness, not pungency. Built like the trunk of a tree, with concentric folds, skins within skins, and a fuzz of leeky hairs, it is a quiet achiever, seldom the hero on a plate, often undetectable and underrated, softening the ambience for other extrovert ingredients to step into the spotlight and take all the credit.

'We must cook before it gets too dark,' Yasmin says.

We are seated around the fire on the sand, the water lapping a hundred metres away, and Yasmin in a few deft moves marvels the space into a makeshift kitchen. From her backpack, she removes a dishtowel and a thin plastic cutting board. Next, she unsheathes a maroon velvet pouch, tied with a silk ribbon. She gives it a tug; the pouch falls opens as if to the favourite passage in a book and there, lined up in perfect readiness, are three chef's knives, with mother-of-pearl handles, nestling from smallest to largest.

'My lovelies,' Yasmin says, touching each one with her fingertips. 'Can we prepare to cook the leek? Fiona, our cooker?'

Fiona rummages and brings out a small gas cooker from her bag and a frying pan which she perches on top.

'We need some boiling water,' Yasmin says.

'Oi, I carried the billy,' Kiri says. She fishes in her pack and hauls out a battered old billycan.

'And you brought the almonds?' Yasmin asks.

'Give us a sec,' Kiri says, delving into the bowels of her backpack. 'Can't see a damn thing in here.' She pulls on a head torch and scratches around again, finally emerging with a packet of almonds. 'Hiding right at the bottom, tricky bastards.'

'Now, we need pistachios,' Yasmin says.

'I got those,' Cate says. She fishes in her small daypack and pulls out a packet of shelled pistachios. 'And didn't you want these carrots?'

'Yes, carrots, lovely. Anyone have the golden raisins?'

No-one answers.

'I think we asked Liz,' Fiona says.

Liz is lying some metres away, head perched on her backpack, lost in a gaze towards the ocean. 'Asked me what?'

'To get golden raisins. Did you get a chance?'

Liz looks wearied even by the question. 'No, sorry. I've never even heard of golden raisins. I thought raisins were all brown.'

'No worries, we will ask the cranberries to carry the story of the golden raisins into the dish,' Yasmin smiles.

Yasmin moves like a dancer, removing items from her backpack and setting them down on the dishtowel. A Tupperware of what looks like cooked brown rice. A ziplock bag of cranberries. A tiny bottle of olive oil, one of orange blossom water, a pinch of pink Himalayan salt. Tiny packets of spices. I recognise the cardamom, cinnamon and saffron. She pulls out the smallest chopping knife from the velvet pouch and picks up an orange, brings it to her nose and sniffs it. She then holds the blade of the knife to the orange's navel, the spot from which it was plucked from its tree and sings the scalpel through the flesh. The blade is so sharp, her motions so unwavering, that it looks as if the peel falls from the fruit by its own volition, an accession, a woman unveiling for her secret lover, not a hint of force or pressure.

I have seen mothers handle their third, fourth and fifth babies with such effortless sureness, a holding that stills the Moro reflex, a presence utter and assured that imparts, '*In these hands, you are safe.*' It is almost as if both Yasmin and the orange know that there is only one way this is going to play out; it is a denuding ballet, an understanding between them of unfraught harmony and rightness. The peel falls away in a seamless spiral.

Yasmin sets the orange aside and cups the rind in her hands, returning it to the armature of its wholeness, an empty husk of fleshlessness. It is a playful gesture, not a necessary step in the preparation of our food, but one I can tell she wouldn't miss. Then she pinches the one end of the spiral and lifts it up, like one of those slinky toys. She does this a few times before she lays the peel out on the board, smooths it down and chops its curls into segments. These she slices finely into the tiniest shards of orange peel splinters. She gentles them onto a plate.

'These must stay a soft minute in the boiling water,' she says, 'to call their bitterness out. Can you sink them in and fish them out, Jo?' She hands me a small set of tongs. I move over to the fire, where the water Kiri fetched is now sputtering, and drop them in. I watch them swish around.

'Don't throw the water out. We can keep it for midnight tea,' Yasmin says. 'With Fi and Cate's honey, mmmm.'

I bring the orange slivers back to her, where she is now crushing the saffron with the back of a spoon in a bowl. She adds a splash of the orange blossom water. She then slices the two carrots into matchsticks. She hands me a Tupperware container.

'We're making Persian jewelled rice,' Yasmin says. 'A dish for special days. Not how my mother taught me, I'm making the recipe dance a few new steps. We use farro not rice, and I've already cooked it,' she says, tapping on the Tupperware. 'It takes too long otherwise.'

'Farro? I've never heard of it,' I say, opening the Tupperware and sniffing.

'Very healthy, an ancient grain, like a nut, and bouncy on the teeth. Taste,' she coaxes.

'With my fingers?'

'Of course, like this,' Yasmin says, grabbing a small scoop with her fingers and sucking off the grains.

I do the same. It is all she says, chewy, nutty, a robust grain, rice with attitude.

'Two nights ago, I had a leek dream – you remember your dreams, Jo?'

'Sometimes.' I have never, I don't dare confess, dreamed of vegetables, and suddenly this seems amiss. I could readily dream of eggplant.

'I invite a question into sleep with me and wake up

next to the answer. You know that is how dreams work? Knowledge is on the inside,' she says, tapping her sternum. 'All the answers are here.'

This is what Frank would call 'flaky' and Helen would deem 'nonsense,' but I am enchanted by whatever is going on between us.

'Then the leek spoke and said, "*Don't leave out the lentils*," so I thought, yes, we must add these for protein and strength. It's good for Cate's muscles.' Yasmin is aglow with sweat and wipes her forehead on her sleeve.

'Oooh, hot flushes.' She lifts up her dress, allowing air to billow and fans herself with it, and as she does, I catch a glimpse of her soft brown belly, its fish-mouth of a navel nestling in a tummy roll. This is not one of those unloved, un-caressed, hidden-under-all-these-clothes muffin tops. It is the bountiful belly of an Arabesque dancer, one rubbed with coconut oil, exposed to the sun, invited to the party – an enhancement, not an embarrassment. The corporeal hospitality she exudes is heady.

When it's over, she exhales contentedly. 'How's your weather?'

'Same as yours,' I say. I know well this burning, roiling arpeggio that works its way up and down the body, hit by lightning, a breathless thunder.

Menopause has been a personal internal summer. Heat waves ripple from my abdomen all the way up to my neck and like a woman-caught-fire, I fling my shirt and sports bra off so my torso can breathe. Skin to air. Even in the middle of my first winter as a menopausal woman, I slept naked, my body sucking at the darkness in search of a chill, sniffing for a shiver. I used to feel the cold. Now I crave it. Urgency is the thing when that hot flush rears in me. I can't pause politely or ask, '*Do you mind?*' I must throw off whatever is touching flesh. I don't mind it – and if anyone else does, tough titty. I've become an inadvertent exhibitionist. If sag is your kind of sexy, knock yourself out.

The last time I remember being so in-furnaced was during my pregnancies. You could feel the warm simmering of mitosis, the fever of quickening.

'I like generating my own heat,' Yasmin says. 'Like solar energy – it's free and it works. I don't use the heater or take long hot showers anymore. I am saving us hundreds of dollars.'

'Perhaps some millennial will invent a way of converting our inner climate into fuel so we could boil a kettle or charge an iPhone off ourselves,' I say.

'Hatch eggs.'

'Heat the swimming pool.'

'Defrost the freezer.'

'Menopausal women – a new source of green energy. What an advertising campaign Liz could pull off.'

We laugh as if after forty years of menstruating, these intermittent bursts of uninhabitable heat that rip through us are a hoot.

'Who taught you to cook?' I ask.

'My mother. Before cooking, she taught me to smell and to taste from when I was a small girl. Between us, there was always a pot, a ladle – they were arms, how she held me. She gave me my nose and my tongue. Now I'm trying to give them to my children, but only Ibrahim is interested in learning to cook. He has my mother's touch. So much is being lost, so many disappearing recipes.'

'My mum is also a wonderful cook,' I feel a tug in me now. Chicken soup. Chopped liver. Pickled herring. Latkes. Kugel. All the Jewish flavours of my childhood she could churn out so effortlessly. And then Africa got its hold on her and she taught herself lamb potjie, waterblommetjie stew, Chakalaka and mielie pap, Cape Malay curry, dishes I have not learned to prepare. These are tastes I didn't know I loved until they were gone.

'She is alive still?'

I nod.

'Lucky. My mother died last year. Pancreatic cancer, so very quick.'

'I'm so sorry.'

'Death is a camel that lies down at every door, isn't that so? I miss her so much. My heart is like a twisted, wet towel.'

'I cannot bear to even think of my mother dying. It must be so confusing.'

'Yes that is a good word to describe it – like a concussion on the heart. Rajit doesn't know, but I still am paying for her mobile phone. I call her number to hear her voice. Every day, I have things I want to tell her, questions I need to ask her. I want to know her opinion. To lose a mother is something you cannot truly believe – you think you have misunderstood.'

I swallow hard. 'Ridiculous, isn't it, to be fifty-two and not ready to lose a mother.'

'But if she was here, you know what she would say? *"I am not lost. You have me. I'm here."* Smell,' she says, bringing the bowl with the saffron and orange blossom to my face. I inhale. It's a sparkle of aromas, an olfactory firework display that lights up something in my brain.

Suddenly I am a child in my mother's kitchen, watching her stand at the stove in an apron, talk radio is on, the pots are sizzling, the peeled onions are lined up, waiting their turn. She is sprinkling, stirring, seasoning. It is the summer of mulberries, and her jam is burping a sticky burgundy storm as she supervises. It is Passover and the dumplings are churning and chattering in the soup. Ruby grapefruits were on special and her marmalade, a blood-red bittersweet honey, is taking deep gulps in the pot while she boils the bottles she will fill that will last three winters. Over this heat, despite all the ways she will be let down by life, including decades later – when I will take her grandchildren halfway across the world just as she has come to learn the pleasures of being a grandmother – she is full of a happiness nothing will ever rob her of; and it is hard to take my eyes off her.

Yasmin has woven me back to my home, to the smells

and tastes of a world I left behind, reminding me how to love. The way to a woman's soul is past her lips, and into her belly, where she nourishes herself first so that she may nourish others.

My mother makes food the way some people sing; it rolls out of her, a generous, boundless creativity. She cooked back then to keep the peace, heal the storm, make us forget that life isn't fair – to soften bruises, cool the African heat, heat the winter Highveld chill, keep us together, simmer in us a memory of home, a place where hunger dies and satisfaction lives. She never thought of herself as an artist, but she could concoct a feast from the simplest of ingredients: an egg, a potato, a tin of pilchards, a bunch of radishes, a leftover chicken carcass. In her quietness, a shyness mistaken for aloofness, she understood how to unlock the hidden masterpiece modesty conceals, the way Michelangelo saw the angel in the marble.

'It's so complex,' I say. 'The flavours are so layered.'

She nods excitedly. 'You and me, we have noses like flies' eyes. We smell the whole lemon, even the soil from the lemon tree. You must look after the nose,' she pats hers like a pet mouse. 'Give it muscles. Make it strong. I so closely lost my nose on the boat. We came from Iran to Australia, packed in like sardines. The smell of bodies without sanitation and water – sweat, urine, faeces, menstrual blood – you can never forget. My mother put rose water and ginger root under my nose to keep me from vomiting.'

'Your family came as refugees?'

'When I was fifteen, we were so lucky. My father wanted a better life for us after the revolution. He gave up his business, our big house, our long history, our huge family, so we could immigrate to this wonderful land. He knew how to sacrifice. Maybe this is something a man knows. He was not sentimental to leave things behind. Not like my mother. Oh, she cried. But he turned his ears away, for a better life.' She shakes her head. She shifts her weight into a hip.

'My husband and I also immigrated when our children were two and four, but not...not like that. We elected to come, on a plane, with a choice of the full or continental breakfast,' I say.

'Immigration is immigration, not so? It's always not home.'

As she speaks, I feel the corners of a wedge in my windpipe. 'After eighteen years, shouldn't Australia be home for us?'

Yasmin makes exaggerated movements with her lips from side to side as if she's chewing gristle and needs the help of all her molars. 'For our kids. We are half-half. We are always stuck in the ditch of memory.'

She gets a wistful look in her eyes. 'I remember,' she inhales, 'the red curtains in my childhood home, the fountain in our garden, my mother's cooking...all the smells, spicy, sour...' She closes her eyes. 'And a dog crying in the courtyard...ah, the light and the dark.' Even with her eyes closed, something in her face changes, a small contortion as if she has been jabbed. She blinks her huge eyes open. 'It was just a mongrel,' she says softly. It is a five-word full stop.

'Fiona, please give us the ears of corn,' Yasmin calls out. Fiona steps towards us from her place near the fire and whisks out six corncobs from her backpack still wrapped in their leafy bridal gowns.

'Straight on the fire?' Fiona asks. Yasmin nods.

Yasmin pulls out a small Tupperware with a spice mixture. She opens it and hands it to me to smell. 'Coriander, pepper, sesame,' I say.

'You have a good nose. Your mother taught you well. It's toasted Aleppo pepper, black and white sesame, and coriander seeds. Once the corn is done on the fire, we'll sprinkle it with oil, dip in the spice mixture and mmmm…'

'Have you ever tried a mixture of mayonnaise, sour cream, chilli powder and lime juice? You brush it on the corn and sprinkle cheese on it. Grill it and serve it with fresh coriander. It's a Mexican dish.'

Yasmin's eyes light up. I don't know how I remember that recipe. I've only made a few times in my life. She brought it out of me. She is a force field, evangelical, a missionary reviving something long lost in me.

'Fiona said it true – once a food witch, always a food witch.'

'Maybe once… '

Yasmin cocks her head and looks at me as if she's

weighing up whether to believe me or not.

'You can't lose. It's here,' Yasmin says, tapping me on my nose. 'Can you lose your history, your parents, your family?'

She bats those outrageous eyelashes in my direction and my assertion that yes, you can lose everything - all you ever trusted, all you ever knew, your identity, your children, your happy marriage – all of it – is in a shambles.

'Now,' she says earnestly, 'let us prepare the leek.'

9

The Burning Woman

'You gonna let me see that blister or what?' Kiri says to Liz. 'Or you wanna walk back on it, get it good and sore? Maybe even give yourself a nice infection as a souvenir?'

Liz sighs and swings her legs around to where Kiri is sitting.

Kiri looks at it. 'So damn short-sighted, can't see a thing.' She switches on her head torch. 'Left my glasses in the car. Didn't think I'd need them out here, hey. Don' suppose we got a magnifying glass with us?'

'It's just a blister,' Liz says.

'Let's put a dollop of honey on it,' Fiona proposes. 'It's

got antiseptic qualities.'

'Pawpaw ointment,' Cate suggests. 'In the front pocket of my daypack.'

'Need to see what I'm looking at first, hey?' Kiri says, holding Liz's foot in her hand and squinting at it.

'I've got magnifiers in my bag,' I say, fishing them out. It's one of six pairs of these slim foldable glasses I keep close at hand – in my bedside drawer, kitchen, car, desk and in two different handbags. It happened in my mid-forties. My eyes decided I was middle-aged and I suddenly couldn't read a menu, recommended dosages on medication, instructions in English on small folded paper inserts or anything in the category of 'small print'. I am illiterate, stupefied and disconsolate without them. I once tried to lather myself with hair conditioner before realising it wasn't shower gel. I reached a low point some months ago when I almost brushed my teeth with the tube of thrush cream I'd left on the vanity. Why are middle-aged women in need of reading glasses in the shower invisible to advertisers? We make all the consumer decisions in the household. Liz really should take up cudgels on our behalf.

I hand them over to Kiri, who slips them on.

'Ah, there it is. Ooh, that's a bastard of a blister you given yourself. Excellent work in the friction department.'

'New shoes,' Liz says. 'You'd think for what you pay for them, they'd make them blister-proof.'

'Money can't buy everything,' Kiri says. 'You get stung

by a bee, it's gonna hurt, whether you Rupert Murdoch or homeless.'

'Tea tree oil,' Yasmin says. 'Fixes everything.'

'We're not gonna pop it. You never pop a blister. That fluid is protective. I'm gonna wipe down the whole area with some antiseptic, and then we gonna cushion it with some gauze and a plaster. Keep it dry.'

Liz nods. 'Not going to argue with the nurse.'

'But hang on, what's this then?' Kiri leans in to examine Liz's calf.

Liz looks down. 'Eczema?'

'You had chicken pox?'

'As a kid.'

'Don't you got some aches, like a burning, tingling pain?'

Liz's expression exposes that she has not come here to be subjected to public wellbeing scrutiny like a patient on a medical students' ward round. Liz lowers her voice in an attempt to privatise the conversation.

'It's a bit itchy. And there's a sharp pain that comes and goes down that leg.'

'Well, mam, you got yourself some shingles is my best diagnosis,' Kiri bellows. 'It's a little bonus when you stressed and such. See how it's just down this leg? Follows the nerve.'

'Shingles?'

'Same virus as chicken pox. You gonna get a rash that's starting there, and then some mutt-ugly blisters. It's gonna be sore, and you need to go see a doctor, maybe get some antibiotics on board. The good news is we don't have to amputate.'

There is a second of silence before Fiona gives out a yelp.

It takes me a moment to catch on. A furious hush descends as Kiri's words drop and settle.

It's Liz who shakes us clean. 'Relax, it's okay. The world doesn't have to censor every amputee joke just because my son lost a leg.'

Kiri pales. She clamps her hand over her mouth. 'Oh dear Jesus, I'm sorry…'

'It's no big deal.'

Kiri drops her head into her hands. 'Me and my big mouth.'

'Relax. Everyone is so oversensitive these days,' Liz says. 'It's ridiculous to censor thoughts and comments based on everyone's personal traumas, for heaven's sake. There are a thousand fates worse than losing a leg.'

She looks drained from her own barrage, a woman who has lost control of more than just a confidential interaction about her health.

Kiri lifts her head. 'I always make jokes about amputation, being diabetic and all, but it's not a joke.'

'Just forget about it,' Liz says. 'Damn shingles on top of everything.'

'Don't let Kiri jump off the hook,' Yasmin laughs. 'She's so bossy. Now she is sorry.'

I look over at Kiri and her face is smashed with regret. I

want to go over to her, rest my forehead on hers and let her know we all make mistakes.

Yasmin wipes the sweat from her forehead. 'Whoo, more flushes.' She stands and begins to shake her body, her wrists, her arms, her head, as if she's a fluttering flag in the wind.

'Aren't you on any drugs for those flushes?' Liz asks.

'No, I won't take drugs for natural things. Not laxatives for constipation or painkillers for headaches. I treat these hot flushes with yams and black cohosh. Are you taking pills?'

'I'm on drugs for Absolutely Everything,' Liz says. 'Yams and black what?'

'Black *cohosh*. It's the medicine herb of the buttercup family, from the Native Americans. But I left my tablets at home. So today, I am a burning woman,' Yasmin laughs. 'I'm going to join Kiri and put my feet in the water to cool down,' she says, fanning herself with her hands. Kiri is standing with her back to us, facing the ocean, her pants rolled up her enormous calves.

'It's just a heatwave,' I say. 'It comes and goes, like labour pains, remember?'

'I had elective Caesareans. And a torturous menopause,' Liz says.

'You had it rough too, didn't you, Kiri?' Fiona calls.

Kiri turns around slowly. 'You talkin' about me?'

'Menopause. You had a tough few years…'

'Can't hear ya,' Kiri says, making her way back to us.

'She had a three-year monogamous relationship with a UTI,' Cate says of Kiri.

'What's that then?' Kiri asks, returning from self-imposed exile.

'Telling them how you kept getting dehydrated cos you didn't want to pee razorblades,' Cate says.

'True story. But that's just plain stupid, worst thing a person can do,' Kiri says. I can almost hear the soundtrack – the way she's beating herself up inside.

'UTIs were light relief from the rest of the nightmare,' Liz says. 'Didn't help, having to go through it all twice.'

'Twice?' Yasmin asks.

'Like double jeopardy.'

'How did you repeat it?' Yasmin asks, blinking her eyes. It could be that her superpower is to make a person do things they don't want to do, even though she may not know it.

'Musta been endometriosis,' Kiri says.

'Exactly, it started fifteen years ago with just that – endometriosis,' Liz says. 'I went on drugs to treat the cysts, heavy periods and cramps. That brought on an early menopause – with hot flushes, insomnia and I even managed to put on some weight. I did come right after a while. But then real menopause kicked in five years ago.' She pauses. 'I got all those symptoms again, just more viciously.'

'Some women do get it really terrible. Not just the physical stuff, but the emotional and psychological stuff,' Kiri says, drying off her feet with a cloth and flicking the sand off. 'We even had one woman stab herself with a fork, right here,' Kiri points to her thigh. 'She said it was to stop herself from stabbing her husband who was keeping her awake with his snoring and farting.'

Liz twitches. 'It felt like a brain injury. I kept dropping things, bumping into table edges, tripping over my own feet. I didn't sleep for more than an hour at a time. Worse than having a newborn. My skin was on fire. I was having up to fifty hot flushes a day. The reflux was horrendous.'

'Zilly?' Fiona says. 'I didn't know.'

Liz shrugs. 'No point in complaining.'

'Sorry, Liz,' Yasmin croons. 'So much hurting, just for menopause to arrive?'

It is barely detectable, but Liz's posture shifts. As if she has stopped bracing against a squall. Her shoulders drop, her demeanour eases, as one's body does, coming in from a storm, shutting the door behind you. It is a softening, not pummelled or tenderised by force, but a slow fascial release of a muscle coaxed from constriction. It affects her larynx; the tone of her voice now changes an octave as she pulls us into something resembling a confidence.

'It affected work. It shattered my concentration. I became obsessed with small things like where I'd sit in a meeting or boardroom. I'd send my assistant in ahead of me to reserve a seat near a window if there was no fan or aircon. I'd have to sit near the door in case I needed to escape. It verged on the paranoid. It's embarrassing to think about but there were days when I'd perspire through one silk blouse after another,' Liz continues. 'It was like being in an illicit affair, keeping my symptoms a secret from everyone. I once had to send my assistant out to get a skirt dry-cleaned before a presentation because the back was wet from sweat. But what took me by surprise, what I really didn't see coming…,' she rakes her hands through her hair, '…was the rage. It was epic. A derangement of sorts.'

The confession slips from her and she pauses to see if she has gone too far. She does not trade easily in vulnerabilities.

'I was unprepared.'

'This is normal, Liz. I have bursting anger in me too since menopause,' Yasmin interposes. 'I call it my dragon breath.'

'My nickname on the ward was Vesuvius,' Kiri laughs. 'They'd see me coming and scatter, like a buncha cockroaches.'

'Zilly, I have been wilting with fury for years,' Fiona says gently.

A concatenation. One hand goes up, then another, then another. This is how a #MeToo movement begins.

'I had to go on medication. I didn't know at the time, but it's what they give to psychotic criminals in maximum security prisons. It worked, though.'

Something lightens in my chest, a hollow-boned flurry of wings. Oh, to be amongst peers, fuming, raging, bellowing women in our middlepause. Maybe I'm just an ordinary shrew, a perfectly normal harridan in her mid-fifties, not a crazy woman unravelling.

'I don't know why you're so angry,' Frank tutted.

'How fucking dare you tell me how I'm feeling?'

His equanimity was baffling. Couldn't he see? Every vegetable in the supermarket – find me an exception – was asphyxiated in cling wrap or polystyrene. Facebook had become a platform for white supremacists, chauvinists and climate change denialists. We were still mining coal in Australia. And who the fuck had eaten my vanilla slice I'd left in the fridge?

'Don't sweat the small stuff. You'll give yourself a hernia,' he'd said, and godhelpme, a cliché thrown in there was like a lit cigarette flicked into a drought-ravaged bush. Besides, none of this was small stuff – I'd been *saving* that vanilla slice.

I'd slammed the door on my way out. 'I'm going for a walk.'

'You do that,' Frank called out. 'And take some nice deep

breaths.'

I strode out, seething. Something in me had ruptured with no assurance that it had finished rupturing.

I had never known rage. Passion, yes, but not anger. I'd grown up with an angry father, and I had made my vows about not repeating history's histrionics. 'A temper is not very attractive on a lady,' my granny Bee would say when I'd express a strident opinion or raise my voice. So I'd adjusted myself. I'd managed my ire with the same tenets I applied to my weight – with deprivation and denial. I starved myself of legitimate fury against sexist jokes and casual misogyny so as not to fuel the stereotypes or be responsible for further anti-women sentiment. I assured Frank that I didn't mind him putting on the TV in the loungeroom to watch rugby and boxing. I accepted these as a matter of taste, as in, *'Not for me, but you go ahead and enjoy it'* – though I'll tell you right now that he never stayed when I was doing meditation, kirtan or yoga nidra.

I became expert at concession, hyper-flexible with my wants, so accustomed to their erosion to accommodate others. All the while, I was erasing myself with every 'I don't mind' I uttered.

But as soon as my periods dried up, my tolerance for my own tolerations ceased and I finally let rip the flatulence a marriage forces us to keep tightly sphinctered in our hearts. As my mercury rose, the world around me seemed to become a madhouse, and why was I the only one who could see how the cling wrap on the pumpkin was connected to the death of phytoplankton in the ocean and the smug Facebook post by a journalist who claimed the feminist movement had gone a little 'too far'?

Also, Frank should have known better. I'm all for a good laugh but there is a time and place.

He contested the preposition, but I know the difference between laughing *with* and laughing *at*. For starters, I wasn't laughing. It was a stinking hot day, which begs the question, why were stockings even in play? I had come back from a meeting in the city, and torn them off, ripping them to shreds. I turned the attack to my blouse, popping buttons, got into a brawl with my bra until I wrestled it to the ground. With naked breasts, gasping free at last, I'd yanked my underwear drawer out of its wooden socket and hauled out every pair of bra and stockings, tossing them like electric eels onto the floor

Who the fuck designs these things?

And that's when he chuckled.

'Are you laughing at me?' I'd yelled.

'Definitely not.'

'You are. You're laughing at me.'

'If it makes you feel any better, I have to wear ties and long trousers,' Frank had shrugged as he'd backed out the door. 'Sorry, my love, I didn't make the rules.'

'Yeah, but all you men love this bloody pornographic lingerie, itsy-bitsy lacy garments of affliction.'

'You can wear granny panties up to your chin for all I care. I'm interested in what's inside them.'

He didn't dare come in for a goodbye kiss.

It can be this simple. A pile of stockings on your bedroom floor and you find yourself addressing No-One In Particular with the solemnity of a blood oath: 'No more torture.' Over that stack of nylon hosiery and underwire girdles, you swear you will never squeeze yourself into anything tight and castigating again. You make a vow against confinement, discomfort or pressure sores. You declare your body a peace zone. You denounce your allegiance to Victoria's Secret. How could constriction of one's breathing be a way to exist, be creative, love the world, love oneself?

I then raided my cupboard like a woman on the trail of betrayal for anything resembling a pincer, *elasticised waist my arse*, snug-fitting, armpit piercing, tummy-flattening, zip or button in the wrong place, trouser. I bagged all that athletic clothing I used to preen in – the clingy, needy Lycra, the body-hugging, claustrophobic yoga gear with straps and ribbons and netting and donated it to the Salvation Army, though why I would inflict such needless suffering on those who are already suffering, shows you how careless I can be when I am in a fury.

Then there was the asphyxiation incident. He was applying his deodorant one morning as he did every morning – but this time, the very smell which would certainly undo me in a widowed state if I brushed past a stranger doused in Lynx Africa, made me bolt from the bedroom spluttering and gagging. *Can you do that in the bathroom?* Suddenly scents I had always loved or at least found inoffensive made me sick, like during my pregnancies. I threw out ten years of expensive perfumes.

I was becoming allergic to my very life.

And yet.

Vagueness, a *not-sure-what-do-you-think?* people-pleasing personality trait lest I not be liked by the average so-and-so, vanished. Everything blurry clicked into sharp focus, like a lens in those optometry frames which turns an O into a D.

My anger, like an arterial stent, purified and cleansed me, not in a holy-mother-of-god-virginal way, but in a near-death-gasping-for-breath-skin-melting apocalypse that stripped me raw. It aroused a dormant voice, an echo stirred from where voice began; it brought the silent war inside out. I was The Burning Woman, not one tied to the stake and set alight by those who feared her, but one with a fire rising from her belly, marking where the kingdom of herself began and where it ended. It became my firewall, a fortification. Admittedly, it was not me at my most amiable or amenable. But it was me at my most powerful and it terrified both me and Frank.

Now listening to these women, I see it for what it is — not an isolating madness, an aberration of the norm. It is an earned life stage, a milestone of mature self-formation. But what are we to do with it when it comes? Do we let it sweep through our everything-working-just-fine life like a bushfire and swallow the lot whole? Or do we remove ourselves from those we love to protect them as much as ourselves while we figure out what to do with it, and what – if anything – it changes?

'I've finally come right,' Liz says. 'I found a doctor who put me on HRT.'

'Really, Liz, is that safe?' Fiona asks. 'There are natural solutions.'

'I had to have drugs,' Liz says.

'What you got? Cancer history like Fi?' Kiri asks.

'My mother died of breast cancer.'

'She was only what? Forty-two?' Fiona acknowledges. Her and Liz trade a glance that has a long tail.

'Yeah, you and Fi should stay away from extra hormones, poor buggers,' Kiri nods. 'I got a hormonal patch. Releases a bit of progesterone through the skin. Look,' she says, rolling up the sleeve of her shirt.

'Camomile tea is good, Liz. Melatonin, even red wine,' Yasmin says. 'Yoga also.'

'Bio-identical hormones,' Cate says. 'I swear by them.'

'Trust me, I needed chemicals. The only time I've lost

my temper in a doctor's rooms was when I insisted that he put me on HRT. The arrogance of male doctors is enough to enrage any hormonal woman. I told him, "I make multi-million-dollar decisions every day about how to spend other people's money, and you think I can't make a decision about my own body?"'

'You intimidated him to put you on HRT?' Kiri asks.

'By any means necessary. It is *my* body,' Liz says. 'I thought women had won that debate, but clearly not.'

'It's her body, bitches,' Cate says.

'HRT saves lives,' Kiri says. 'It's true. I've seen it a hundred times. You just gotta be careful with your history.'

'I don't have the BRCA gene,' Liz says. 'I did my research, became an oestrogen expert, and it's not just a fertility hormone. There are oestrogen receptors all over our bodies, in the brain, the amygdala, the hippocampus and the hypothalamus. Our serotonin, dopamine and other hormones depend on it. We need it for brain function and cognition. Without it, we're a blurry mess, a danger to ourselves and everyone around us. Menopause should be a legitimate, bona fide murder defence.'

'It's been argued in some cases,' I say. 'I've been doing some research for a new book.'

'Tell us 'bout that,' Kiri says.

'We all know that when a woman ends up in court, sexist stereotypes follow her. We're forever clawing for credibility, arguing against our hormones.'

'Like in rape cases where they go into her whole fucking sexual history as if she's somehow asked for it,' Cate says.

I nod. 'It's astonishing any woman ever lays a rape charge. If we're not stereotyped as virgins, then we're whores. If we're not menstrual, then we're pre-menstrual. If we're not peri-menopausal, then we're menopausal. Menopause has mostly been used against women who've brought claims to blame them, deny or devalue injuries and the compensation they'd be entitled to.'

'Like what?' Kiri asks.

'There was a case where a plane had to make an emergency landing and a woman sued for emotional and physical distress. The defence argued her symptoms were menopausal and had nothing to do with the trauma of the landing. Same thing happened to a woman who drank a bottle of Pepsi which had a rusty, used razorblade in it. They argued her distress was due to her hormones. Menopause is where sexism meets ageism.'

'So we doubly fucked?' Kiri asks.

'Everything gets twisted against us in the end,' Yasmin says.

'It's just really hard to control the narratives of our bodies,' I say. 'In the wrong hands, they become weapons against us.'

Courtrooms aside, menopause is never going to win the Ms Popularity Award. Not many women I know feel neutral about growing facial hair (proper stick-out of your face whiskers, not the fluff beauticians wax off your upper lip) or a menopausal tummy easily mistaken for a five-month pregnancy. The rolls of back fat take getting used to, as growing unnecessary extra body parts would. Your lushest places desiccate as the heat rolls through you, a brickfielder wind from the Outback, your own personal sirroco or khamseen, leaving you slick with sweat, slippery with anxiety. We become nervous, erratic and according to a medical journal I read, 'subject to the powder keg of emotions slowly smouldering somewhere in the hypothalamus.' Drought season turns us finally into a termagant, which any dictionary will enlighten you is a 'violent, overbearing, turbulent, brawling, quarrelsome woman; a virago, a shrew.'

But I for one will not bewail this 'change of life'. It came and freed me from my enslavement as Oestrogen's Bitch. It broke the cycle of bleeding in which I'd been caught since I was thirteen and my life became a sequence of monthly anxieties and shames: *Have I bled through my skirt? Do I have sanitary pads on me? Can I swim at the school carnival?* I survived four decades of bloody-cramp-acne-bloating management. Until menopause arrived.

I finally relaxed about contraception after a lifetime of avoiding unwanted fertility with some form of *oh-no-you-don't* (the pill, the loop, the Mirena). I've financed and carried my own stash of condoms because whose life would really be at stake if he didn't have any? Frank didn't like condoms. I considered tying my tubes. Until, eureka – '*How about you have a vasectomy?*' The story of my body could be entitled: *Bleeding and Breeding.*

In perimenopause, fibroids began to mushroom inside me, squashing my other organs. '*I recommend a hysterectomy now that your family is complete,*' the specialist suggested. I opted for a myomectomy to excise the biggest fibroids. I plugged myself with super-duper tampons and three overlapping sanitary pads and still could not risk leaving the house on day two and three of my period. I changed arrangements, flying plans and planned my life around my cycle. I pretended I was sick.

So I will not badmouth menopause, whether it makes me a crazy bitch or not. I'd take being a hot mess over a bleeding, breeding vessel any day of the week.

'I actually don't mind menopause,' I say.

'That is just plain weird and wrong,' Liz says. 'Have you had any symptoms?'

'Plenty. But for the first time in my life, the Red Cross lets me give blood because I'm not anaemic. I overheat, I need lube, I'm angry. But I can live with all that.'

'Have you tried HRT?' Liz asks.

'I don't need it. Happy to sit it out.'

I've always erred on the side of not interfering with my hormones or body's natural rhythms even as I've felt bullied by them at times. I want to believe my body knows what the hell it's doing even though it made a few mistakes during childbirth; and if it could fuck up then, when I really needed it to come through for me, who's to say it can't fuck up again?

I want to believe the moon has some pull on my body. I'd

rest my faith on Her any day over a man-made Big Pharma chemical someone is earning dividends from. I don't want a synthetic block between me and any greater energy that I may or may not understand, because that would be like telling my body, in yet another way, 'You're not good enough. I don't trust you.'

'HRT is a medical breakthrough, like the Pill,' Liz says. 'It's precisely to help us get through all this. Where would you be without epidurals? Caesareans? Anaesthetics? Chemo?'

'I'd be dead, that's for sure,' Fiona says. 'A routine mammogram saved my life. But HRT…it is risky, Liz.'

'We've fought for women's rights to choose the Pill, abortions, gay marriage, elective Caesareans, bottle feeding, and now we're telling each other how to manage menopause? I don't think so,' Liz says. 'And you know who perpetrates this scaremongering propaganda? We do. Women. The damn sisterhood. We harass each other into believing our way is better than your way. You take your black cohosh, and I'll take my HRT. It's as if we've learned nothing from the patriarchy except how to oppress one another.'

'Of course, we should each have the right to choose how to manage it,' Yasmin says. 'But maybe the remedy is influenced by how we think about menopause. Is it a problem to be fixed? Or a natural threshold?'

'Kinesiology, acupuncture and flower remedies help control all the symptoms for me. And my favourite, Tantric dance,' Fiona says.

'We don't live in tribes where we menstruate as a communal activity into the earth anymore,' Liz says. 'Some of us have to get up in front of the boardroom no matter what's going on inside our bodies. We can't delay a five-million-dollar presentation because we have cramps or the sweats. I don't get this whole "grit our teeth and manage with the odd vitamin" to be "natural". It encourages female suffering – as if we don't have it bad enough – and it strikes me that we would consider this level of pain inhumane if men or children experienced it.'

'Some cultures, like Japan, don't even have a word for hot flushes,' I say.

'Is that true?' Kiri asks. 'Do they, like, not have hot flushes?'

'It's their diet,' Yasmin says. 'All the vegetables and soy products which are full of phytoestrogens. It mimics oestrogen. Food is always the cure.'

'We have so many intelligences in our bodies,' Fiona says. 'All those neuro-networks in the heart, the gut and maybe even the womb. We're all in such a hurry to try and "fix" something when it's not broken – it's just changing.'

'My heat is uncomfortable, but unbearable? No,' Yasmin says. 'Do I need hormones to stop two hairs growing from my chin when I can pull them out? Do my moods hurt someone? Maybe Rajit. He wants me to go on medicines, but as we say in my culture, "You don't ask the donkey, '*When is Wednesday?*'" His opinion is irrelevant.'

Fiona sits in a yoga pose with her feet impossibly resting on the opposite knee. 'Since menopause, I feel more grounded. I want my body to stay connected to the rhythms of our Mother, Gaia. The thought of chemically overriding them would feel like an assault on my body. And I can't help wondering,' she says softly, 'what the generational impact will be of altering our hormones – especially during childbearing years. Don't you think the rise in breast cancer has something to do with the onset of oral contraceptives?'

'You blaming yourself again for your breast cancer?' Kiri asks.

'I was on the pill for twenty-two years,' Fiona muses. 'You can't tell me that doesn't count for anything.'

'Would it make you feel better if you thought you caused it?' Liz asked.

'I want to take full responsibility. For everything in my life. Not just the good stuff.'

'Not everything is your responsibility,' Liz says.

'If it's turned up in my life, how can it not be?' Fiona asks.

'You know what's really good for managing menopause?' Cate cuts in. 'Adrenalin. Read some research that if you do something batshit crazy and risky that gets your heart racing, you don't need drugs. Parachuting, bungy-jumping, paragliding, scuba diving, kite-surfing, skydiving, swimming with sharks. I did them all, and even if it doesn't cure the hot flushes, you can tick it off the list, and say, "I fucking survived that."'

'Swimming with sharks, no, that's not for me,' Yasmin says, covering her eyes. 'Maybe dolphins.'

'Every time you come back alive, it makes you braver, hungrier for more of life.' Cate chuckles. She picks up her ukulele and begins to strum, holding it like a small creature under her breasts. The sound is pure and gentle around us. But suddenly, it falls from her fingers, as if scaldingly hot. 'Oh fuck,' she sighs, trying to retrieve it.

Fiona picks it up and hands it back to her. She squeezes Cate's forearm.

'Catey, are you afraid of anything?' Fiona asks lovingly, rhetorically.

'Right now, I'm afraid of pissing myself. Anyone want to join me for a pee-funnel contest?'

Fiona jumps up and reaches out her hand to help Cate stand. Yasmin grabs her other one and together, they pull Cate up. Cate almost creaks as she straightens herself out, her hinges rusty and raw. This long walk has taken its toll on her.

As I watch the three of them head off in the direction of the water, arms linked like teenage girls excusing themselves to go to the Ladies' and leaving a trail of footprints on the beach, I remember how it felt. My feet in the sand. My toes, curled like bird's claws, gripping its safety, Wedding Cake Island far behind me, my body clanging with adrenalin.

A vicious hunger in me awakened.

10

Activated Pussies

Kiri rummages in her bag and brings out a large plastic Coke bottle with clear fluid inside. She hands it to Liz. 'Peace offering, quick before the others get back.'

'Thanks, I've got my own water,' Liz says.

'Take a swig,' Kiri winks.

Liz opens the bottle and sniffs. 'Tequila?'

'Si, but not just any old Tekkie, this is the finest of the fine…but let's keep it our little secret – just outta respect for Fiona's wishes. Her dad was a bit of a heavy bottle-hitter,' Kiri says in hushed tones.

'That he was,' Liz says. She puts the bottle to her lips and takes a generous mouthful, closing her eyes as she swallows. 'Aaaaaaahhhh... Whoa...'

'You're welcome,' Kiri says. 'Have another. It'll keep the mozzies off you too. No burn, right?'

Liz shakes her head and hands the bottle back to Kiri who wipes the mouthpiece with her t-shirt before taking a swig herself. She brings the bottle over to where I am crouched over the gas stove.

'Not for me,' I say. These days I can't stomach anything but a small sip of high-quality whiskey. I've never been a notable drinker, but I could keep up with Helen. At that first sleepover, we powered our way through a tub of strawberry daiquiris, with chasers of Butterscotch schnapps. These days, one glass of red wine or bubbly and I'm a torment of wide-eyes-at-the-ceiling through the night and cradling a blistering headache for the next twenty-four hours. Frank grumbles that he hates drinking alone (it hasn't stopped him) as if I'm deliberately trying to be un-fun by drinking soda water instead of gin. But it's a damning fact of midlife that just as we have the time and resources to enjoy our libations, the body doesn't cooperate. If I've been saving up my excesses for the post-motherhood era, it's a little late.

It is a choice; I recognise this. My allegiances are torn. That's what happens when you've inadvertently made promises in two directions. But I can't see how Fiona will ever know. She's also one of those maddeningly forgiving types. Liz has a badass blister *and* shingles. It's a vicious add-on, a cruel 'but wait, there's more'. She needs all the help she can get.

I fish out the flask of whiskey from the bowels of my backpack, take a long private sip and feel the heat whistle down my gullet before I take it over to Liz who is examining her blister with her headlamp.

She breaks into the first genuine smile I've seen on her face all day. It's heavenly to see her eyes light up more blue than grey. I wonder if she knows it. How breathtaking she is when the cynicism recedes.

'*Le'chaim*,' she says taking a swig. She closes her eyes. 'Now that is classy,' she sighs, handing it back to me.

'Keep it.'

'You trying to get me sozzled? I'm not a quiet drunk, just so you know.'

It could be that I've just made matters worse, which is where trying to be helpful often gets you. Ask any mother.

'Shall we bless the feast?' Yasmin reaches out to take my hand to her left and Fiona's to her right. If I needed a sign that the ritual is upon us, here it is – a group handholding. Everyone in turn reaches out to hold hands until we form a ring. Even Liz concedes to the closing of the circle and gives her hands over to be held. Everyone closes her eyes, so I follow.

'Seriously,' Liz mutters, 'are we going to pray or something?'

Yasmin continues. 'We offer gratitude in this moment, as we give appreciation for this food, for the earth that grew it, and the rain that nourished it. We give thanks for our hunger and appetite...'

'...and the hands of all those who worked to bring it to us, especially Yasmin,' Fiona adds. 'You are such a feeder.'

'Jo also helped,' Yasmin inserts.

'Of course, thanks, Jo,' Fiona says, though it feels like cheating to be overthanked for the most menial of tasks, unlike motherhood, where the labour is endless and the gratitude, miserly. Fiona beams at all of us in what feels like a longer than comfortable silence. Finally, she speaks.

'I always thought there was something different about Alice, my mum. But I only realised what it was when I became a mother myself. She had no girlfriends. She was an only child. She knew nothing of a big, raucous family, full of cousins, aunts and grandmothers. She didn't understand why I wanted to spend all my time with you, Liz, when we became friends.'

'Pinkie sisters forever,' Liz holds up her pinkie finger.

Fiona copies her gesture. 'We had such an adventure in India and Mexico...'

'We ticked off over a hundred *first times*,' Liz concurs.

'When I had postnatal depression after Gabe was born,

that's when I understood friendships with women are not add-ons to life – they're not secondary relationships. They make everything else possible. They sweeten the most bitter of circumstances. They bring light and laughter into the darkest, most desperate of places. Yasmin, I'll never forget how you'd arrive to the PND support group with something delicious for us to eat, and always with the brightest lipstick on, no matter how exhausted and broken you were. Remember that day you insisted we all paint our lips and kiss each other's cheeks?'

Yasmin chuckles. 'Lipstick makes your brainwaves dance.'

'Then Jo, we met at the kids' preschool. That sleepover was epic – you and Helen went to so much trouble to feed us and make us feel like we were the most important people in the world. It's rare to feel safe enough to tell your deepest secrets and know they won't become gossip.'

I must remember to tell this to Helen. I have a reason to call her when I get back.

'Catey, you'd come with Sally to the breast cancer support group and paint our bald heads, even when you knew she was terminal.'

'I'd sing for you metastatic bitches,' Cate says.

'Sally was Cate's girlfriend,' Yasmin whispers to me.

'That voice…it's been part of my healing journey. And I know it soothed Sal, especially in those last days.'

Cate lowers her eyes.

'Kiri, you helped me through chemo, the best nurse I

could ever have asked for. I don't know how you made us all laugh while we were being pumped full of poison, but somehow, you did. Then, you insisted on being there through hospice, and Ben's dying.'

'S'why I'm here,' Kiri says bashfully.

Fiona pauses and wipes her eyes with the back of her hand. 'When I look at you all, I see my life, defined by circles of kindness and care. I know my mother would have been a different person if she'd only known about girlfriends – you have all been my salvation.'

Fiona bows her head.

A deep ache builds inside me for Helen, for all the girlfriends I have loved and lost, some to distance, some to death. In my mind, I begin to pan the waters of memory, and sift them out, each gold fleck of friendship. Kirsten who painted me watercolours and gave me ee cummings, Ilze who picks me up from Cape Town airport and drives me straight to the water, Emma who ran me a bath and plumped my pillows when I had pneumonia, Tracey who reminds me it is full moon and how about a dance? And my sisters, Carolyn and Laura across the ocean, who know my ring size and who cry when they see me.

Cate clears her throat. 'That's a goddamned hard act to follow. So lemme say thanks a shitload to everyone for the support to get here. I screwed you all by not carrying my own weight.... you know how frigging hard that is for a tough old badger like me. Cheers to all of you for not laying a guilt trip.

You carried the weakest link, and that's the only reason I'm sitting on my bony arse right here – but I wouldn't want to be anywhere else. Sorry to be such a drag.'

'You're anything but a drag,' Fiona says.

'Hoi, I'm the ultimate drag queen.'

'You don't drag,' Yasmin tuts.

Kiri purses her lips as if she's preparing for a long sermon and puffs out her enormous chest like an accordion. 'Fiona, my friend, you thought it was the end when your boob went bad on you. But it wasn't your time and I told you so, and I won't remind you of that. Then it was Ben's time – and it's as it should be – he was older. It's the right order. He had his three score years and ten.'

She wipes her brow and exhales. 'I'm chuffed I was in the room when it happened, grateful is what I mean. Seen lots of people die, this way and that, and truth be told, it wasn't an easy death he had. Hard for you and Gabriel. But looking on the bright side, all that suffering is over. So let it be over.'

Fiona reaches for Kiri's hand. Kiri lowers her gaze and nods her head.

It is now just me and Liz who remain ungrateful.

'Um…I feel like a bit of an add-on to this special gathering, so thank you for including me,' I swallow. What I am really thankful for is that I am not a widow, that I am not waiting on a diagnosis that could be a degenerative neurological condition, and that my son did not have his leg amputated. I squeeze these silent gratitudes into my chest, and tuck them under my ribs.

'I'm grateful for the chance to reconnect with you, Fiona, and Liz, after fifteen years. What a coincidence it was to bump into you last week.'

'Meant to be,' Fiona smiles.

Now it is Liz or nothing. The silence runs between and among us. She seems to be delayed, caught in a reverie. We stay with her.

She finally clears her throat and says, in a somewhere-else voice, 'It was just a leg. For all it could have been…it was just a leg.'

I am uncomfortable. The limber years of sitting cross-legged, feet splayed with a plate on my lap are behind me. I need a backrest. I dig into the sand and scoop out a hollow for my butt and build a mound of sand against which to lean. My body sighs as I nestle in. 'What a good plan,' Cate says.

'Want me to make one for you?' I ask.

She is about to say no, when she changes her mind. And nods. 'Yeah, that'd be good.'

I scoop out a seat for her and pat the sand into a sturdy backrest.

She gives me a nod. 'Ta.'

'You sure you don't want any food?' Yasmin prods Liz.

Liz peers at the pot of Persian jewelled farro and shakes her head in what can only be a complete denial of desire. This food is an invitation to every life-affirming instinct. Then there's the fire-cooked corn, the smell of popcorn everywhere as dusk begins to settle around us, and the sounds of where we are become a white noise of the wild.

'It will make you feel good.'

The whiskey has given Liz flushed cheeks, and elicited a tender confession, but it hasn't inspired an appetite. The aromas are melodious, so clear and single-minded. I am suddenly ravenous.

'Food isn't going to make me feel good.'

'What would make you feel good, Zilly?' Fiona asks.

Liz's eyes half close. She pinches the bridge of her nose as if willing a memory of where she left something she can no longer find: *Was it the kitchen counter? The entrance hall? The backseat of the car?*

She sighs deeply. 'A call, from Chloe, to tell me something inane about her day – what movie she saw, what band she's going to see, no big reveals, just an ordinary mother-daughter chat.' I sense the wobble in her discourse, the slight misalignment that becomes a perdition at speed.

'Your daughter isn't speaking to you?' Yasmin asks.

'She cut off all contact with me on her nineteenth birthday. I believe she had a cut-the-cord ceremony with some friends. So it's been, what, two years, seven months and fifteen days.'

'I didn't talk to my mother for years,' Cate says. 'It's normal, I'd say.'

'She'll come back to you,' Fiona says. 'She'll need you at some point in her life. She'll want her mother.'

Liz shrugs. 'I can't force contact. I'm the one who left.'

'She does ask about you,' Fiona says softly.

'Does she?' Liz seems surprised to hear this. 'Got one thing right in making you her godmother.'

'It's just a phase she's going through,' Yasmin says. 'Fatimah doesn't talk to me anymore about her life. I have to fish, fish, fish, and then I pull up a sardine.'

I could swap stories here. I won't, but I could. A parent must expect to be exiled at some point. Deportation from our children's inner worlds is both inevitable and excruciating but is not meant as a personal punishment in the good old Catholic excommunication and banishment tradition.

For over three years Jamie hasn't shared a single detail about her life. I used to know she was menstruating because our periods were in synch. Menopause put an end to that. I'd taught her to say no to drugs, insert a tampon, cover up pimples, get rid of dandruff, ignore bullies, gift wrap with perfect corners, dose up on vitamin C at the first niggle of a scratchy throat, write a thank-you card, apply for a job, never drive drunk. But a mother can't possibly cover all the bases. Contraception, I was led to believe, was covered by sex education at school. Mothers teach by modelling. *Look, this is how it's done*. We are here as examples. *Copy me*. Until we are dismissed. Same. Until different.

'Do not stalk her,' Frank had warned.

I'm all for Privacy at Some Point. Within reason, and with the same kind of exceptions that ought to apply to 'immediate family only' signs at hospitals which cannot possibly be interpreted to exclude girlfriends and same-sex partners.

'Instagram is a public forum,' I'd said.

There were gaps I desperately needed to fill.

I discovered that she frequented a club called The Ghostly Tail, she'd been part of a team that won a platter of cold cuts in a trivia competition, that her drink of choice was something called a Tom Collins. She'd been to student balls in gowns I'd never laid eyes on, had acted in a production of the early feminist masterpiece, *Trifles* by Susan Glaspell (didn't she want us in the audience?), a Halloween party, a concert, the opera – since when did she like opera?

I know better than anyone that life and writing don't match perfectly. Still, I scoured the photos for any sign of him, the one in her prize-winning short story she calls the 'cummunist'. I didn't recognise anyone with their arms slung comfortably around her. Who was that bearded fellow with his tongue in her ear? Was he the one? Or the bloke with a shaved head and a tongue-stud? In the comments on her Facebook feed, she referred to these strangers as her 'family'.

'Maybe feeling good is not the right way to measure our lives,' Fiona's voice is delicate.

'You would say that,' Liz says.

Fiona pauses. 'We have to adjust our expectations of this time of life. Pleasure and comfort are important, but maybe there are other ways to soulfully experience our lives.'

'And that's why you sleep on the floor, is it?' Liz asks.

'You sleep on the floor?' The right moment to ask has come to me at last.

Fiona nods.

'By *choice*,' Liz elaborates.

'Like on the floor floor? Not on a futon? Or a mat?'

'On the cold, hard floor,' Liz comments. 'The colder, the harder, the better.'

'You're exaggerating, Liz. I do use a blanket.'

'Why?' I ask.

'It's a stance,' Liz continues. 'She's making a point.'

'No, not exactly. I did make a lifestyle decision after my breast cancer treatment. I'd received so much care and kindness from nurses like Kiri and some of the doctors over the years. When I went into remission, I wanted to give back. So I began to volunteer at hospice one day a week where I got to sit with people at the end of their lives. There, you learn a lot about who you are and how attached you are to comfort. Dying is mostly uncomfortable – it can be excruciating.'

'Always? Is it always painful?' I gulp.

'Can also be peaceful,' Kiri says, 'depends, how and when.'

'I've seen some people let go as lightly as a kite string in a strong wind, and others wrestle so hard, as if it were a tug of war. Those who battle to let go at the end are struggling to surrender. Our obsession with comfort is often the cause of our suffering.'

'So Fiona goes out of her way to put herself in uncomfortable situations,' Liz says. 'Hence this overnight in the middle of…I don't know…where are we again? Sitting uncomfortably, with sand and dust everywhere,' Liz shudders.

'You love the outdoors. What about your gardening?' Fiona asks.

'What I appreciate about a garden is precisely its attachment to a house. And what I value about a house is its attachment to a flushing toilet, shower with hot water, bed with linen, table and chairs. We romanticise Nature like we do with marriage and motherhood. It's crude, wild and uncomfortable.'

'But it's called the Great Outdoors for a reason,' Kiri says. 'Nothing so bloomin' fantastic about the Great Indoors, is there? Loungeroom, kitchen, laundry.'

'We need to re-wild ourselves,' Fiona says. 'We're

supposed to sleep under the stars, bleed into the earth, make love in the forest.' She trails her fingers in the sand.

Yasmin, eating her food with her fingers, licks them one by one. 'I wish I could have sex outside. I've always done it inside. With closed doors, windows and curtains.'

'I once made love on a bed of pine-needles in a forest,' I say.

'Oh, I want to lie with pine-needles on my back and trees as my walls,' Yasmin says. 'You are lucky your husband is so romantic.'

'It wasn't with my husband. It was an ex-boyfriend.'

'You can't have it all,' Cate says. 'Would you rather be cherished or ravished?'

'I am tired of being cherished,' Yasmin says. 'I want to be ravished,' she sighs. I am certain she would have a long line of volunteers for this job.

'Sal and I were hiking in Yosemite once,' Cate says. 'Gawd, we were horny as hell. I lost track of how many orgasms she'd had. She could come five, six times. When I finally came up for air, there was a group of four hikers watching the whole thing. They started clapping. It was an impressive performance. Sal was a screecher.'

'Is it not illegal to be doing such private things in public?' Yasmin asks, her eyes wide.

'Yeah, but who's going to report that?' Cate smiles.

'Ben and I had sex on a beach when we were on honeymoon. But it wasn't romantic. A seagull pooped on me, and he got stung by a wasp on the butt.'

'That is good luck,' Yasmin says.

'Give me satin sheets, a pillow and a firm mattress any day,' Liz shudders.

'Cate, you lost your virginity on the beach, didn't you?' Yasmin says.

'Brighton as it turns out.'

'You would'a got chafed something terrible,' Kiri says.

'That I did,' Cate says.

'I pretty much seen it all,' Kiri says. 'People shagging wherever, using whatever. We once got a woman come in – a nanna in her sixties. She'd lost a bullet vibrator, never heard of such a thing before. Not even where you'd expect. Up her backside. Took a team of doctors to extract it. The bloomin' thing was still buzzing when we pulled it out. You just wonder what people get up to.'

'Nothing weird about that,' Cate says. 'All in a day's fun for your average lesbian.'

'People are pretty out there about their sexual preferences on Tinder,' Liz says.

'Tell us about Tinder,' Yasmin says. 'Please, I want to hear sexy stories.'

'You can hook up with anyone you want in twenty minutes,' Liz says. 'It's an all day, all night a la carte sex menu for whatever you're looking for.'

'I missed out. There was none of this in our day,' I sigh.

'It's overrated,' Liz says. 'It's good for turnover, and

variety. But that breeds an appetite for the insatiable, until you find someone you connect with beyond the physical. I mean, if you're on Tinder, it's strictly about sex.'

'Are you going to use Tinder, Fiona,' Yasmin asks, 'now that Ben is gone?'

Fiona shrugs. 'It's too soon to think about anything like that. But maybe I'll experiment with women next.'

'I also want to kiss a woman. Catey, when did you know you were gay?' Yasmin asks.

'Always knew. But only came out to mum in my early twenties. Funny thing is, she didn't believe me. I came out and she put me back in. I told her, "*That friend, Isobel, I've been flatmates with for the past two years, she's my girlfriend, Mum. I'm gay.*" And she said, "*No, you're not. Don't let one bad experience spoil everything.*"'

'I don't know how a parent can't tell,' Fiona says.

'Sometimes things slip through the cracks. Can't blame a parent for that,' Kiri says.

'We're all on the bisexual spectrum, aren't we?' I ask.

'I'm a hetero, through and through,' Kiri says. 'Top to bottom, one side to the other. Head to toe.'

'Maybe if you met the right kinda gal,' Cate teases.

'Not me.'

'You having such great hetero sex then?'

Kiri starts to laugh. It begins as a small chuckle and then bubbles over into a full-bellied laugh. 'Let's see, last time I had sex with Jim, gotta be over a decade ago. Even then, he had OMPS,' Kiri says.

'OMPS?' Fiona asks.

'Old Man Penis Syndrome. Couldn't get it up.'

'More than ten years? That's an outrage to your pussy. It's basically abuse, starvation-style,' Cate says.

'Ah, it's all overrated, sex'n'stuff.'

'That's cos you not getting any of the good kind,' Cate says.

'Best sex I ever had was with my ex, and he was a piece of dirty work. Bastard. Try to run me down with his car. That's where I busted my scapula. Still get pain there,' Kiri says.

'But then you met Jim,' Fiona says.

'Yeah, but still, we've had our fights. We once had one of those Deep and Meaningfuls about divorce and I said, *"You have an affair, it's over."* He told me, *"If you get fat, I'm outta here."* Then he had an affair and I got fat.'

'But you're still together,' Yasmin says.

Kiri nods. 'We share a bed, he passes wind in my direction, I make dinner for three. Take care of him and his old man. I don't even remember sex.'

'Well, you have a lot of…history…' Fiona says, putting her hand on Kiri's enormous forearm.

Kiri shrugs. 'Yeh, maybe time to move on from all that, hey?'

'Nurse, you need a vibrator urgently,' Cate says. 'Paging Vibrators, please come to Emergency. Nurse Kiri needs a good pussy activating.'

'Too late,' Kiri says. 'Mine's flatlined. Call the undertaker,' she chortles. 'You can't flog a dead clitoris. If I never have sex again, it wouldn't make any difference. And don't feel sorry for me or anything like that. That part of my life is over, and you know, sometimes you just gotta accept that some things are done for good.'

'You shouldn't give up,' Fiona says.

'What, you and Ben had such great sex, didya?' Kiri asks.

'For a while,' Fiona says. 'But then it changed. After my chemo, it was like he lost his way with my body. He started to hold me differently, like I was a small, strange mammal he was trying not to harm. As if a woman who'd had breast cancer had to be made love to differently. He did weird things he'd never done before. Like he'd thrum my thighs and press me in places that were just – wrong. But I didn't say anything. I just kept on having disappointing sex.'

'Right there,' Liz says, 'is one of the reasons I left Carl. Sex has to be varied. The day it becomes a habit, you might as well pull the plug.'

It's a perplexing manoeuvre of the mind, jealousy. I wouldn't trade Liz's life with mine, not for a moment. But the variety argument, I get it. I should know – I've been eating the same item on the same sex menu for the past twenty-four years.

When Hallmark praises couples celebrating crystal, china, silver, pearl, ruby, sapphire, gold, emerald and diamond anniversaries, it doesn't compute the decades, quarter and half centuries of the exact same fucking of the exact same person. Someone has to volunteer for The Variety Committee to keep things interesting like the entertainment planner at Club Med, because Bingo on a Monday and water polo on a Tuesday in perpetuity is a grind for all concerned.

Frank and I've had every season of sex there is. The early spring years of all-night fucking, the summers of wild panty-pulling and mouth-seeking greediness as if our crotches were magnets, frantic to find the opposite pole. We've had the late summer, the rushed exhausted perfunctory copulation of early parenthood, with stifled moans so as not to wake sleeping babies. We've been through the autumn decades of doing it exactly the same because it works in between menstrual cycles, bouts of flu and migraines sex, to the wasteland of monthly stretches between feel-like-a-bit-of-action-tonight? intercourse I could either take or leave.

But the chasm between forty and fifty wrought a slow extinction on my healthy libido. As menopause swept in, the place where I once was moist became a fearsome wasteland. We had to call in special lubrication services. But dependence on a tube to mimic a natural bodily function invokes infirmity in the way a permanent catheter or a walker must. I got libidinal amnesia – even my ability to fantasize disappeared. I missed craving cock and really desiring someone, when truthfully, all I wanted was an early night with a book and to sleep uninterrupted.

For the past few years, this is how our sex goes. Frank reaches out for me. I think, 'Does my vagina still work?' I am mortified to the point of outright denial that my sexual hunger has been replaced with maintenance considerations. Not that I'm treating Frank like he's a handyman or anything. It's just that he's so willing. It's a miracle he still wants to fuck me.

'What about your Tantric powers?' Cate asks Fiona.

'Ben never knew about all that. I told him I was going off on another yoga or meditation retreat. It was my secret.'

'God, what was the point, then?' Liz asks.

'I learned to experience my own pleasure. It was for me, not him. Most of us don't know how to give ourselves permission to feel pleasure,' Fiona says.

'I read in a book about menopause that we must have sex, maybe a few times a week. Quickies. To keep the pelvic floor up,' Yasmin says.

'Therapeutic fucks work just as well as any other kind,' Cate says. 'Any reason. Except pity. No pity fucking. Though, come to think of it...'

'Yes, sex is medicine,' Yasmin says. 'So now I have sex with Rajit once a week, on Thursdays.'

'Bit of a passion vampire, isn't it?' Liz asks. 'Pencilling it in, like a hair appointment.'

'We have never had passion. In an arranged marriage, this is hard. So I drive the sex bus. I don't rely on him for sexual pleasure. I get excitement from getting wet up to my elbows in dough, from mixing new spices together, from seeing chocolate oozing from my cake when I cut it down the middle. What about you, Jo?'

'Frank and I still have…satisfying sex…'

'Sounds thrilling,' Cate says.

'Least they're still having sex,' Kiri says.

'Sometimes no sex is better than bad sex,' Liz says.

'It's not bad. It's just…what I'm used to.'

I sigh. Really? Is this what I've come for? Is it even appropriate on this sacred *yatra*, which was supposed to be in silence, for me to discuss the fact that I don't know what satisfies me anymore, not even when it comes to sex? Surely, Spirit doesn't need to know that what used to work down there, doesn't anymore. That my pussy has become both indifferent and fussy, as if it's developed a personality disorder. I just never know what to expect from it: intense mood swings, extreme reactions, impulsive behaviours.

It is surely not the right place and time for me to be sharing that the best part of being over fifty is that my boobs don't hurt anymore. Now that they droop and have gotten slack, I can smack them, squeeze them, flap them around. I have to tuck them in. I do not find them sexy and cannot imagine Frank does anymore, though, bless him, he tries. He's always tried.

'Tell me what you want. I'll do whatever you want.' Frank's face was between my thighs, his voice imploring.

'I don't know. I don't know my own body anymore.'

I would have directed him if I could have. If I knew, I'd have said, *'Press harder right here, use your tongue, move more slowly, go faster,'* but I would only have been guessing. My body had changed all the rules on me, and I was new to myself, as if I had only just met my vagina and clitoris and we needed to be introduced all over again.

I feel pressured to say something to these women who have all shared intimacies of their sex life around the fire.

'We make an effort to have sex a few times a month,' I say. 'Though he says, if it's an effort, something's wrong. But I don't know about that. Exercise is always an effort, and it's always good for you.'

'The test, darlin' is, do you talk dirty to each other?' Cate says.

'Really?'

She nods.

I have tried. But it gets weird and corny.

I sometimes say, 'Fuck me with your big cock.' It's a universal turn-on for a man to hear the adjective 'big' as a description of his penis. It would be entirely un-sexy to say, 'Fuck me with your medium cock,' or godforbid, 'Fuck me with your teeny cock,' though I have read that there are women who really do love men with tiny weeny wieners for a range of personal and anatomical reasons.

'Ooh, that feels so good.' I can also manage, when he's deep inside me, because, well, it does feel good. But again, this does sound hackneyed, lame and lazy. Everyone wants to hear, 'I love you,' but it isn't sexy, as fight-fucking proves.

Frank, on the other hand, can really go for it, with talk of *tasting me, loving my wetness, eating my pussy, licking my cunt and fucking me hard.* Not original, but so what? I love it when he speaks like this, because it's so un-Frank. He becomes a stranger, not the person I call about the dry rot or my latest cholesterol results. It wouldn't qualify as zipless, by Erica Jong's standards, but it does create the illusion of delectable remoteness.

I try to follow his lead. But the words feel weird, forced. I get shy as if I'm being overheard; that it's laughable, ridiculous. I question the sincerity, although what in the end is sincere about sexual hunger other than the urge to have it satisfied? Before Frank, I was uninhibited; my love affairs were torrid. I sprouted obscenities with ease. But that sex was going nowhere except towards the next round of copulation. The sex I have with Frank is good sex, between people who love each other. It would make for yawn-inducing pornography. It's kind. Respectful. Decent. Well-mannered. Baby-making. With a history. Safe.

The night I came back from the concert with CJ, Frank was already asleep. But as I crept into the bed, my head hammering with alcohol and adrenalin, he reached for me across the bed. It wasn't a cuddle or hey-you're-home vibe. There was animal in it.

'Sorry, didn't mean to wake you,' I whispered. 'I'm a bit sozzled.'

'I'm coming for you. You better get those undies off before I rip them off,' Frank had said, groping at me.

'I'm exhausted, Frank. And these are my most comfortable undies. Don't rip them.'

'Who's Frank? I'm a dangerous stranger, not your husband.'

I let out a small snicker. 'Dangerous?'

He sighed. 'I'm trying something here. But you don't take my cock seriously.'

'I do,' I'd said. I reached for it and stroked its stiff, silky warmth. 'It's just been a hectic night. I mean, it was...'

'Pretend I'm Robbie Williams.'

He'd nestled at my crotch and pulled aside my undies. Then I felt the heat of his mouth and the sleuth of his tongue.

'God, but you're beautiful,' he growled. He kissed the folds of my flesh, stopping in between to inhale.

'The smell and taste of you,' he sighed. I could still feel the pounding of the Robbie Williams concert in my veins.

He parted my lips with his fingers and gently inserted a

finger.

'Oh god, you're already so wet…' his voice trailed off.

And my heart nearly stopped. 'Am I?'

'So wet… Robbie Williams did all the work for me.'

'Fuck me,' I said.

'Not yet.'

'Fuck me…like a slut.'

He'd stopped and looked up at me, his lips slick with my wetness. 'I will never fuck you like a slut. You are my wife and the mother of my children.'

I'd sighed. 'See, that's the problem.'

'We have good enough sex,' I say to these women. 'But I don't know what makes me feel good anymore, or what turns me on. Nothing works like it used to.'

'Climate change,' Yasmin says. 'Us too, not just the earth.'

11

Making Our Daughters Afraid

I could choose to be defeated. But at some point, with enough failures on your side, a stealthy competence sneaks up on you. You can perfect a headstand – my yoga teacher insists this is the case. However, if I don't get it right this time, in the interests of personal hygiene, I'm reverting to the good old ancient-as-childbirth-on-your-haunches squat.

I press the squidgy plastic siphon against my vulva and aim it at a tree. I've gone for generous clearance, so my pants and underwear are knee-height. This posture seems a world apart from the casualness of the unfurled penis through an open zip, where the butt retains its dignity and cover. Exposure from navel to patella surely ranks higher on the ledger of commitment. I thrust my hips forward. I tentatively unclench my pissing muscles and try to control the stream that trickles out. In. Short. Little. Bursts. It all hangs on the seal – so much as a crack and you're dribbling all over, but you dare not stop for fear of further seepage. Without that perfect airtight lock, my bladder and the whole vaginal kingdom of which it forms part will leak beyond my jurisdiction.

Suddenly I hear rustling sounds from the brush close by. I drop the funnel midstream and hike my pants up, sloshing as I go, as I feel my shoe warm and wet.

'Shit, what is that?'

We are, geographically speaking, trapped on this small beach if a wild cassowary were to make its way down here.

'Hey,' I yell into the thick brush. I read somewhere that ferocious noises can scare away predators. You have to act like you're scarier, which if you think about it, is basically parenting in a nutshell. I brace myself, ready to confront the mysterious behemoth, my heart a jackhammer in my chest.

I hear the sound of footsteps crackling in the brush.

'Ello, ello…'

'Who is that?' A woman's voice.

She arrives as a tousled mane of Botticelli Birth of Venus curls bearing a hefty backpack. A young woman with auburn hair steps out from the brush. Her wide toothy smile reveals the gums of her upper teeth. She glistens with sweat and fatigue.

'I'm so happy to see a person.' She holds out her hand to me. 'Emilie.'

She is a willowy creature in well-worn boots, with bright pink neon laces in one of them. A red and white kerchief acts as a buff around her neck. A small furry made-in-China koala bear dangles from her backpack, the kind tourists buy in souvenir shops in the cities, together with a grimy rag which started life as white lace. She is dazzled with freckles and has a foreigner's sunburn on her nose and cheeks, signalling the limits of sunglasses.

'Oh, you don't want to shake my hand,' I say. 'It's...'

'Ah, I see you using the...?' she laughs, pointing to my funnel on the ground. 'I have my own too. A Shewee. I like mine, it's very useful.'

I bend down now to retrieve my pee funnel. Bits of grass and sand are stuck to it.

'Emile, you're surely not out here all on your own?'

'Yes, it is just me. I was meant to have a short four-hour hike, but I made a mistake and couldn't find the way back after eight hours. But so lucky for me, I saw smoke from the beach from up there,' she says, pointing to the escarpment, 'and so I knew people must be here. This is why I came down.'

Her nonchalance jars alongside this explanation, as if she's misplaced appropriate apprehension. I have experience with such prefrontal cortex deficits. Jamie's still paying off her *thirteenth* speeding fine but seems on the brink of a breakthrough. Aaron's recent tattoo of Sienna's thumbprint on his wrist is a giveaway that he's still light years away from the basic math of consequence. Motherhood often feels like a long, anxious wait for the human brain to fully wire itself. I feel a stern lecture coming on, but I am not Emilie's mother.

'Eight hours is a long walk in the sun. Are you okay?'

'A bit tired and thirsty. I've finished all my water and most of my food by noon.'

'It's going to be dark soon.'

'I was just going to stop and wait for sunrise. I have a one-man tent. I can pitch it, do you think? It looks good here.'

'What about food?'

'I have a few nuts left.' She pulls a small plastic packet from a pocket in her shorts and offers them to me. 'Are you here on your own?'

'God no. That would be idiotic. How old are you, Emilie?'

'Twenty-one.' Two years younger than my Jamie.

'Does your mother know you're out here wandering around in the Australian bush on your own?'

'Ah, no,' she shakes her head.

'She'd be worried about you. Maybe you should let her know where you are, you know, when we get back in mobile phone range.'

'I don't have a mother anymore. She's passed on.'

These words land between us, lightly from her side, an

isthmus of bereavement. She is bereft of the one person who would worry for her safety, wait for her call, track her every move, demand a text to say, '*Landed safe.*' She is too untethered for my heart.

'Oh, right…sorry, I…'

'It's okay. She's gone many years now.'

'What about your father?'

She shrugs. 'He doesn't know I left Germany five months ago.'

'Do you have any family?'

'A brother, Jan. But…we have lost contact.'

There is no-one waiting for her.

I'm not trying to be an inquisitive and intrusive stranger, yet I've just about forced a confessional of personal information from her.

And I haven't even told her my name.

'I'm Jo, Emilie. I'm glad you found us. Come, follow me.'

'Everyone, this is Emilie,' I say, presenting her. Everyone is sitting around the fire on the tarpaulins, now bundled into rain jackets and beanies. 'She saw the smoke from our fire from up the top of the ridge while she was hiking, so she came down for some company and a bit of help.'

Emilie stands next to me, jostling from one leg to the other.

'Wow, this is a cool place,' she enthuses. 'Rose petals…lights…' She is enchanted. 'Hello, everyone. I don't mean to crash.'

'You on your own?' Kiri asks.

She nods.

I make my eyes big, hoping Kiri will see that I have already cross-examined Emilie and now's the time to attend to her. 'She's been walking all day and is a little low on food and water. She needs to rest for the night.'

'Shouldn't be on your own,' Kiri says. 'First rule…'

'You're very welcome to stay with us,' Fiona says.

'Are you hungry?' Yasmin asks.

Emilie grins. 'If you have leftovers…I would love some.'

'Course, we do,' Yasmin says. 'Plenty, come help yourself.'

'Thank you, yes. I am firstly needing…how can I say it…I am bleeding.'

'You injured?' Kiri asks. 'I'm a nurse.'

'I am…excuse my confession, having my menstruation.'

'Well, that's bad luck on top of bad luck,' Kiri says.

'Yes, and I have only a scarf, inside my pants, folded up.'

'No pads or tampons?' Kiri tuts. 'That's bad planning on top of double bad luck.'

'I used up all my pads two nights ago. It was leaking from rain in my tent,' she laughs. That prefrontal cortex couldn't come quick enough.

'Damn, young missy, you really thought this all through,' Cate says, shaking her head.

'I have pantyliners,' Fiona says. 'Not sure how absorbent they are though. You might need a few.'

'I have some spare too,' Yasmin says. 'I'm sorry I used my last pad just now.'

It's been close to a year of carting around spare sanitary items, three tampons and pads for my leaky bladder in my Menopausal Survival Kit.

'I think I can help,' I say.

Emilie is hungrier than she thought. Now that she's tamponed up, secured with sanitary pads, rinsed herself off in the ocean, dried herself off and sanitised her hands at Kiri's insistence, she sits cross-legged at the fire, in our circle, tucking in to the last of the farro and the corn Liz passed up. A radiance settles on her, from being among others, safe, warm, welcomed. Kiri notices a bite on the inside of her arm she doesn't fancy and administers a dab of antiseptic and a small bandage. 'Gotta watch that doesn't get infected.'

In the past twenty minutes we've learned that she's been travelling around the world. She came to Australia as a waitress on a cruise ship and since arriving has survived doing odd jobs, fruit-picking, dish-washing and casual waitressing. And yes, maybe she did run out of water, sanitary items and just about all her food, but she proudly tells us her phone still has juice in it, thanks to a solar-powered charger.

'Millennials,' Cate shakes her head.

Emilie shows us selfies on her Instagram account of herself in Darwin, Uluru, and the Great Barrier Reef. Her phone passes from hand to hand. I recognize my own hungers as I flip through her feed. She has amassed a capital of adventure in five months. Even if I started now, I could never catch up. Admiration stirs in me.

'It is fun to be with other people,' Emilie says. 'It's nice to have friends.'

'It's actually my birthday,' Fiona says. 'This is our celebration. Don't you have any friends you could travel with?'

'Everyone is at university, or in jobs,' she shrugs. 'Rushing, stressing for…what? I am wanting to see the world, before…'

'…you're old like us?' Kiri finishes.

Emilie laughs, 'I was not trying to be rude.'

'Oh, luv, don't worry about that,' Cate says. 'We're relics.'

'Also, before the world is changed and things disappear,' Emilie says. 'Your reef, the coral is bleaching. The acid in the ocean and the heat is causing it to die. This is one of the most horrible sights I have ever seen. Ja, it makes me very sad.' She tears up.

'I've been twice to the Reef,' Fiona says. 'Once when I was a teenager, and then about ten years ago. The difference was devastating.'

'Been up there a few times to do some research,' Cate says. 'Been tracking the reef for a few decades.'

'It's on my bucket list,' Yasmin says.

'I've been meaning to go for a while,' I join in.

Emilie gets a wild and frantic look in her eyes. 'When? When will you go?'

'Maybe next year, or the year after,' Yasmin says.

'Time is running out. You must go soon.'

She pierces us with her eyes, waiting for a promise.

'I'll go,' I say. 'Sometime next year.'

'Maybe we can go together?' Yasmin says.

'Let's all go,' Kiri says.

Emilie nods, though she has no idea what a miserable record of promise-keeping I have. I promised Helen we'd see each other once a year when she left. I'm not to be trusted.

Emilie wipes her mouth with the back of her hand as we all watch her eat.

'It's brave of you to be travelling all on your own,' Fiona says.

'You are my Fatimah's age, but never would I be happy for her to be doing such alone business,' Yasmin says.

'Why not?' Emilie asks.

Yasmin sighs, 'Is it safe for a woman by herself?'

'I am careful.'

'Dunno 'bout that, young lady,' Kiri says. 'Mean, here you are and it's dumb luck that you bumped into us. Besides, it's not up to you, is it? Screwballs, oddballs, psychos, sociopaths – they're everywhere. The world wasn't made with women in mind, so you gotta be extra careful.'

'I am loving *Waldeinsamkeit*, to be alone in nature, so close with forests and birds and wildlife,' Emilie says. 'Nature is not trying to hurt you. Maybe you get in an accident, but this can happen anywhere, in your own home even.'

'She's not wrong,' Cate says.

'People are sometimes meaning to hurt you. I am more scared of people than animals or weather. Some men...' she trails off.

'What's a bloke gone and done to you?' Kiri asks.

'It's really none of our business, is it?' Liz asks.

I turn to argue with Liz, for we are a makeshift coven of mothers for this motherless young woman. But Liz doesn't have much practice with parenting a young woman. Surely, she can see Emilie is now our responsibility?

'*Once is a mistake. Twice is your own fault,*' Emilie says. 'My mother used to say this. I made a mistake, but now, I will never open a door unless I know who is on the other side.'

'Bloody oath, I don't like what I'm hearing. Who's done the dirty on you then?' Kiri asks, her brow furrowing.

'A stranger.'

'What happened?' Yasmin asks. 'Tell us.'

'We want to know,' Fiona says.

'Okay, so I arrived in Darwin. This is where I got off the cruise from being a waitress in the dining room. I am excited to be in Australia, and I get off at Fort Hill Wharf, and I am going to a motel. I am asleep in my room and there is a knock on my door. When I opened it, a man is standing there.' Emilie's eyes grow wide. 'His face is familiar and I remember, I have seen him in the dining room on the cruise. "Why are you here?" I ask him. Then he pulls down his pants and shows me his *schwanz*, you know, his ... penis,' she shudders.

'He followed you from the dock to the motel?' Yasmin asks.

Emilie nods. 'And then he grabbed me here,' she says, gesturing to her long hair, 'and here,' pointing to her breasts.

'Motherfucking bastard,' Cate spits.

'Bloomin' outrage,' Kiri says.

'I shouted for help. I pushed him and kicked him. I got the door closed and locked.'

'This is a terrible welcome to Australia for you,' Yasmin says sadly, shaking her head.

'Were you injured?' Kiri asks.

'Just some bruises and a sore neck from where he pulled my hair.'

'Did you see a doctor?' Kiri asks.

'No, it was a small hurt. I took painkillers.'

'I'm talkin' about the emotional trauma, young lady. S'not just about the marks on your body.'

'Did you report it to the police?' I ask.

'What'd be the point?' Cate says. 'They're useless as a box of crocheted condoms.'

'Ja, I did report it. The woman who owns the motel drove me. The policeman took a statement. But all I know about this man is that he was on the cruise, his hair colour and beard. And his grey and purple shlong.' She shudders.

'Bet nothing came of that,' Cate says.

'Two days later, the policeman calls me. He tells me they are investigating and working on the case. Then,' she pauses dramatically, 'he asks, "*Are you free for dinner tonight?*"' She laughs thinly.

'Ah, fuckit. Men are bigger dicks than we could ever give them credit for,' Cate heaves.

'That is such a violation,' Fiona says, putting her hand on Emilie's back. 'Are you okay?'

'I am feeling fine about it,' Emilie says.

'Did you report him?' I ask. 'The policeman, I mean.'

Emilie pauses, swallows and doesn't meet my eye.

'No, I don't want him to get in trouble. And I was afraid if I did, they would stop investigating the case. And he was kind of cute. But still, I am thinking this is not how a policeman should behave.'

'He should lose his job for that,' I say.

'That's a series of serious professional conduct rule violations,' Liz says.

'And he'll probably do it again to some other woman,'

Fiona adds.

'Guarantee you that's not the first time he's done that and gotten away with it,' Kiri says.

'You were feeling unsafe from the assault,' Yasmin says, 'and the policeman made it worse.'

'Did you get his name and rank? My brother's in the police force. I got a good mind to take it up,' Kiri says.

Emilie looks around at each of us, a chorus of *how-dare-he?* and *you-didn't-deserve-that* and breaks into a huge grin. 'I have all his details. I have heard nothing about this investigation of the shlong-man from the cruise. Thank you, it is good to speak about it with other women.'

'Men are toxic as shit,' Cate says.

'C'mon, Catey. Is Gabriel toxic?' Fiona asks.

'Not counting the exceptions, mostly raised by feminist mothers.'

'Only one of mine is a write-off,' Kiri says. 'It's the temper on him that's made him rotten. His dad's genes. Blake, on the other hand, is a top bloke. Pure gentleman.'

'Farouk and Ibrahim are good men,' Yasmin says. 'We have raised them to respect women. But my Baba had this virus of a temper. See this?' Yasmin points to her forehead. 'When I was ten, my father hit me with the back of his hand. His ring caught the side of my eye.'

'That's outright child abuse,' Fiona says, aghast.

'In Australia, yes, we call it by this name "abuse". But in Iran, my father was something like a king, highly respected

– everyone came to him for business opinions. He was clever with money. But I heard the neighbours on the streets whispering about the curse on our family. Baba's anger and violence were well known in Bushehr. Neighbours became deaf and mute around us – they turned their ears away. Sometimes this is even worse than violence – how others watch and do nothing. I know people say violence is in our culture, but it is the same – even Australia, the land of the fair go, and *everyone's the same.*'

'Women and children are abused everywhere,' Fiona says. 'But to be hit by your father, the one man who is supposed to protect you, my beautiful friend, my heart aches to hear this.'

'Ai, thank you. For me, Australia is my home because when we arrived here, my uncle told my father, *"Albazi, you have to stop. No more hitting. They don't like hitting in Australia. You can get into big trouble. Even jail."* Imagine this welcome to Australia for me, my mother and my brothers. My father never used bad language – he thought it was vulgar. But he had one swear word – *DOCS*, Department of Child Services. He would shout that DOCS is like a witch's spell – it takes a man's power from him. He would make his finger like this,' Yasmin says, holding up a drooping forefinger. 'Australia is a land of limp men who make laws against a man's nature. He believed it was a man's right as head of the family to do whatever he wants.'

'He hit your mother too, then?' Kiri asks.

Yasmin nods. 'She tried to protect us, but she was a housewife with no skills to make money or stand on her own two feet.'

'It would have been so hard for her to see him hurt you,' I say.

'Yes, but she had magic powers. Not to stop the beating, but to return us to our happiness. She would make food to sing soft songs into us. She made jewelled rice with nuts and dried fruit, or rice with dill and beans. Butter and saffron, maybe raisins, almonds, barberries, fava beans, chunks of lamb. I took my lessons from her. I cook to make my sons gentle, to keep the peace, to bring kindness, the way my mother used to. Wherever there is poison, there is a cure. A calming soup. A soft dessert. A kind bread.'

As Yasmin speaks her story into the night air, under the emerging stars, I feel a small ache under the sternum, a cavity of regret. I circle back to that moment where I wish I'd found the right remedy, grabbed my chance. I should have told Aaron – the army decision aside – I'm proud of the man he's becoming.

Maybe he needed to hear that from me.

But it's too late now.

'It's common. Lots of men cheat on their wives,' I'd said.

Aaron was telling me about his friend Toby's father who'd abandoned his wife of twenty-six years. It was so classically clichéd. He'd left her for his PA and, who was, in gratuitous mathematical irony, twenty-six years his junior.

'Not real men. I'd never do that to Sienna. It's such a dickhead move.'

That was pure fathering by Frank, slowly seeped into him. He's self-sacrificingly and forswearingly loyal – the epitome of the non-cheating sort.

Here was my chance to praise Aaron. Nothing gushy or mawkish. Some breezy positive feedback on his character: *'You're a good bloke,'* or something equally low-key and Australian. I'd prefer to claim it as a careless omission, but it was more calculated than negligent. We were within earshot of Jamie and the last thing I felt like was an argument about why men need endless applause just for being decent human beings, which, she maintains, is why the average man has an inflated sense of self-worth and the average woman, low self-esteem.

When put it like that, who could argue? My hesitancy is a symptom of a deeper illiteracy as I strain to decipher the new tyrannical regime of Unacceptable Behaviours and Other Forbidden Acts of Mothering in our home. These include telling Jamie she is beautiful, how fabulous the pink jumpsuit looks on her or how perfectly the new haircut frames her face. Comments on her physical appearance are 'inappropriate,' 'intrusive' and 'offensive,' even those that celebrate her beauty. I cannot exaggerate the extent to which this has confused my mothering instincts. The 5G interference has nothing on this disruption of the world as I knew it.

I responded to Aaron's 'not real men' comment with a feeble, 'Women also sometimes cheat on their husbands.'

He too recoils if I falter into spontaneous exhalations about his 'handsomeness' or dapperness but for entirely different reasons to Jamie. 'You would say that,' he objects. 'Listen to yourself, mum.'

'Just an objective observation.'

'You're a Jewish mother. By definition, I can't trust you. You shouldn't even trust you.'

No-one likes to be religiously stereotyped, even less, belittled by a millennial in a perplexing reversal of roles. It may be a perceptive bias, but it's also a maternal right to rescue flecks of brilliance from our children's mediocrity, in much the way Blake saw a 'world in a grain of sand.' Isn't this how all mothers' eyes are made?

Aaron also gets his sense of humour from Frank. But again, I'm constrained on the limits of permissible mirth. I dare not laugh too hard or too long.

'Settle down, mum. It's not *that* funny,' he says.

'He really is averagely humorous. At best,' Jamie pipes in.

I can barely breathe right now thinking about how much I will miss my son when he's at the mercy of the military.

Frank had meant it light-heartedly.

'He probably wouldn't have needed the real thing if you'd let him play with toy guns.'

I banned all plastic weapons in our home, in stark contrast to my friend Ilana who let her son Steve collect real weapons when he began to show an interest in them. He was five years old. When I once picked up a samurai sword in their playroom, Steve warned me, 'Be careful, it's dangerous.' Ilana's philosophy was to let Steve learn to handle dangerous objects responsibly and let him 'grow out of it.' I thought it was feeding a bad habit that could only go from bad to worse.

My problem was that I never got the 'play' in 'play-play' violence. Instead, I redirected Aaron's attention to activities that didn't maim or end in death. I thought of it as a toilet training of his spirit. I became a diversion artist. Cookie baking. Jigsaw puzzles. Ceramics. Books. I didn't trust the world to teach him what it means to be a man. Perhaps he took it to mean that I didn't trust him to work out what it means to be a man. I see now how that might inspire a mutiny. And Steve is now studying botany with a focus on rare orchids.

'You backed me up, didn't you?' I asked Frank.

'I didn't want to undermine you. But I played with toy guns. Just saying.'

'You didn't have Call of Duty, and all those violent video games.'

'It's better to pretend to kill than actually kill, isn't it? It would let him get it out of his system.'

He said it as if it was the most natural impulse in the word to want to 'pretend to kill'.

Frank had had no choice – he'd been conscripted into the South African army for two years where he learned how to iron, make a bed with hospital corners, sleep standing up, and load and shoot a real gun.

You build a careful track of values one sleeper at a time, only to raise your gaze and find your kids on the express heading in the opposite direction.

Even love, it turns out, is its own form of carnage. It's either too little or too much, not in the right way or in the way we want it, a little to the left, no higher, over to the right. Its execution is a blunder by the person doing the loving and an intrusion on the person being loved. As we scramble to repair the historical deficits of our own impoverished childhoods, we seem only to slip up in another way. Overcompensation is just another form of disfigurement and ironically often has the same outcome as the easterly wound we were trying to outmanoeuvre by going west.

'Aaron has to take responsibility for his own choices.

Only offer your opinion if he asks for it,' Frank had said.

If there is any value to having parents, it's for their tendency to interpose, intervene and forewarn, based on all that bonus life experience. What kind of parent permissively shrugs their shoulders and says, 'Oh well, my work here is done, good luck with that life choice'? This is how people marry narcissists, become strippers, join cults.

Frank seemed braided with certainty when I was a bouquet of misgivings. I took his directive.

Aaron used my computer to print out his application form. He asked if he could borrow my car for his medical.

But he never asked my opinion.

'Ah, just forget about it. You're passed it,' Cate says to Emilie. 'You've survived. Anyone here not have their own #MeToo story?' She looks around. No-one raises a hand. 'Can't live your life cowering. Fuck it, something catches up with each of us in the end. We just have to run a little faster than the thing that's trying to kill us.'

I feel a ticking in my chest.

'But Cate, it's not the kind of world we want. Not yet.'

'Please promise me you will never walk by yourself alone at night,' I'd implored. Jamie's eyes narrowed as I spoke.

It had been all over the news that day. A young comedian, Paige Ellis, had called her housemates to let them know she was on her way home after performing in a show the night before. Before she could get to safety, a man stalked her from the train station, raped and murdered her. 'Paige should never have been walking at night on her own. You know that, right?'

'FOR FUCK'S SAKE, MUM! Paige did everything she was supposed to do to be safe. Have you spoken to Aaron? Have you told him not to rape and murder? Why's it always the victim's fault?' I'd never experienced Jamie's fury before. She was incensed by me. *For my collusion with the cultural narratives. My victim-blaming mentality.*

I wasn't trying to engage in a debate about gender politics. All I wanted was for Jamie to assure me that she would never walk alone at night. I wanted her to use that word: *never*.

'I won't be dictated to by male violence. I will walk where I want, when I want,' she yelled.

She refused to talk to me for days.

Weeks later, I was just falling asleep when my phone rang.

Jamie's number. 10.18pm. My heart leapt.

'Hey mum, I'm just calling you because I'm walking through a park…on my own.'

I waited.

'I just wanted to keep talking to you on the phone until I get to the car…'

'Sensible. How far away is it?'

'Quite far…' She was talking in a tone I hadn't heard before. It was consciously jaunty, the way someone speaks when they sense they are within earshot. Someone trying, putting on a brave face, pretending to be fine about walking alone through a dark park at night.

I slowed my voice down. I spoke calmly. 'Where are you? What's the name of the park? What suburb are you in?' I forensically collected details.

I memorised them. I kept her talking. 'How was your day? What did you do?' the way a mother does to take her child's mind off a bad dream or an upcoming medical procedure. I distracted her with gentle inane murmurings.

When she was finally inside the car with the doors locked, we said goodbye. I exhaled.

It was a sickening victory. I had prepared her for the world we're in. But I had to break something to get there: the woman she was before she ever feared for her safety.

Now, Emilie smiles at me through her food. 'I always feel my mother is looking after me.' She arches her head and looks up at the twilit sky.

'Pepper spray works better,' Kiri says.

'Done any self-defence, luv?' Cate asks.

Emilie shakes her head.

'What protection do you have?' Fiona asks.

Emilie erupts in an unexpected and chilling scream that seems to fill the cove and inflame the fire. It stuns us. Cate coughs in surprise, Yasmin blinks and Kiri's dentures are dislodged as if she's been punched in the mouth.

'Damn, girl, you're a fire alarm,' Kiri says, rearranging her jaw.

'That's not going to help you if you're gagged,' Cate says,

'Or drugged,' Liz adds. 'What if someone spikes your drink?'

'We are not making jokes with you,' Yasmin says.

'What would your mother say if she was here?' I ask.

She blinks at me. '*Let everything happen to you, beauty and terror.*'

'Rilke?'

'She always quoted him. He was her favourite writer.'

'Do you really think she would want *everything* to happen to you?' I ask.

Emilie shrugs. 'Not...everything.'

'Don't let us infect you with our anxiety,' Liz says. 'The only way to get through it all is to refuse to carry your mother's fears. They're nothing but a burden, and you're right to be travelling light.'

I catch Liz's gaze, and through the weary glaze in her eyes, her defences are shorn. I glimpse the young girl who lost her mother too soon, the Liz she was before the goals, the boardroom, the perfect haircuts, the manicures and the moratorium on pleasure and food. In the dimming light, she looks so breakable, someone famished for the kind of affection a child gets from a mother, and a mother gets from her child. It's an intimacy I took for granted when my children were small and hugging was a daily staple, a way of knowing who you are and what you mean to other people.

12

The War on Hugs

Emilie sits hugging her knees, resting her chin on them. As we speak, she turns eagerly to each of us, soaking in every word.

I wonder when last she was held by someone who only wanted to keep her safe, the way a mother does. She looks like she would accept an embrace from just about anyone – unlike my own kids, who were saturated with physical and emotional attention from me all their lives, and who have surreptitiously declared a war on hugs.

I've been starving for the hugs of my children for years. If you have to request a hug, it's not the hug you crave. No-one throws themselves into my arms after a hard day or rests their head on my shoulder to have a meanness annulled. Through the teen years of contempt, I learned to decode their day by navigating silences, closed doors, insolence. I've had to wean myself off the bodies of my children, like a bad habit. Unlike the justifiable deprivations one suffers to lower cholesterol and reduce the risk of stroke, this withdrawal is a swindle – it's as if you opened your bank account on physical touch one day and everything you'd been saving over the years, your entire retirement fund, had vanished.

It's not a mystery. I know exactly when the hugs from my children stopped. I remember the squeal of tyres, a terrible crashing, crunching noise, the thud of impact, spinning my blood cold.

Frank and I ran outside to find the wreck of a car, curled around a truck, its backend compressed and collapsed in folds, like a squashed Coke tin, the truck driver already on his phone, his hands in his hair.

A young man was bent over, his hands on his knees.

No blood. No body parts. Thankgodthankgod.

'Anyone hurt?' I asked.

The young man who looked no older than twenty straightened and looked at me with wide eyes, pale. He was unshaven, wearing a Pink Floyd t-shirt. His whole body shook convulsively.

'N…no…no…'

'Are you okay?'

'He nodded,' shivering with adrenaline.

'You sure?'

And yes, I know this isn't protocol, but I hadn't had much practice in being the first one at the scene of an accident, and so I did the only thing that seemed right in that moment.

'Do you need a hug?'

Frank frowned at me. 'Leave the poor bloke,' he whispered.

'I think you need a hug. Can I...?

He didn't disagree. I took that as my cue.

Frank reached for my arm to stop me, but I shrugged him off.

I put my arms around him, gathered him in. I leaned my body into his and felt the shuddering of his shoulders, the breath in him shallow and shaky, and I held him. He gingerly returned my hug. I let him rest against me. 'It's okay,' I cooed. 'You're okay. You're going to be fine.'

I have since read that friendly hugs shouldn't last more than three seconds and that heart-to-heart hugs that last up to twenty full seconds cause oxytocin to be released. Right then, I was ignorant of the science but clear on what I had to do. I don't know how long we stood there, this lad who knew he'd somehow slipped through the noose of death. I was not going to be the one to let go. I felt a sob escape him. I rubbed his back, as I might a small, frightened child.

I didn't care who was watching or whether it was appropriate. I was entirely myself, riding instinct. Days later,

I would still be able to feel his terror-trembling bones, the heaving of his heart against my chest, the smell of his sweat, and the way I lent him my strength. He was just a stranger, on his way to who-knows-where, who could have died and didn't, and who would forever circle back to this moment of walking away unscathed when there could have been so many other possible endings. This was a story he would tell on occasions when we speak of our narrow escapes, our lucky days, our brushes with death, about how he'd dodged a bullet, used up one of his lives and how a crazy woman hugged the shit out him.

When we broke apart, he gazed at me with a look filled not quite with gratitude or embarrassment, but it hovered close to the edge of that vulnerability. It was a complete acknowledgement of whatever had passed between us.

'Sorry about my wife,' Frank intervened, manly. 'Would you like us to call someone?'

'Can I borrow your phone? I think mine's somewhere in there,' he said, pointing to the mangled wreck. Frank produced his phone, and from that moment, I became invisible. The NRMA was called, the young man's girlfriend came to pick him up and the cars were towed. The only evidence of the crash was broken glass that lay on the road for the next ten days. I never got his name, but I've never forgotten him and how he let me be my open-armed self.

That night, over dinner, Frank told the kids. 'There was a car crash outside our house today. And you know what your mother did? She went up to the guy who'd just written his car off and *hugged* him.' He made it sound like I'd socked him in the face or given him a blowjob.

'Mum, what if he didn't want to be touched?' Aaron asked. 'Creepy much.'

'Did he ask you to hug him?' Jamie asked.

'No, but I asked if he wanted one and…he needed it.' I felt less sure now.

'He could have had internal injuries and you could have made them worse,' Frank said. 'We'll know when the lawyer's letter arrives.'

'You're so inappropriate, Mum,' Jamie tutted.

I felt small shifts around me, alliances forming, like the *Survivor* contestant quietly earmarked for elimination. I became the Family Freak. I started thinking twice when any of them was around, about bursting into my natural instinct. Could I say this? Could I laugh at that? Could I wear this?

And I withered.

In the months that passed, the wound burned inside me. I was trapped in a rip that kept taking me back to the scene of that accident, unable to reach the shore of my own clan.

Then the estrangement turned to anger: I didn't need to be told how to behave. Not by my children and not by my husband, as much as he loves me. I didn't require advice, approval or review, least of all permission. All I wanted was the space to erupt into my own version of myself.

Once, when I was in my late twenties, I was driving my car when a terrifying sound churned through it – as if its innards were being ripped from its chassis before it came to a dramatic standstill. The mechanic informed me that this was due to a crucial driveshaft that had come loose. Who knew what a driveshaft was or that cars had them?

'Why did it come loose so suddenly?' I asked the mechanic.

He surveyed me with the mild disaffection reserved for stupid questions by people we will simply be invoicing, not dining with later. 'These breakdowns are never sudden. Things loosen over time due to multiple stresses and factors. What we're seeing here is where the slack finally let go.'

He was speaking as a blue-collar worker, an oil-grimed tradesman who had engines and probably driveshafts on his mind. But this was some of the deepest and most profound philosophising about the human condition I had ever heard.

Not all awakenings are precipitous and bubble bursting. Psychological truths are deft and delicate. They work the slow shift, spawning like fungus in nuance, miniscule dial shifts in tone of voice, appetite and sleep patterns, like emotional asbestos, one breath, one filament at a time. They inch up on us from the inside, one cell metastasising after the other, *shhh,* while we are sleeping. They ooze in under the doorframe, between the pot plant and the window ledge. They pull up silently, no high-pitched wailing nor ambulance siren.

Pick one out at random, and it means nothing. Piece them together, place them side by side, and you get a picture.

A contamination.

An unravelling is spiral. One loop beneath another, a stack of coils unfurling. Mine had been happening for as long as I could remember.

'Sorry, they're cluttering the hallway. Please, can you take these to the Salvation Army?' I'd asked Frank the day before I left.

'You getting rid of all these books?' Frank asked. 'Done with all that self-help, have you? Become a better person?'

'Fuck you, Frank, at least I've tried.'

Despite all the personal development I'd undertaken over decades, I hadn't apparently become the best version of me, unless being a fifty-something author with writer's block was in fact, all there was. Worst of all, I'd failed as a role model for my children. One cannot be self-appointed;

one must be chosen. To them, I was the roadblock to 5G. A needless hugger. A mistake of a human being. Someone to avoid becoming.

Right then, Frank spied his Roosters mug in the box. I felt bad. The look of hurt on his face was genuine.

'How could you? It's *sacred.*'

An overpriced bit of merchandise made in China you pick up six beers later when your football team has won? Do you see what I'd been tolerating?

Mountains out of molehills. Blowing things out of proportion. Storm in a teacup. Chuck all the clichés at it you want. Granted, it's not bloodshed. It's not fraud. It's not a human rights violation to mangle a word like 'sacred'.

But if I had doubted my decision to go (and I had); if I'd felt guilty about leaving Frank for three months (I did), there it was. The universe couldn't have been clearer.

'Turkish delight?' Yasmin asks, passing around a container. 'Homemade with cornstarch, not gelatin, so it is vegan-friendly.'

Emilie claps her hands like a little girl. She picks up a piece with her fingers and holds it to the dying light. 'This is the special treat my mother bought for me once after she came back from Prague. She went to see the ballet of *Swan Lake* with her girlfriends. I was so upset for her to be away for three days, and because she did not take me with her. But she came home with a box of Turkish delight. I love this name. I always wanted to taste it since I read *The Lion, The Witch and The Wardrobe*. Do you know this story?'

'Of course, C S Lewis's *Chronicles of Narnia*,' I say. 'The forbidden delicacy the Queen feeds to Edmund to lure him over to the dark side.'

'Greedy boy,' Emilie giggles.

I imagine Emilie's mother, surely a long-haired, fine-boned woman, returning fun-wearied from a weekend away with her friends after three blissful, unfettered days, nursing a well-earned hangover from too much bubbly and too little sleep. Seeing those dancers, almost airborne, bones as light as birds. As the taxi shuttles her back towards the dinners she must prepare, the homework she must check, the backlog of laundry that will need doing, she remembers. She asks the driver to pull over outside a store. She scans the shelves to find the offering that will make everything right, the one that tells a child, '*See, I never stopped thinking about you. You were always with me.*'

For years I never travelled anywhere without spending half my time away searching for gifts to bring home. With Aaron, it was easy – some kind of ball always sufficed, a pack of cards, chocolate. But with Jamie, it was different. I searched for objects, symbolic and meaningful only between us: a book by Amy Tan. A hand-made wooden box with a secret drawer.

Peonies, I had taught her – the queen of roses.

I stopped this overcompensation for absence, or 'parenting by retail', as Frank calls it, when I knew I'd lost it - the understanding of what delights and inspires her. She found her own things without telling me. Once an old-fashioned typewriter turned up with a courier at the door. A polaroid camera. A book of Hafiz's poetry she hadn't noticed I already had on my bookshelf.

I get the gist of a spring clean, I do; but still, it was scalding to find treasures I had bought her in boxes to be given away, some unopened and unused. We can't expect our kids to become hoarders simply because our love language happens to be 'gifts'. 'Knowing' our children is not synaptic, a groove we can rely on. They outgrow our knowing of them. They change, just as we do. We wanted them to be themselves, didn't we?

Appreciation is an alignment between giver and receiver; otherwise, gifts become burdens, as fraught as secrets and as manipulative as conditional kindness.

Of all the losses of the empty nest, this one may be the most unexpected – how travel changes. I return to the nest without fat worms to nourish my babies.

I miss the part of me that combs the world, hunting for trinkets to announce my homecoming.

My leaving heralded no drama or curiosity. No-one asked where exactly I was going or why, or when I was coming home.

They responded to my WhatsApp message in the family group:

'See you when you get back.'

'Have a great time.'

'Can I drive your car while you're away?'

No-one signalled that they remembered the accident outside our house and the young man I had hugged. No-one acknowledged the rupture.

Frank and I left the house early for the airport, before either of them woke up.

'May I have another?' Emilie asks. 'If you have enough?'

'Of course, yes, please,' Yasmin encourages.

Emilie reaches for the second last piece of the soft, sticky, pink rose-petally treat.

I watch her face as she deepens into the sweetness. Her hair falls around her face. Those curls remind me of Jamie's when she was little, jet-black, not auburn. I used to plait them into a French braid while we talked of things she wished for, like a sleepover with the genie from *Aladdin* and a tea party with Willy Wonka from *Charlie and the Chocolate Factory*.

'You have such beautiful curls,' I say. Jamie would have a feminist apoplexy. I instantly regret the remark.

Emilie reaches up to touch her hair.

'I get it from my mother. She had even more hair, thick and full of curls. She wore her hair long, to hide her hearing aid.'

'Was she deaf from birth?' I ask.

'No, from a skiing accident when she was ten years old. She knocked her head and was unconscious for many weeks. It was lucky she only lost her hearing on one side. And also her front tooth, but this was fixed.'

I sense Liz's body language beside me as she tunes in to our conversation.

'My son was in a skiing accident last year. He lost a leg. He's just learning to walk again, with a prosthetic.'

Emilie clasps her face in horror. 'Oh no.'

'We're over the worst. He's walking again. The technology these days for artificial limbs is futuristic.'

'Yes, we have so much new developments with robotics and computers and 3D printers,' Emilie says.

'They're using 3D printers for implants and prosthetics,' Liz says. 'I've actually invested in a company that's using bioprinting for burn victims to regenerate skin cells. We're on the verge of advanced gene-editing technology which will transform how we treat diseases like cancer and HIV. Soon we're going to be able to cure just about all illnesses and disorders.'

'What about mental illnesses?' Yasmin asks.

'We already have neuroprosthetics like retinal chips and cochlea implants. With advances, they'll develop ways to manage memory and other parts of the brain, including the parts affected by mental illness. They're already using digital tattoos to monitor and diagnose heart arrhythmia, premature babies, sleep disorders and other brain activities.'

'Eating disorders?' Yasmin asks.

'Who knows?' Liz shrugs.

'Leah, my daughter, has anorexia. It is a frightening, invisible illness,' Yasmin says.

'That's a tough one,' Liz concedes.

Suddenly a brisk wind arrives and the salt from the sea reaches us, a fine mist of brine.

'I used to eat and then vomit,' Emilie says.

'Bulimia?' Kiri asks.

Emilie nods, abashedly.

'Such a waste of good food,' Yasmin says, 'when there are so many starving children in the world.'

'I know. It was wrong to do it.'

'Why did you do it?' Yasmin asks.

Emilie holds her hands up helplessly. 'I don't know. Maybe because I came too early as a baby, and nearly died. I was very small and skinny, and my mother always wanted to make sure I was finishing my food.'

'Least she was watching,' Kiri says.

'She never took her eyes off me,' Emilie says. 'I could

never hide anything from her. She saw everything.'

We all have our fantasies. Here is one of mine: someday my kids, sitting around a fire with friends, find themselves saying, 'My mother is the one person who really saw me.' This is a fantasy both hubristic and wasteful, for I know I've warped them with my over-mothering. Then again, perhaps an absent parent is so much easier to romanticise than a living, demanding, ageing one.

'I got the other kind of mother,' Liz says. 'She only saw and thought about herself. If you were eating a biscuit, an ice-cream cone, a slice of cake, she'd say, "You know where that's going? Straight to your thighs," before berating you for messing on her carpet.'

'She was a bit of a stickler, wasn't she?' Fiona confirms.

'Is that what they're calling narcissists these days?'

'Your bulimia is better now, Emilie?' Yasmin asks.

'After my mother died, yes.'

'That's because you didn't have anyone breathing down your neck and watching you eat anymore,' Liz says.

'I watch Leah eat all the time. Am I making it worse with this watching?' Yasmin asks. 'I just want to help her.'

'I don't know,' Emilie says.

'A little less scrutiny wouldn't harm her,' Liz says.

'I keep asking myself, *What did I do wrong? How did I cause this problem for my child?* But I cannot find an answer. Even after many prayers and books,' Yasmin says.

'Or you could just let your kids work things out for

themselves?' Cate suggests.

'Leah is too sensitive. She saw a program on TV about starving children in Ethiopia. You remember that photograph from *National Geographic*, the one that made all the news? After this, her anorexia started. She asked me, how can she enjoy her food if others are starving in the world?'

'It's dangerous to be an empath in this pain-stricken world,' Fiona says.

'It's nonsense,' Kiri says. 'She cannot starve herself because others are starving. How is that helping the starving people?'

'It could be epigenetic,' I say.

'What is epigenetic?' Yasmin asks.

'Ancestral trauma. It's like an echo in our DNA,' I explain. 'It's a new field that's developing, around intergenerational suffering. It suggests that whatever happened before us, is passed down to us as a memory.'

'It's bad enough that we have to deal with other peoples' tastes in décor and jewellery when they die, but their memories too?' Liz asks.

I admit, this does seem an oversaturation of inheritance. I'm still grappling with what to do with my granny Bee's full dinner service of silverware which I schlepped all the way from South Africa to Australia at great cost after she died. When it comes to intergenerational legacy, silverware is easy. At worst, it creates a storage problem. It's the insidious, invisible hand-me-downs that slip through the knot of our DNA and cannibalise our children's souls that we have to watch out for.

My family's story has tributaries traceable to gas chambers, young mother's graves and children's graves. No wonder I am a parenting wreck.

'They're finding success with addictions and anxieties. You know how sometimes therapy doesn't help, and drugs don't do the trick, and a change of diet makes no difference? People work so hard to overcome these issues and feel like they've failed. What seems to aid healing is an understanding that they're holding on to someone else's story, not their own.'

'Can this be true?' Yasmin asks.

'There have been experiments with mice, who are given electric shocks timed with the whiff of cherry blossom. Five generations of mice later, those poor little rodents released cortisol, the stress hormone, when they smelt cherry blossom,' I say.

'This is a fascinating discovery,' Yasmin says. 'For sure we know that we pass down history from grandmother to mother to daughter.'

'Maybe there's some ancestral trauma with food, or starvation, in your family that explains Leah's addiction,' Fiona says.

'Yes, I must explore this,' Yasmin says.

'We each gotta do the sorting, what's our stuff, what's ancestral stuff,' Kiri says, 'like separating the whites from the colours in the wash so that the colours don't bleed into the whites.'

Emilie scans from one face to the other, as if watching

characters in a play –amused, fascinated. *So this is what women become as they age.* She is in the first act of her life; we're in the second, possibly final, of our own. Shorn of maternal reminders to stay away from the edge, be careful and never talk to strangers, she is surrounded by women who quietly want to drape an arm around her shoulders and bring her in for the kind of hugs we wish we could dispense to everyone desperate for comfort.

Liz turns to face Emilie. 'I also lost my mother young.'

The two of them gaze at each other for a while.

'I was eighteen. She was diagnosed with breast cancer when I was fourteen. I knew she was going to die for about two years. Still, it shook things up when it happened.'

'Mine passed three days before my sixteenth birthday,' Emilie says. 'It was a car accident on the autobahn. My brother was driving. Me and him got not a scratch. This is why I am never learning to drive.'

'That's a backhand of a backstory,' Cate says.

'Oh honey, I'm so sorry,' Fiona says.

'My heart hurts for you,' Yasmin says.

'Yes, it was a big shock. I think it is better to die slowly. Not here this morning and gone in the afternoon. It is hard to understand.'

Gone-ness. The brain keeps trying to absorb it, but an impermeable repelling membrane gets in the way.

'Here,' she says, pulling on the bit of dirt-stained satin and tulle attached to her backpack, 'is the dress my mother was working on for me. But she never finished.'

Liz peers over to look at the bit of material Emilie is fingering and Emilie leans towards Liz. It is so obviously an invitation. I wait, holding my breath. My body twitches, like a mother's engorged breasts on hearing a baby cry. Right now, despite myself, I really do give a fuck about what happens next. My arms were made for moments like these.

Go on, Liz. You can do it. You have the medicine she needs.

But Liz leans back, widening the distance between her and Emilie, her arms folded across her chest. I can almost see her left-brain lighting up, her heart-light dimming.

Emilie sees she has misjudged the situation, and folds back into herself, like a sea creature shrinking into its shell.

And I see how things fall apart and fail, when two people try to reach across the ravine of skin, to touch with tenderness the very thing they need.

13

The Tear

From down the far end of the beach, I hear the sound of Cate clapping her open palm onto her ukulele, calling us all back. I make my way up the sand, clutching a curl of paperbark with my offering resting in its fold. When Fiona sent us off with the guidance to 'let something find you', Emilie, bustling with eagerness had asked, 'What are we meant to do?'

'Do you know what a scavenger hunt is?' She seemed unsure. 'Bring back something – a little treasure from Nature.'

'Ah, yes.'

'I'm not pulling my boot on over this blister,' Liz

muttered.

'I can find something for you,' Emilie smiled.

Liz's face had frozen. 'Oh, no…that's…I wouldn't expect…'

'It's easy for me.'

Liz couldn't bring herself to make eye contact. '…okay.'

'She's just not used to people helping her,' I'd explained to Emilie as we headed for the water.

'Why can't I live In This World?'

Jamie was four years old when she'd asked me the question I'd never been able to answer. It had been a lucky detour to break a long road trip. The kids were floppy and feral with boredom strapped in their car seats in the sweltering heat. The sign on the highway for Butterfly World meant a toilet stop, a stretching of legs and maybe, if they behaved and didn't fight, an ice cream. Any kind they liked, yes even a Drumstick with chocolate chips.

As soon as we pushed our way through the plastic flaps and stepped into the cloying humidity of the breeding enclosure, hundreds of butterflies encircled us, a winged confetti, warm, flickering, breathing. I left Frank in charge of butterfly welfare as Aaron ran around, trying to grab them with his sticky hands. But Jamie stood wide-eyed in the teeming scintillation of colour. Then she twirled, arms open, her face lifted. A butterfly landed on the warm starfish of her open palm. *'Look, mum, it chose me.'* She cried when it was time to leave. For years she drew and painted butterflies. They became her doodle, the mark she left everywhere.

In our absence, the fire has been rejuvenated and is a bubbling, spitting cascade of flame. As I arrive, Fiona picks up Cate's beat with a cupped palm to her chest. Kiri bangs the billy can with a stick and one by one, we're aroused to a ceremonial counting in.

'The time has come,' Kiri announces, 'for sacred business.'

'Ooh, I'm excited,' Emilie whispers next to me. 'This is my first time.'

Something starts to happen deep in Cate's throat, indistinguishable from a wailing, keening, Gregorian howl, an elongated 'ohmmmm' as if she's been quietly hoarding all her breath just to let it out. In it I hear the girl who sang in the church choir, the one who belted out A-ha's *Take on Me* in the shower, the intoning meditator, an unbroken thread of pure deep sound. Fiona, Yasmin and Kiri catch the billowing mantra, which is hymn and carol and psalm, looping around and around the same words which echo and refract like a fugue until I find myself lifted into the chanting too.

When the ancient singing subsides, my head is light; my brain, soft; my bones, loose.

Kiri speaks. 'First, we welcome all our relations – the fire, water, earth, air, and trees, and all the ancient spirits and guides of this land.' She folds her hands across the savanna of her breasts and her speaking rolls out of her like a preacher, a soul singer, an elder. 'We carried our troubles right here to the edge of the world, and now we share our grief in songs, in dance, in stories.'

I stroke the paperbark in my hand, this little happening of sacred flimsiness.

'Give an old fart a hand up, will you?'

Kiri and Fiona help Cate to her feet. She steadies herself, turns her back to us and spins around. A large palm leaf is a mask. She peekaboos from behind it: *Here I am, now I'm gone;* she fans herself with it, an empress; rotates her pelvis in a seductive, silent dance. You don't need her history to understand that she once owned the dance floor, that her bones were made for rhythm. It is a wordless eulogy to her weakening limbs, as they argue with memory.

And just like that, she is out of breath and it's all over. She drops the frond in the fire to hiss and smoke and choke us as it's eaten up.

She takes a dramatic bow and slowly sinks back to her knees.

Yasmin sings us into a Persian lullaby, a coil of perfect folds of melody, unintelligible. There are so many things I do not understand, but its comfort abides through the bars of my own limitations.

'From my childhood,' Yasmin says. 'My mother's lullaby to whisper, "Go away," to night terrors. This is what I sang to her as she lay dying. When I could return to the kitchen again, I knew grief was growing up from a bud to a branch.'

She snaps a Y-shaped twig in two. 'Separation, ai, we do not believe we can survive such breaking.' She shakes her head. 'But this is too simple. Things can also die if they cannot go their own way.' She tosses her stick into the fire.

The fire nuzzles then guzzles it.

'This here's from the Illawarra flame tree,' Kiri says, holding up a pod. 'Still got most of its seeds inside. Makes you think of all kindsa strange things, don't it? S'a funny business you turning up here like you did, Emilie. You're not so far off from my Tiffany. Same gumption, forgetful as a pup. She'd be wandering here, there and everywhere without a sensible thought in her head, her mind up in the clouds. It'd be getting dark before she knew it.'

Kiri picks out one of the seeds.

'Now me, I'm not a big reader, guess that's not something to boast about, but I reckon I got some undiagnosed dyslexia and so I prefer me some Netflix. S'pose that's one of the reasons I've never forgotten it – *Jesus Wants Me for a Sunbeam*. Don't ask me to remember who wrote it. One of the few books I finished. Gist of it – the little girl has leukemia. How that story turns out is the father takes his own life,' her voice breaks, 'so he can be there "on the other side" to meet her.' Kiri exhales as she plops the pod into the fire. 'But what if you're needed on both sides? Person can't be in two places at once, that's just a fact.' She hands Emilie the salvaged seed. 'Now it's time for you show us what you got, Emilie.'

'I found this pinecone,' Emilie says, holding it up.

'This is a symbol of fertility,' Yasmin smiles.

'Ah, I like it because the dinosaurs used to eat them. They remind me how old the earth is.' Emilie lets her cone drop, a dazzle of light, and the fire slurps it up.

'Any sorrow you wanna let go of?' Kiri prompts.

'It was long ago that I lost my mother.'

'How about your brother?'

Emilie looks puzzled. 'He is still alive.'

'So why you gone and lost him then?'

Kiri stares into Emilie's face for what seems like a long log-flickering minute. She reaches out and takes both her hands in hers. 'You never done something that needs forgiving, then?'

Emilie shifts uncomfortably. '*Doch*, of course.'

'There's lotsa things you can't change – for one thing, he's your *family*. Someone's gotta forgive him, else he'll never forgive himself.' This moment hangs, like a seagull clutching the wind, with nowhere to go and nowhere to land.

Kiri's tone softens. 'You didn't ask for this story, and neither did he. He's the only one who lost a mother same time you did. You were in the same car together when it crashed. No stronger bond than what two people both lost.'

Kiri brings her face to Emilie's so their foreheads touch.

'How 'bout you, Liz?' Kiri says. 'You got something to offload here?'

Liz holds up the bright pink sea-fig flower Emilie brought back for her.

'You can make toffee and jam from the fruit pulp of Pigface,' Yasmin says. 'Also delicious pickles from the leaves, like salty kiwifruit. Jo would like this flavour.'

Liz flips the flower into the fire and looks around at us.

'Wanna share what you carried all the way here?' Kiri says. 'And I don't mean in your backpack.'

From the north side of the cove, where the ridge looms, deep in the rocks, cicadas begin to stir in the heavy stillness.

'Make a wish, if that's easier,' Fiona whispers.

Liz gapes into the fire. She twists the cocktail ring on her finger. 'Last time I made a wish, I asked the Tooth Fairy for Fantales rather than cash.'

'What is Fantales?' Emilie asks.

'You gotta taste Fantales,' Kiri clucks.

'Chocolate-covered caramel lollies,' Liz says. 'Iconic Australian brand. Each one comes with a celebrity biography and trivia on the wrapper. I used to trade them at school. Collected hundreds of them. Maybe thousands.'

'I remember another wish,' Fiona says.

Liz meets Fiona's certainty with a slight tilt of her head.

'That your mother would see you graduate, remember?'

Liz nods. 'So we know wishes are for children. Still, I wish for your next birthday, you'd let me take you to the Sheraton.'

Fiona smiles, 'I wouldn't miss it.'

Kiri gestures to me. I unfurl my paperbark to reveal bright blue and black wings.

'A Ulysses butterfly.' Cate is impressed.

When I first saw it on a rock, I thought it was alive, but as I bent down, I saw its quiver had left. I wondered if I should leave it to rest where it chose to settle in its last moments. Lifelessness is always an electric shock: *gone*.

'Why does a butterfly die?' Emilie asks.

'Females die after they lay their eggs,' Cate says. 'She's done what she came here for, her job is complete. No such thing as a menopausal butterfly.'

'May I see?' Emilie asks.

I pass the paperbark around the circle. Emilie holds it in one hand and touches the wings of the butterfly with her other. In that simple gesture, the one wing tears right off and sticks to her finger. 'No no no no...' She looks at me panic-stricken.

'It's okay. We can't hurt her anymore.'

Emilie holds her finger out to me so I can pull the wing off and I lay it in the paperbark with the rest of the butterfly.

I look up at these gentle faces and I am churned backwards like Alice down the rabbit hole. I am at Jamie's bedroom door watching as she rubs coconut oil into her tattoo and my daughter has made two irreversible decisions without me.

Please shut the door on your way out.

I pluck both my children into consciousness. I try to see them, but I cannot get a clear image as they flicker between child and adult. My brain won't let me seize or freeze them. Did I dream them? Are they real? What are they doing right now, at 6.36pm on a Thursday evening?

Everything is leaving too soon, and I am not ready.

I tip the butterfly into the fire.

I don't say it out loud. I speak it down into my cells, the ones that Jamie shares.

I'm sorry I couldn't make that world for you.

Fiona begins a dance with oyster shells in each hand, to music Cate pulls from her ukulele. A backwards bend, a wrapping of arms around her body, spinning and twirling. The oyster shells are breastplates, earmuffs, castanets. Finally, they are two halves of one whole.

She kneels down at the fire, placing only one of the shells into its flames.

'My sisters, I brought you all here so I didn't have to be alone on my birthday. But the truth is, I've been alone for the past ten years.' She looks up at us, reckless with confession. I can see it in her eyes – something she has been storing that is ready for release.

'I was planning to divorce Ben.' She pauses. 'I had a lawyer. I was just waiting for the right moment. And then he got sick.' She seems stunned by her admission.

'Why didn't you say something?' Yasmin asks.

Fiona shrugs.

'You hid that like a pro,' Liz says.

'I should have left a long time ago.'

'Toss those *shoulds* into the fire, my friend,' Kiri says.

'I was unhappy for so long. I put up with so little joy for years. Ben was forever away on business. We seemed to argue about Kirsty all the time. She was his blind spot – we could never see things the same way.'

'Blended families, you need a bloomin' medal,' Kiri says.

'He kept giving her money. In the past six years, she's borrowed over $50,000 from us. But she hasn't paid back any of it. That money would have helped save my business. There's no record of what she's borrowed, so when it comes time to dividing up the estate, Gabe won't get his fair share.' Her lips quiver.

'Can't you document what Ben gave her?' Liz asks.

'He hid some of the transactions as business expenses and gave her cash too. I've honestly got no idea how much she's borrowed. Fifty thousand dollars is what I can trace. But I don't want to talk about money or desecrate Ben's memory.

What I needed was to tell the truth, to have witnesses. I want to let it go and get on with my life.' She exhales as if she's been holding her breath a long time. 'The hardest part is owning my hypocrisy. I pretended we were happily married all the way to the end. He died thinking I was still the love of his life.' She drops her head into her hands.

'Ai, Fiona, you protected Ben from heartache,' Yasmin says.

'I've been living a lie for the past two years. It's made me feel crazy.'

'We all just marking time,' Kiri says. 'Anyone you know in a happy marriage?'

'Mine is an arrangement,' Yasmin says. 'We don't expect happiness.'

'I am.' These words jump from me.

'What, Jo, you didn't get yourself a disappointment called a husband, then?' Kiri asks.

'Frank is a lovely man.' Not an asshole. Not a swindler. Not a drunk. Not cruel. Not irresponsible. Not selfish. I shuffle through the card deck of Frank's personality traits like an emotional croupier. 'Of course he has bad habits…we all do…'

'Porn, I'll bet,' Kiri says.

'Gambling?' Yasmin offers.

'Cocaine?' Cate suggests.

'Prostitutes?' Liz asks.

'God, no, nothing like that.' I feel ridiculous as I divulge, 'He's a stickler. He does not stray from the list.'

'What list is that?' Yasmin asks.

'The shopping list.'

'A man who can follow instructions? Clone him,' Liz says.

'Why is this a bad habit? Kiri asks.

It's admittedly not a crime to only see what's directly in front of you and completely overlook that strawberries are in season and they're practically giving them away, three for the price of one. How can a marriage fall apart because one party never notices the serviettes or cat food are down to the dregs? It's surely forgivable to stroll past a new limited edition of caramel yoghurt or lychee chocolate. But what I am doing – proclaiming dissatisfaction with my husband to strangers – is both disloyal and misdirected, like filing a complaint to the wrong department. It is one-sidedness at its most unscrupulous. Frank is not here to defend himself. But the personal has ruptured into the political, right here, amongst others who flounder under a similar avalanche of mundane discontents.

'Men don't understand how to be gatherers, only hunters. They go out to catch one fish, they come back with one fish,' Yasmin says.

'You saying that's his worst fault?' Kiri asks.

Frank had looked bewildered. 'It's a once in a lifetime invitation, an international writer's festival. Just think of the exposure, the publicity, the career-defining opportunities. What's it been about, otherwise?'

'I just can't... I feel like a fraud, talking about my writing.'

'You've written ten books.'

'I haven't written anything in over two years. I don't know what to say anymore.'

'Talk about your successes.'

'I've lost it – that thing I used to be able to do, with words.' It seared me to say this out loud, but these were my undeclared truths.

'Nonsense. It's like riding a bike.'

Really? Had he ever written anything? And he knew I can't ride a bike.

I'd given as much to my writing as to motherhood. I'd devoted myself to characters, plot lines, transformation arcs, grateful for meagre advances and paltry royalties. I'd watched my best books flounder and sputter for life on Amazon, and bewilderingly, the book I was least proud of become a minor bestseller. Books of mine had been pulped. I'd won no awards, been overlooked for writers' festivals, had none of my books optioned for the screen. I'd abandoned my writing, only to recommit to it, avoiding the obvious similarities to an abusive relationship. When I'd stood back to appraise my life's work, what I saw was a career in jealousies and doubts, failures and disappointments. Then the writer's block hit – a paralysing void whenever I sat down at my computer, emptying me of the ability to do one of the two things that made sense of who I was.

By the time the offer arrived celebrating my achievements as an author, the longing for this kind of success had dissipated in the waiting.

'Besides, you're so good at public speaking. You've done so many of these presentations, just recycle one of your old talks.'

I'd done such a great job of pretending that I'd fooled even the man in front of whom I fart, belch and cry.

'Where's the woman I married? She could do this in her sleep.'

Right then, something between us tore, just like the wings of a Ulysses butterfly.

When someone was just trying to touch me and meant no harm.

I turn to Kiri and say, 'Yep, other than that, he's pretty alright.'

'So how come you've left him, then?' Cate asks.

'Oh, I haven't left him. Not permanently,' I say.

'You're thinking about it, though,' Kiri says.

'Of course, she is, yes,' Yasmin says. 'Every woman is thinking about it.'

No, I'm not. These words line up. I open my mouth. The sentence tiptoes to the tip of my tongue and then slides back down my throat. I scratch the soft inside of my left elbow.

'She's not,' Fiona intervenes. 'She and Frank are soulmates.'

The fire sizzles. A log falls, giving off neon orange dust, a cascade of molten heat.

I understand what she's doing. She's protecting me, standing up for me like the feisty girl with the bruised knees does for a kid being bullied in the playground.

These women know nothing about me or Frank. Fiona's interfering.

But she is wrong.

'I need to go away on my own,' I had finally mustered up the courage to say to Frank. He'd paused *Who Wants to Be a Millionaire*. It was a question for $50,000 and of course, he knew the answer.

'For how long?'

'I don't know, maybe two months.' I had paused. 'Maybe a bit longer.'

Frank had reached out for my hand. Now I had his attention. His eyes flickered back to the television screen. *Is it A…B…C…or D?*

'I need to be alone for a bit. You know, after everything

that's happened.'

He nodded. 'Don't take the short story thing personally.'

'How else can I take it?'

'Impersonally?'

It didn't implicate Frank the way it did me. For starters, I'd had to explain to him what *dystopian* meant. Jamie's prizewinning short story, *The Right to Life AB* is set in 2045, when foetuses can elect to terminate their relationship with their mothers just as pregnant women can choose to abort their pregnancies. Communication is done through ultrasound, and if a foetus chooses, it can be surgically removed and grown in an artificial womb. The AB in the title stands for 'After Butterflies.' 'No-one remembered having ever seen a butterfly,' is the first line of the story.

'It's not just the story. It's been one thing after the other, CJ, Paige Ellis, David Attenborough…everything.'

'David Attenborough? Thought that would calm you down.'

All my bingeing on wildlife programmes had been a mercy to my heart. I'd made the switch from the news, CNN, politics, planes crashing, war in Syria and the climate crisis. It was medicinal, to connect me to the glory of our planet, give me perspective. But I hadn't reckoned on how heartbreaking Nature really is.

I'd been drawn into the lives of creatures in jungles, mountains, caves, oceans, entranced by their endless quest for food, water and procreation. I found myself sobbing at the fate of tiny tree frogs, fruit bats, meerkats, and animals I'd never even heard of – the sengi and the ibex – and baby reindeers separated from their mothers who spent weeks searching for them, but they'd already been killed by vultures.

'I have to be on my own for a while,' I said.

This was supposed to be the time in our marriage to find each other again, as a child-free couple, to reignite whatever flint had brought us to this co-tending experiment in raising people. Like two scientists engaged in a mutual research project, we'd shared the responsibility, playing to our strengths. He's mostly provided the finances and me, the emotion. Our collaboration has been expressed through text messages and conversations: *How should we handle this? We need to talk to him. Who should speak first? You want to be good cop or bad cop this time? Let's call a family meeting.* We'd canvassed behind closed doors, him usually calming me down, reminding me not to panic. We'd confided the unutterable to each other: *I don't like who she's hanging out with. He's a selfish shithead. Fuckin' animals.* He'd comforted me when I'd cried over them, the kind of tears children should never know a parent has shed, borne from the heart-arresting angst for your child's emotional wellbeing. *I don't think he's coping. Should we get professional help? Do you think we should get a doctor to check that out?*

Frank's finger twitched on the remote. But he turned to face me.

'Then you must go.'

'Really?'

'Absolutely.'

Tears sprang in my eyes,

'Is that the wrong answer? Do you want me to beg you not to go?'

'No, of course not.' I wasn't playing a hard-to-get game. This wasn't a trick, or a test. I didn't want him to freak out and tell me he can't live without me. Or get suspicious and imagine I was going off to have an affair. Frank is self-sufficient. It's one of the reasons I'm with him. I am not a wife-in-your-pocket and he is not a husband-in-your-handbag. Over the past twenty years we've taken turns to go away by ourselves, leaving the other to take care of the kids, as we've each pursued our own careers and he, an international cycling obsession.

But this was different. This was a sabbatical from our marriage, from who I was as his wife and as a mother. I knew it was a big ask.

I also knew he would miss me terribly, and that I would probably miss him too. But I wanted to feel that – what it feels like to miss and be missed. I missed being missed.

'Are you not happy?' It was a sad question, without an A, B, C or D option.

How could I explain it had to do with the linen? Maybe not when he'd vetoed the purple towels. Or when he said, 'You've got to be kidding,' to the red bedspread. But when he shook his head at the forest green sheets, I began to fray. 'I don't mind grey,' he'd said. White it was then. The colours of peacekeeping and marital treaty. I kept brightness for my wardrobe. For all

I knew, he secretly flinched whenever I threw on an emerald shawl or stepped outside in my fiery pink coat. It does the reverse of wonders for your sense of self, to know you are a source of unmitigated sensory overload to the person you live with. Frank, bless him, had learned to smile and say, 'You look lovely,' because that's what good husbands say to wives who have applied lipstick and chosen earrings.

Then there was the waiting. I'd wait for him to come home before eating dinner, even though I prefer to eat early. I'd wait for him to wake up before going for a coffee, though all I wanted was to have one down at the beach at sunrise. My own rhythms broke, reset artificially, like a woman on the pill.

'I have happy moments,' I'd said. 'But there's something in me I can't access while I'm in this life with you, and I need to work out what it is.' I paused. 'I didn't think it all through – like what was on the other side of motherhood. Getting here was the whole purpose of my life and now that I'm here...'

'...you have no use for me?'

'No, it's not that. I have no use for the identity that got me here. I have to figure out all over again who I am.'

I could see Frank's bafflement, but through it, also his strength.

'I have to go inward, and to do that properly, I have to be alone. But,' I paused, 'I'm afraid that if I go, things will change between us. I'm scared it will shift something in me, and I don't want to do anything that will hurt us.'

Frank reached out to wipe my tears. They were the truest

words I'd ever spoken.

'You can't not go because you're afraid of what might happen. We'll figure it out when you come back. You have to go. I don't want to stand in your way or stop you. I'll take you if I must and come get you when you're done. And we'll work it out then.'

See, this is why I had chosen him.

True to his word, he dropped me off at the airport. 'See you on the other side,' he'd said, hugging me. 'I love you. I hope you find what you need.'

But as I turned and wheeled my bag away from him, I felt traitorous to us.

Ours was never a Heathcliff and Cathy–like passion. It had none of the drama of fervency, the rapture of Plato's twin-souls. Neither of us ever bought the myth of 'the one'. We both understood the magic recipe of timing, compatibility and intellectual equality as the ingredients of our connection. Such practicality had leached our relationship of romance but had grounded it in the firm soil of abiding friendship and respect.

So no, I would never say that Frank and I are 'soulmates', and if we are, it is not what I imagined it would be. We have made a life together with as much esteem and lightness as any two people I know. He knows me best because he has seen me at my worst. More than that, he has loved me at my bitchiest. He is funny and smart. He tells me I keep him on his toes. His particular way of corralling me and immunity to the provocations of my moods makes him the only person who could ever put up with me. He is goodness and kindness and loyalty.

And with all of that, I still craved more. More of what? I couldn't say. I'm not interested in an affair, or trading in one husband for another. If Frank can't give it to me, it can't be given. If we cannot have it, it cannot be had.

I had left him to finally make peace with this fact.

14

The Point of Children

'Don't fancy this wind,' Cate says, zipping up her windbreaker.

The sudden breeze causes the sand to skitter. The fire gyrates in its stone-enthroned pit, lapping at the gust, and stuttering as the air around us chills. The spaces between us have shrunk, and we huddle close as the optimisms of day are corrupted by darkness.

Kiri sniffs the air. 'Reckon we oughta put out the fire and head up to the cave. I feel a change coming.'

'Not rain, surely?' Liz startles.

'That'd be a miracle, but it's what my nose is tellin' me,' Kiri says.

I worship rain in just about all circumstances, except right about now. God knows we need it. The preferences of middle-aged women to stay dry are irrelevant. I've been caught in thunderstorms – one in my youth, while climbing Mount Mulanje in Malawi. Rain changes where you are and what you can trust – landscape, water levels, visibility, safety. It makes everything slippery. Scaling the incline back out of here will be a mudslide after a downpour. The stirrings of anxiety about how we'll all manage tick loudly in my chest. Cate, especially.

Suddenly, I hear a splat. Spittle on my cheek.

'Run for the cave,' Kiri calls. 'I'll put out the fire.'

Fiona and Yasmin each give Cate a hand up, and everyone gathers what they can, including the flickering fairy lights draped over the driftwood, before making their way up the beach towards the cave.

I follow Kiri's lead, scooping handfuls of sand onto the fire until it puffs and splutters, smothered by the pelting rain.

'Who would like some Persian love cake?' Yasmin offers as she peels back the tin foil to release the waft of cardamom, nutmeg and orange.

We are huddled in the cave, our head torches and the overly bright lantern scatter light in strange arcs, throwing shadows. We've unfurled our sleeping bags to mark where we'll surrender to the overnight part of this adventure. It's going to be a close affair of elbows and heads. Apart from the first sleepover and reunion with Helen and girlfriends, I haven't slept in such proximity to anyone other than Frank in fifteen years. I stand at the entrance to the cave where the fairy lights now twinkle and listen to the soft singing of the wind and the rain.

'This is the cake my mother baked for every birthday. I bake it for all my children's birthdays too. It is a tradition,' Yasmin says. The cake is dusted with dried rose petals, pistachios and icing sugar. She inserts a single candle into the centre.

'Oh, Yasmin, sweetheart, that's just lovely,' Fiona says, pulling her close to give her a kiss.

Cate offers her lighter, and Emilie cups her hands around the candle so that it springs to life.

'Happy birthday to you,' Yasmin begins, as we all join in, even Emilie and Liz. Fiona sways helplessly into this singsong before blowing out her candle.

'C'mon and give us a piece already,' Cate says, ferreting in her backpack. From a leather holster, she pulls out a large hunting knife.

'We are not slaughtering a dog,' Yasmin gasps.

'You need protection when you go out into the wild,'

Cate says, unsheathing it with unsteady hands.

'Rule number one,' Kiri says.

'You don't need a sledgehammer to swat a fly,' Yasmin says, removing a cake-cutting knife from her velvet pouch. 'Put that killing weapon away please.'

Cate sighs, returning her machete to its holster.

Emilie receives her slice with glee, her fingertips embedded with dirt around the cuticles and under the slivers of nail. 'My mother never baked cakes for my birthday. She bought cheap cakes from a supermarket,' she says between mouthfuls, her lips glistening with syrup.

It edges close to a complaint, the kind we all have against our mothers before we become mothers ourselves. I never baked cakes for my kids either. What a relief it would be if that were their single grievance against me. I'd consider it a win for them to bring their confectionary disappointments to the therapy couch.

'Then you will make cakes for your children,' Yasmin smiles.

'*Nein*, I am not having children,' Emilie says, wiping her mouth with the back of her hand.

'Ah, Emilie, you are young still. When you meet the right man,' Yasmin soothes.

Emilie laughs and shakes her head. 'I am never getting married.'

'Maybe you'll change your mind someday,' Fiona offers.

'No. Marriage is so…weird. I don't know whose idea it

was. Anyways, I'm… I like both men and women.'

'Bisexual?' I ask.

'Ja, and not just a couple, sometimes three or four even.'

'Open? Polyamorous?' I ask.

She nods. 'It's not natural, just one. I can never choose just one.'

'Talk about having your cake and eating it, hey?' Kiri says, chomping on her piece. 'Delicious cake, Yas. You're a damn diabetic's nightmare.'

'What about jealousy?' Yasmin asks Emilie, her eyes big.

'Maybe there is a little, sometimes, but okay, even in marriage, you also get jealous, I am sure. I am hearing lots of unhappy stories from you…'

When I was Emilie's age, people were straight or gay, married or single, had kids in or out of wedlock. Like the either/or of economy class meals (*the chicken or the pasta?*) it simplified things. Relationships these days are a smorgasbord of pansexuality, demisexuality, thrupple-dom, polyamory, transsexuality, swinging – and these are just the fashionable ones. I had to ask Jamie to explain what she meant when she said she was in a 'polycule'. It refers, to my genuine enlightenment, to the group of people in a polyamorous union. I didn't freak out as she predicted, but gamely drew her attention to the mathematics of STD infection given the numbers.

I once travelled business class on my way to a rare all-expenses paid international conference. I felt naïvely misplaced, two-people deep at business class check-in, as the line for economy snaked five, six, seven times around the crowd-controlling barriers. The customer service officer leaned conspiratorially towards me and pointed at a door. 'You can head through that gate to get through customs quickly.' I'd never noticed these secret passageways to short-circuit the mayhem of the stumbling, swerving, sweating masses. The outrageous convenience, far from soothing, infuriated me. All my life I'd been excluded from this knowledge, forced to follow the throng, lose myself in the mob while the already privileged few leapfrogged ahead to the buffet in the business-class lounge.

This strange and lovely young woman licking syrup from her fingers, with a fraction of our life experiences, has somehow unearthed a shortcut to an understanding I'm only slowly reaching now, after an exhausting wait in line.

I don't know what it says about the kind of woman I am, that I agreed to a partnership with Frank in nuptial real estate although the architecture suited neither of us. Not every compromise is a cop-out, especially those girded with sacrificial undertones. I'm not laying it on the kids when I say we got married for their sake soon after we immigrated – for all they knew, we were having a party with a colour scheme. We grabbed the security handles of convention, huddling like penguins against the snow blizzard, seeking refuge in the pack. We bought into the Family McMansion where our kids could shelter through the storms of life. But we both knew it was a flawed plan upfront.

By the terms of this arrangement, Frank and I became doorways for one another. I held myself open exclusively to him, and he did the same for me, gratifying our egos' clamour to be the only one, special, chosen. I suspected the lease on our union would naturally expire, when in the throes of teenage narcissism, the kids didn't overly care whether their parents still loved each other. Without children to complicate matters, I'd never have contracted out of my rights to waywardness nor would I have acceded to the monogamous, unsexual, self-sacrificing martyrdom of motherhood.

I once made a list of my heroes – Frida Kahlo, Oscar Wilde, Virginia Woolf, Freddie Mercury – and noticed, with a start, that few of them were parents (by design or default). And those that were, were probably quite horrible at it.

How did I stumble? Why didn't I ask all these questions before I stood a chance of hurting someone I love?

'I don't believe you.' CJ had shaken her head, leaning forward so that I could smell the pineapple on her breath. The music in the bar was intrusive and we'd had to shout to hear each other. 'You're saying you've never been unfaithful?'

I'd sipped my pink gin. 'Not to Frank.'

CJ had leaned back and given me a sizing-you-up glance. 'You are so not a one man til death do us part kinda woman.' It felt like a challenge.

'What kind of woman am I then?'

'You're...' she'd cocked her head and narrowed her eyes, '...dangerously curious.'

'You can be curious and faithful.' I sipped my drink. 'That's why I write.'

'And how's the writing going?'

CJ could be a sassy bitch when she wanted to.

'That's what happens when you stay in one place for too long. Stagnation.' She'd slugged back her martini. 'You think about that while I get us another round.' She'd slipped off her barstool.

'I don't want...' but she'd already gone. My drink was still half-full. I twirled the straw in the gin. The ice cubes clinked against the side of the glass. I chased the ice cubes around the inside of the glass until I cornered one. It burned the inside of my mouth as I sucked on it.

Frank and I had always been upfront about our shared misgivings about marriage. Good on the swans, gibbons, bald eagles, barn owls, wolves, octopus and beavers for mating for life, but humans are a less easily contented species. Humans are sexual omnivores. When you understand that, it makes mind-easing sense, the kind that relieves shame and guilt. Monogamy is a preference in service to a higher good – like the quinoa-eating vegan who salivates at bacon, the nun who chants a thousand Hail Marys while her clitoris throbs, the bodybuilder who lingers outside McDonalds for a whiff of those fries.

CJ plonked a shot glass down in front of me. 'You know what I see when I look at you?'

I was intrigued.

'Someone who is not for the taking. You don't want to belong to just one person.'

'I do belong to one person for life – that's what marriage is.'

'You know why I fell in love with Kito? He's into punk music, heavy metal, reggae, country, the blues, Gregorian chanting, even fucking Mongolian throat singing – have you ever heard of such weird shit? It's the sign of a deep and rarefied intelligence, to have a range of taste in music, books, movies, clothing, food. So why not when it comes to sex with other people?'

'A vow is a vow, CJ. Don't get married if you want to fuck around.'

'You know where I'm going next year? To Yunnan in southwest China. I'm going to spend a month with the Mosuo. Ever heard of them?'

I hadn't.

'It's a matriarchal society, one of the few that's left. The women never commit to one man. They have what are called *walking marriages*. There's no social stigma attached to the number of men they sleep with, they don't live with one man, and it doesn't matter who fathers the children because the women help each other raise the kids. Imagine if you could have as many one-night stands as you liked, or regular hook-ups with different lovers, that could turn into life-long partnerships – or not.'

'Southwest China, huh? Who'd have thought?'

'You can't tell me you don't fantasise about other naked bodies, the sounds of other people's pleasure. Don't you wonder what strange sexual act someone new might get you to experience? How you might feel with someone else's tongue between your legs? Whether you've already experienced the range of orgasms you're ever going to? And whether all you've had, is enough?

I used to. 'After what Tom did to you when you were pregnant, never thought I'd hear you be an advocate for screwing around.'

'Tom's problem is that he got caught. And anyway, I'm over it. I've forgiven him. We're friends now.'

'You're kidding?'

'Friends who fuck occasionally.'

'Does Kito know?'

'We have an open relationship,' she'd laughed. 'And besides, the one thing Tom never lost was his fuckability.'

'So he's not TFB anymore?'

'*That Fucking Bastard* had become part of my inured vocabulary. What was I to use now that TFB was off the table?

'I got over myself. All that inner work, therapy and meditation paid off.'

'Bullshit! Meditation? You were always so dismissive of all that spiritual stuff.'

'Kito got me into it. I've become the queen of chill. If I'd kept holding on to my anger towards Tom, I'd have gotten cancer, like Fiona did.'

'Fiona?'

CJ had raised her eyebrows. 'What do you think that kickboxing was all about?'

Kickboxing, come to think of it, had seemed out of character for someone as earthy and green as Fiona was. But contradictions are what make people surprising, fascinating. Maybe I couldn't read people after all.

'If you repress it, it will erupt. Monogamy is a man-made rule – to keep us gals oppressed, Mrs-Fucking-So-and-So. That's not your vibe. That's not who you are.'

If there's one thing I hate, it's people telling me who I am.

'You can still have kids without getting married,' I say to Emilie. Frank and I only got married when our kids were five and seven.

She shakes her head. 'I am never having kids.'

'Why not?' Yasmin asks.

'We are too many on the planet. There is no point to having children now. More people are only causing more problems.'

'I've never understood the point of children,' Cate says. 'They take root inside you like a parasite. They suck the life and money out of you...'

'Don' forget the teeth,' Kiri adds.

'Motherhood is like the Mafia. Once you're in, you can never leave,' Liz says.

'But isn't that what makes it so poignant and uplifting?' Fiona asks. 'You have a lifelong relationship with someone that can never be severed. It's the deepest soul contract you can enter into with another human being. You keep growing and learning – about them and yourself. You never stop worrying about their stupid choices or the people they're hanging out with, or whether they're physically and mentally well, but it keeps you connected to something beyond your own petty needs and wants. You can never be carefree. Not about them, or the planet, or the future. You're always invested in this world. Children raise the stakes and make everything worth fighting for.'

It is a stirring pro-motherhood rhapsody, excellent marketing copy.

'I'm a closer. I sign off jobs, deliver the goods, pass the parcel. When it comes to kids, you're indentured for life.

Beholden for…ever,' Liz says. 'It's too…endless.'

'You make it sound like Groundhog Day,' I say. 'It does go on and on, but what it asks of us, changes. There are seasons. We're not parenting the same way now as we did twenty, fifteen, ten, even two years ago.'

'The rules keep switching,' Yasmin says. 'It is hard to keep up.'

'Kids force you to evolve,' I say. 'You're caught in another person's life cycle, their childhood, school years, teen angsts and adult decisions. You get to be an extra in someone else's story.'

'Who wants to be an extra? Lead role or nothing,' Cate says. 'I watched my mother give her life to her five kids, and what good did it do her? Were we grateful? Pffft. We drowned her. She spent her life fighting the tide of us, spluttering for breath, a frustrated musician who barely got to sit in front of her piano. That was the only time she was happy. She once told me, "You kids stole my life." What could I say? "I'm sorry, mum. It was a shit deal for you, no question." But that's parenting for you. If you're not giving up your life for your kids, you're not doing your job. Why anyone does it voluntarily is a mystery.'

'But she chose to be a mother, didn't she?' Yasmin asks.

'Who chooses to have five kids under the age of seven?' Cate asks. 'That was too much church and too little birth control. And I tell you what, you can't console someone when you're the reason they're suffering.'

'Where's she now?' Liz asks.

'Rotting away at a snail's pace in a shitty aged care facility in London, with tea at 4.30pm and lights out by six. One of my brothers rocks up on Christmas morning with a mince pie, and that's only when he's on parole. She's as bitter as old vinegar, and who can blame her? She gave her life for us and got fucking sing-a-long Thursdays in return.'

'She got you, though,' Fiona says. 'And look how you turned out.'

'What? Bit of alright thrown in with the damnable and the decrepit.'

'Oh, come on, Catey, you're a champion,' Fiona says.

Cate laughs out loud. 'We're too damn sentimental about our value as people.'

'What about Rilke, Rumi, Frida Kahlo, Albert Einstein, Nelson Mandela, Greta Thunberg?' I ask. 'We've produced some astonishing human beings, haven't we?'

'A handful, maybe. Most of us plodders are polluters and oxygen thieves. Don't get the fuss every time a mother goes into labour. Chances are, she's pushing out another psychotic, narcissistic addict, as if we're running short of those. My two pence worth? Those of us with the privilege of an education have a moral duty to draw a line in the sand and say, "No more." Biggest contributor to climate change is fucking relentless motherhood.'

'No, Catey, that is unfair,' Yasmin says. She looks genuinely injured.

'Don't take it personally, Yas. I'm talking science, not sentiment.'

'Motherhood is marketed for everyone, like cigarettes were in the fifties. And once you start, there's no way out,' Liz says.

'Liz, why did you have kids?' Yasmin asks.

'Same reason wives give blowjobs.'

'To wiggle away from sex?'

'To be a good wife. Carl, my ex, comes from one of those massive, sprawling Greek families. All he could talk about was "when I'm a dad..." Didn't help that he had such a happy childhood, and two quite fabulous parents, suspiciously perfect role models.'

Suddenly I am swept back to that fight under the umbrella on the beach. I had been so certain Frank was obfuscating. Was he, in fact, *protecting* me? He'd never wanted kids. He'd conceded, for me, like Liz did for Carl. Did fatherhood teach him that he didn't want to be a father after all? I sink my head into my hands. In retrospect, saying Hurtful Things might be the slightest of my crimes, when you add jumping to conclusions and misreading the situation to the list.

'But then when the kids came, you must have got some joy from motherhood,' Yasmin says.

'I had moments, splashes of oxytocin, but it was mostly a suffocating relentless labour. And that was *with* the best help money could buy.'

'It's a sacrifice marathon, eh,' Kiri says.

'Always, the children should come first,' Yasmin nods. 'But this is what makes my life meaningful. It is not just for and about me.'

'I can't fathom how I'd make sense of life if it was just about having a good time,' I say. 'I'm not built to be Caligula, to do nothing but travel to new places, looking for the next great glass of Pinot Noir or truffle-infused goats' cheese.'

'That's where we part ways,' Liz says. 'How's it reasonable or empowering for a woman to put herself second in every decision for the rest of her life? What are we role-modelling for our daughters?'

'We live in such a selfish, narcissistic world, there's something to be said for service. Sacrifice can be a great act of self-actualisation,' Fiona says.

'Why should women always be the ones to sacrifice? It's men who routinely leave their families,' Cate says. 'Single mothers are raising most of the children on the planet.'

'Yeah, Liz, you flipped it,' Kiri says, warming to the idea.

'Carl was a brilliant hands-on father. We had warm and mothering nannies. All of Chloe and Brandon's needs were being met. So when the opportunity came to head up the second biggest advertising agency in Europe, I grabbed it. I had no skills and no passion as a mother. In business, you don't put the person with admin skills in marketing or the creative person in finance.'

Emilie leans in. 'When I say I don't want kids, people are looking at me like I have a mental illness. Like only a crazy person can choose not to have babies.'

'Imagine the looks you get when you *leave* your kids,' Liz says.

I know the biting gossip Liz has weathered, as a *heartless bitch*, a *Lady Macbeth, a Lilith*. I'd never labelled her ungenerously, but Helen had had some mean things to say. And I hadn't challenged them, not once. Sometimes loyalty is no more arduous than registering your disagreement at the right moment.

'You'd think I'd left them in a shoebox on the church steps or threw them over a bridge, not with a devoted father. Still, people don't forgive the *leaving* part.'

'Don't be so harsh on yourself,' Fiona says. 'You stayed in touch, you came back several times a year, you flew them over during holidays…'

'Doesn't inoculate you against regrets.'

'Do you?' I ask. 'Regret that you had them?'

Yasmin doesn't wait for Liz to answer. 'No, she's not sorry, are you, Liz? For your two children?' Yasmin pleads. 'Now they are here?'

Liz thinks. 'I'm sorry I hurt them. It would probably have been better for everyone if I'd never had kids.'

I've never heard such a candid expression of remorse, the kind whispered at confession if at all. Procreation is exclusively a liturgical discourse of the 'miraculous' and the 'blessed' – a child is the 'treasure' salvaged at the end of a shipwrecked marriage or the postpartum 'gift' of a disfiguring birth or even one in which the mother dies. Having kids is a life choice, like any other. We don't crucify people who regret their marriages, career choices and other life-altering decisions. Why is motherhood a protected species?

'But then you were happy when you left, yes?' Yasmin asks. She is working relentlessly to discover Liz's happiness, a devotee.

'When I wasn't feeling guilty.'

'Sounds like you were screwed either way, luv,' Cate says. 'I don't know why we think it's unnatural for a mother to leave her kids. It happens in Nature all the time.'

Liz rubs her feet. 'I can't imagine they've developed the anti-depressants I would've needed if I'd devoted my life to raising a family. Someday you just have to look in the mirror and face the truth about yourself. I love my kids. But I chose myself over them.'

I, by contrast, kept choosing my kids. Right here, I'm thinking, might be where I failed. Of my many errors of affection, the one that has returned to cut me most deeply is that I over-wanted a family.

While most kids hunger for more time and attention from their parents, mine probably would have preferred less. I don't know how to love anyone casually, or just enough. Everything I do is over the top. I hadn't considered how that might make a child feel. I spun my love into a technicoloured dream coat, too weighty for everyday wear. As much as a child needs to know they were wanted, perhaps it's exhausting to be *that* wanted.

This parenting gig screws you, whether you take the left or the right turn. Pursue your own dreams, and you've abandoned them. Stay and you're overbearing. Liz left, and Chloe doesn't speak to her. I stayed and Jamie hardly talks to me. It's inevitable – we will burn the rice whether we watch it or walk away. It's perplexing, really, why I don't feel more liberated.

This here is a new conversation, the kind I have longed to have. Among these strangers, it feels safe enough to wonder aloud why we assume living in packs is what humans were made for. Or why we pretend one size fits all when anyone who has ever wept in a dressing room knows this is gaslighting of the most pernicious kind. It seems natural to outgrow a nest and to keep moving when we've exhausted the land, like indigenous people do to give it a chance to regenerate. Maybe families should have expiry dates, like medication and processed food, so we know 'This is good for a while, but be warned, it may go funky.'

For years, I've showered with other peoples' underwear, swimmers and cycling shorts hanging over the tap. I've sighed silently over milk left on the counter to spoil. I've cursed at peaches in the vegetable crisper bruised by beers plonked on top because 'there was no other place in the fridge'. I've lived with dumbbells under the coffee table, a toolbox in the dining room just as Frank has put up with piles of books next to my bed, and the clutter of cosmetics by the sink. I ate beef sausages and spaghetti bolognaise once a week for fifteen years when they were all Aaron would eat. I said, 'Sure, why not?', when everyone wanted the 77-inch flat-screen TV and sat through *Mission Impossible 13* because that's what everyone else wanted to see instead of *A Star is Born*. Frank still wakes me every single night when he comes to bed after midnight, pilfering my REM sleep as if it were sidewalk furniture for the taking.

My efforts with Frank have been valiant, if not flawed and disappointing in ways neither of us could have predicted. A family is the Milwaukee brace on our free spirits. But it's fair because everyone is compromising, shaving themselves down so that the alignments don't cause nerve pain in others.

I'd always regarded my pliability as a strength, not a weakness.

Adults compromise. Grown-ups cooperate. Only toddlers and teenagers can't or won't share. The middle ground, devoid of non-negotiables, is a sturdy foundation on which to build a family. I've bent willingly, lovingly, to make room for what makes Frank and the kids come alive.

But these small refrains from asking myself, *Is this okay?*, have accumulated like a build-up of cholesterol in the arteries. My identity has begun to sag. And now, in my midlife, the self against whom these questions might have been measured – the person who at one time might have said, 'Hell no, I fucking hate curtains. I adore French shutters,' and 'I'd rather have a piece of Aboriginal art as the centrepiece in our living space than an enormous flickering screen' – that person is no more. I reached in one day, and my hand moved straight through her, as if she were a ghost. The neural pathway of 'I want' has died and all I know now is 'I'll have what they're having.'

And this is why I'm sitting in this circle in a cave, in a cove god knows where, instead of in front of the TV while Frank guesses the right answers to *Who Wants to Be a Millionaire?*

Liz turns to Emilie. 'But don't listen to me,' she says. 'Don't use me as a role model. I'm not good-family material.'

'Yes, don't listen to Liz,' Yasmin says. 'Children are the sugar of life. I don't understand what "Yasmin" is without them. Everything I do, everything I am so excellent in, comes from being a mother. Taking care of people. Cooking to feed my family. Loving them. Being a mother is the most important job in the world. And this I got from my own mother. She taught me everything. She looked after me until she got sick. Then I looked after her til she died surrounded by her children and her grandchildren. We sang all her favourite songs, brushed her hair, massaged her hands. She died, smiling. Everyone deserves this kind of death – full of love, music and family. Of course, I baked a Persian love cake, but she never tasted it. The mourners enjoyed it, though.'

'Not the kind of goodbye my mum's got in store,' Cate says.

'Maybe you must go back to London to look after her?'

Yasmin asks.

Cate hangs her head. 'Yeah, that would be the fucking decent thing to do, wouldn't it?'

Fiona rests her hand on Cate's arm. 'Maybe once you get your results...'

'Yeah, let's wait and see...'

'Don't think about us,' my mother had said, when I weepily told her we were emigrating to Australia. I saw her blink, snuff out the howl of every mother separated from her young by force or fate. 'Your primary responsibility is to your children. You must do what's right for them.' Yes, I coached myself, *Think of my children*, like my great-grandfather Nachum did in 1924, shepherding my grandfather Akiva to board the ship bound for South Africa for a better future, knowing he would never see him again. Eastern Europe was no place to raise Jewish children. I imagine my great-grandfather clinched in a hug with his precious only surviving son the fingers of smallpox had failed to filch. Beard to cheek. Jacket to jacket. Heartbeat to heartbeat. I do not know who let go first, or how a parent unclasps from a final hug.

'No matter how bad a parent has been, a kid still wants to be there when they're dying,' Kiri says. 'It's where all the forgiveness and healing happen, when the parent is like a newborn, can't speak, and time is running out, and the child becomes the parent. Seen it a thousand times.'

Liz removes a beanie out of her backpack and pulls it

over her head. She tucks her hair under and pulls it over her ears. Her voice, when it comes, is close and warm, like she's been drinking hot chocolate.

'In the last days of her life, my mother didn't want us kids to come into her room. It was messy, the vomiting, the nappies. The nurse and my dad took turns looking after her. Two nights before she died, I had a joint but no matches, so I stole into her room to look for a lighter – she always kept one in her vanity. She looked so small and helpless, like a child's doll in a bed. The noise of me opening her drawer woke her. She held her hand out to me and said, "Is that you, Elizabeth Frances? Paint my nails." Like a little girl asking her mother.'

This revelation folds out of Liz, an origami of grief in reverse.

'She loved that shade, Mercury Rising,' Fiona reminisces.

'That's the funny part. She asked for Boogie Nights.'

'The deep orange? The one she said should have been called Cheap and Whorish?'

Liz nods. 'Yeah, my favourite colour. The next day she fell into a coma. We buried her with Boogie Nights on her nails.'

Liz's eyes thin into sickle moons as the memory softens through her.

'This is Mercury Rising. Must be getting sentimental in my old age,' she laughs, holding up her hands.

15

Why Bees Swarm

'You know why bees swarm?' Fiona asks.

'Menopausal rage?' Liz suggests.

'When the colony outgrows its hive and it's getting overcrowded, it prepares to separate into two smaller hives. Nature understands claustrophobia. Our children are born to leave.'

I know this – it's inevitable for a family to outgrow its hive.

Jamie and Aaron have left emotionally, but they still occupy space in the bathroom, use up laundry cycles and chew through the WiFi. The fridge empties itself at odd hours. Ten packs of two-minute noodles loaded with MSG – the kind of product I banned from our kitchen when they were little – find their way into the pantry. All of this makes for an ambiguous emptying. No-one knows who anyone is anymore.

One morning Aaron was making himself an omelette. 'Excuse me,' I said, reaching for the kettle to make my morning cup of coffee. He bristled, as if my very presence in my own kitchen was an outrageous invasion of his freedom. I knew we were off kilter when I checked with Jamie if it suited her for me to take my car for the day as she's the one who usually drives it. But the madness came to a head the night of the Soccer World Cup final. 'Would you and dad mind staying in your bedroom while my mates are here to watch the match?' Aaron asked. I had to turn away so he couldn't see my hands clenching into fists. I can't explain why Frank and I then stayed in our bedroom.

'Eventually you have to kick 'em out, or they'll cannibalise you, the very mother that gave birth to them,' Kiri says. 'I'm not sayin' I'm proud of it, but I reported Jackson to the police, anonymously of course, when I knew he was doing ice. Could not, would not, have that under my roof, no sir.'

'Is he okay now?' I ask.

'Who knows? When he's not in rehab, he's welcome for a feed, and to bring whoever his new woman is. I don't ask any questions anymore. When he wants something, he knows exactly where to pull in. You gotta love the bad with the good when it comes to your kids. No way out of it.'

'When they make you feel small in your own home, it is time for them to fly away,' Yasmin says. 'Sometimes I think they are pushing to see how far they can go before we will say no. Some of my jewellery went missing a while ago. We found out Farouk got into trouble with a $15,000 online gambling debt. My own child was stealing from me,' she shakes her head. 'Rajit refused to help him. So I took the money I was saving for my own car to clear it. I told him, "This is the last time."'

'How many times does a parent say, "This is the last time"?' Kiri tuts. 'He stopped with the gambling?'

'I don't know,' Yasmin says. 'I preferred having small children with smaller problems. I don't trust him anymore. This hurts. I miss how I used to love them and how they used to love me.'

'Get a dog,' Cate suggests. 'Only unconditional love there is.'

I think now of Stewie, that big silly grin he'd get when I'd come home, his tail swiping madly like a conductor's baton. The pirouette he'd dance on the kitchen tiles, and how sometimes he'd lose his grip and slide into the fridge in excitement. The love between parent and child is set up to be unrequited. We insisted on them, did we not? Inveigled them into our lives without their consent. It's very possibly unreasonable to expect under these circumstances for them to love us back.

Once, long ago, when I said a Hurtful Thing to my mother, she got a distant look in her eyes and said, almost to herself, 'You were just the sweetest, most loving child.' It kicked me hard, the grief in her words, the soft subtexted yearning, 'I don't recognise you. Where have you gone?' I felt that sad question tucked in there. She was reaching across the years to say to me, 'We loved each other so much back then, remember?'

Of course, I do not remember. Those are memories only a mother has. I was four years old when she loved me like that. That little girl grew up and came back to berate her mother in a voice that did not honour the snugness of the past. Now it is my turn to be spoken to like that by Jamie.

Words between me and the kids have become heavy-duty and usually involve me either censoring my love, disappointment or anxiety. I would never dare say, 'I love you more than I can bear,' or 'How many more traffic fines do you think you'll need before you slow down?' or 'That short story is a work of sheer brilliance.' They, however, don't seem similarly constricted. They express exactly what's on their minds such as, 'If I'd wanted the opinion of a middle-aged woman, I'd have asked you,' and 'Can I borrow some money? I'll pay you back next week.'

We've reached it – the toxic proximity of parent and child.

There is a tipping point where you want your child gone. You do, but of course, you don't. You want them to go so you can begin to bear what it is like with them gone, the rooms they leave behind filled with their childhoods. You need to practice being the parent of a fully responsible grown-up. It gives you the chance to tidy yourself up a bit. Until they actually leave, you're always in a halfway zone, a twilit space of not quite there yet. It will ruin you, the longing for those romanticised years when they were little.

There comes a time when adult children who should, but simply cannot afford to, move out will treat their home as a hotel, a halfway house between dependence and independence. We make do with being treated cordially, in passing, like a concierge at reception, or worse, like children who should neither be seen nor heard. I don't want to be the centre of their world anymore. I want to be replaced. I'm limp with relief that Jamie and Aaron have lovers and boyfriends and girlfriends and friends to confide in and get them through the day. Thank Christ they are lovable by someone other than me and Frank, who were conscripted in our affections.

But goddamnit if I was meant to forfeit my right as a parent to ever be seen as a human being by my own children, it was in the fine print. I never agreed, and I want to renegotiate the terms.

Someone had to break the spell. Someone had to go first. So, I left.

As soon as I opened the door to Penny's house, the years of compressing myself, hugging emotional corners, pinching myself down so as not to be too spiritual, talkative, loud, exuberant, sad, anxious or naked, flaked off me. I sobbed for all the ways I had whittled myself away, just so that they had space from me, when they were with me.

'Don't they owe us anything,' Yasmin asks, 'for all we have given?'

'Our kids don't owe us anything. Not a second thought, not their time, company, information about their lives, a duty to care for us when we're old, not even the occasional phone call to check in on us,' Liz says.

'I don't agree,' I say. 'We bloody well owe those who have paid our way into this life some measure of courtesy, respect, consideration and gratitude.'

'Good luck with that,' Liz says.

'What about the occasional Mother's Day card?' I ask. 'I don't expect to be nursed through illness or have a child change my adult diaper – I'd prefer a professional who knows what they're doing and who charges for their time anyway. But asking if you'd like a cup of tea or need some shopping done is the human thing to do – child or not.'

'I don't think a child owes a parent love,' Fiona says. 'Love isn't transactioned that way. With love, you always want choice. Otherwise, it's a perverted emotion, a mangled synaptic tangle of residual affection, fear, resentment and antipathy.'

'Yeah, better to expect less,' Kiri says, 'though they do come back to you after a time.'

'Do they?' I ask. 'What happens if they don't?'

'Then you'll have wasted a lot of time, money and energy and have zero return on your investment,' Cate says. 'What's the fucking point?'

'Are we all doomed to wonder what it was all for in the end?' Yasmin asks sadly.

'All I want is for Jamie and Aaron to like me and Frank as people, not only tolerate us as parents. Maybe someday they'll choose to spend time with us, not because they have to, but because they want to.'

'Listen, we're lucky if they leave us the way they s'posed to – move out, start their lives, forget about us.' Kiri ventures.

'It is a sad happiness when they go,' Yasmin says. 'I hope someday Leah can stand on her own two feet. She is a little bird with a broken wing. I wonder, when me and Rajit die, what will happen to this starling who cannot fly?'

'Her sister and brothers will take care of her. That's what families are for. Looking after,' Kiri says, looking at Emilie. 'Kids must take care of the old folks. That's how it's meant to be.'

I cryogenically froze the thought, when we immigrated, of my parents as old people who might need my help through infirmity. I packed it into a not-for-now box. *I'd cross that bridge. I had to think of my own children first.* I had to. Otherwise, how else could I have stepped onto that airplane and left them?

'Is it fair to expect that from our children? They have

their own lives to get on with,' Liz says. 'At some point, we have to stop re-mortgaging our relationship with our kids and filling up on what we get from them.'

I sigh. There is truth right here. As parents, we have to plug the emptiness with our own self-love, instead of tapping from the well of our children's life force. There comes a point – too many self-help books later – when we grasp that no amount of therapy will ever change the past. We outgrow the grief for the childhood we longed for that would have enabled us to grow into a different kind of adult, one with fewer or alternative hang-ups. We arrange the furniture of our emotional life in the feng shui of our heart space – we see how we cleverly made exits and escape hatches in tricky places, how we crowded hollow tracts with comforts to mask the vacancies. We determine what is ours and what isn't.

Since I've been away from my family, I haven't wasted a single moment worrying about where Jamie and Aaron are at 3am. I don't obsess over whether they've eaten today. Five veg and two fruits are theirs to tally. Constipation, insomnia and traffic fines are their own problems to sort out. I haven't imagined terrible things happening to them. I've readjusted my expectations, reeled back my unlived life from the spool of my children's destinies. I can finally see them differently, not close-up, but from a respectful distance. And what I see is two young adults who are not afraid of disappointing their parents.

I value my children above all other humans.

But I no longer wish to take on their lives. I am grateful to be unburdened from the responsibility for how things turn out for them. I'm ready to stand back and let them fly or fall. I will not take their glories and failures personally.

We have done together what we came here to do together. It is time for them to fuck off out of my life and into their own.

I can no longer say that I belong with them.

But then. Where do I belong now? With my ageing parents? After immigrating for the sake of the kids when they were little, is it time to return to the land of *ubuntu*, to spend the last years of my parents' lives with them?

Do I belong with Frank?

Do I belong alone?

'I have had the thought,' Kiri says, 'that the problem these days with kids is that we don't expect enough from them. They have way too much bloomin' freedom to be who they want. Everyone wants to be a rock star, a YouTube celebrity, or a gamer – whatever useless job that may be. In Maori culture, old people are the responsibility of the whole family. We don't outsource them to old age homes – no disrespect intended, Catey. It's just not our way.'

'None taken,' Cate says. 'It's fucking admirable.'

'There are other options,' Fiona says. 'Where we don't burden our kids, and we don't age alone. I've been exploring something called *co-housing* – it's huge in Scandinavia.'

'How does this work?' Yasmin asks.

'A group of people, say, like the six of us, might invest in a property together so that as we age, we don't become isolated – we're part of a community. We'd have rosters for shopping, cooking and cleaning. We'd have companionship as well as privacy and even medical care if we needed it.'

'I'm in for this plan,' Yasmin says, clapping gleefully.

'Anything to avoid institutional care,' Kiri says. 'Those places are just living graveyards for the old folks.'

'What about you, Catey?' Yasmin asks.

'Uh…yeah…' she says. 'If you lot don't mind wiping my arse. I expect no complaints, a steady supply of espresso martinis, and lasagne once a week.'

'These are not just old-age communities. The idea is to have people of all ages living together so that young people get to spend time with older people, and parents have built-in babysitters. Maybe our kids would come live with us,' Fiona says.

And there it is – a wish we know will never come to pass. But it is her birthday and we will let her have it.

Yasmin passes around wet wipes for sticky fingers in the wake of the cake-eating. 'I expect one call every week from each of my children, and they must come home for festivals and celebrations. I also expect some grandchildren, like Kiri.'

'With four kids, you've got good odds,' I say.

'No guarantees – my cousin Lakshmi has seven grandchildren from one daughter. And my other cousin Esta has five children and only one grandchild. You cannot rely on lots of children for lots of grandchildren. How are your grandkids, Kiri?'

'They're growin' up. It's worth having kids just to get there. They're so much better than your own kids in every way. It's the purest love there is, distilled to perfection. If only we could skip the main course and just get to the dessert, hey?' she chuckles.

'Do you have pictures?' I ask.

'Yeh, course. What kinda Nanna would I be without?' She pulls her iPhone out of a pocket from her pants and begins searching for pictures. She hands me her phone and there is a photo of her with three small people draped over her. A little girl with tiny arms flung around her neck, a boy on her lap, another leaning his head against her shoulder.

'Oh,' I inhale.

'They're a handful. You can't take your eye off them — not for a blasted second. But they make up for everything. The boys are alright, dirty little scoundrels. Little Willow is my favourite. She's a princess.'

'They're gorgeous,' I sigh. Are you allowed favourites? I pass the phone around.

'Your day will come,' Kiri says.

'I don't know. There are other things mine want to do with their lives,' I say.

'What are your kids up to?' Liz asks.

'Aaron is,' I pause, 'pursuing a public service career, and Jamie is a budding author. Having kids is not on their radar.

What about yours, Yasmin?'

'Fatimah is doing a medical degree, Farouk, economics and Ibrahim, engineering. Maybe someday Leah will get back to teaching, but now, we hope she will just eat her dinner. Children must be better than their parents. This is what evolution is. Fatimah is the first girl in my family to have higher education. It's my dream come true.'

'Did she always want to be a doctor?' I ask.

'She is still not sure she wants to be a doctor. But it's the right profession for her. She is smart enough. It is a good career, lots of respect. She will become a gynaecologist.'

'Don't tell me you and Rajit forced her to become a doctor?' Cate asks.

Yasmin puts her hands on her hips. 'When you are eighteen, what do you know? If you leave dreaming to them, this generation, they will look for the shortcut. They want things to be easy and quick. We have to parent our children and teach them how to look into the future and make decisions to protect it.'

'A woman's gotta have a career and earn her own money. It's the first rule of life,' Kiri says. 'Wish I'd studied medicine rather than nursing. Been the person giving the orders, rather than changing the bedpans.'

'Come on, Emilie, what are your dreams?' Fiona asks.

Emilie tries to run her hands through the thick knot of her hair, but her fingers get stuck. She shakes them loose. 'Me? I don't have...dreams.'

'What are your interests and passions?' Fiona asks.

'Maybe travel and hiking guide?' Yasmin suggests.

'Something to do with the environment? Maybe the ocean?' I offer.

'I don't know. I want to see as much of the world as I can.'

'Choose a career that takes you places,' Liz says. 'There are dozens of options – become a flight attendant, a pilot, a tour guide, a travel blogger, an international aid worker, an au pair, a scuba diving instructor, even a diplomat. Imagine where you want to be in ten, fifteen years' time, and then reverse-engineer it.'

Emilie's eyes narrow for a moment. 'When you were young like me, what future did you see?'

'I wanted to own a house in a good suburb,' Yasmin says. 'And afford private education for our children so they can have many opportunities in this lucky country with so many freedoms and sunshine.'

'Not to mention the racism,' Kiri mutters.

'Yes, after 9/11 it was very bad. But nowhere is perfect,' Yasmin concedes.

'I had it in my head to have a family, lotsa little ones,' Kiri says. 'And helping folk, s'why I did nursing. Didn't exactly plan on ending up in palliative care. Grief work's not something you daydream about. Life leaves it on your doorstep, and then it's yours to take care of.'

'I chased romance,' Fiona says.

'There was a time when we were shag-a-holics,' Liz chuckles.

'But men were always on the side for you,' Fiona says. 'You always spoke about having an international career, flitting between Berlin, Paris, Vienna, Luxembourg. I mean, you were nineteen when you said, "I'm going to run my own company in Europe."'

Liz sighs. 'You just set a goal and you take one step towards it every day.'

'Yes, but in my twenties, I envisaged being a mum, but I didn't know the first thing about postnatal depression or how motherhood would warp my sense of myself,' Fiona says. 'And then the future changed for me again after cancer. I stopped planning far ahead. Now each moment is a blessing.'

'I imagined being a famous author, a human rights activist, doing something meaningful and important,' I say. 'But now I'd settle for being a grandmother someday. Being ordinary seems like quite an achievement.'

Cate shakes her head. 'No-one's answered Emilie's question. She's asking us why we fell asleep at the wheel, aren't you, luv? How we managed to royally screw up her future while we were busy planning how to afford houses and run companies and have families. Am I right?'

Emilie nods, wiping her mouth with the back of her hand.

'Sometimes, I close my eyes and I think of the future – maybe five years or ten years from now. And I am trembling.

Like a dark storm over my heart. I feel…hmm, what's the word?' She rummages in her backpack and removes a small English-German dictionary. Using the light of her iPhone, she flicks through the pages. '*Grauen*…what is it in English?'

'We didn't realise the earth was in such trouble,' Liz says. 'Not until recently.'

'We worried though, din' we?' Kiri says. "Bout nuclear war and all that…'

Emilie finds what she's looking for. '*Grauen*, it's…*dread* – *dead* plus an *r*,' she laughs. 'I have dread.'

Her sentence settles on us, a dark portentous cloud. The how-it-is for a young woman with her whole life ahead of her and an ailing world in which to live it.

I remember my granny once describing to me how as a new mother she'd sobbed when the Second World War broke out. 'What have I done? What world have I brought my child into?'

'Every generation has its terrors,' Liz says.

'My grandparents worried about anti-Semitism and fascism,' I say.

'And we all fear terrorism,' Yasmin says.

'I have nightmares about 5G, enforced vaccinations, state surveillance and encroaching power over our lives,' Fiona says.

'You gotta watch out for viruses – bird flu, mad cow disease, SARS, ebola,' Kiri says. 'Any day a pandemic can break out. And then we'll be in trouble.'

'That seems a little far-fetched,' Liz says. 'Climate change is what's on all our minds.'

I catch Cate's expression. I see a rough edge she has beveled, something botched she has sutured that this conversation is needling. 'No matter which way you look at the future, Leonard Cohen called it. It's murder.'

'Cate,' Fiona admonishes.

'She already knows. She's way ahead of us on this one.'

We all gaze at this young woman who has stumbled into our midst. She is on the crest of her life, with courage and *chutzpah* and early grief hanging off her like that cheap koala bear, as we are settling into the soft armchair of disappointment and regret.

In the glow of the lantern, she blinks at us, a mirage of all the children each one of us has brought into the world, the innocents forced to fight a war they did not start, when the odds are stacked against them. She has no kin to come home to – no mother waiting for her and no children-to-come calling her to any prospects. She is stranded on the sandbank between her past and a future that has slipped from her grasp. Hers are the eyes of one who has been told, *I'm sorry, there's nothing more we can do. Put your affairs in order for it will all be over soon.*

'This is why I am not having kids. I don't want to pass life on. I will be the full stop,' Emilie says.

She is unafraid of endings.

I cannot bear it.

'There is a chance we can turn it all around, isn't there Cate?'

Cate's eyes glaze over. She sees what I'm doing. I am standing at the mouth of the terrible truth, shielding this young woman from what's coming. But Cate doesn't trade in pretense or condescension. She is deeply unmotherly in this way.

She begins to strum her ukulele.

'Let's sing *Hallelujah*, shall we?'

16

The Story of the Cake

'When last did we have rain? I couldn't have asked for a greater miracle on my birthday,' Fiona says.

The plashing beyond the mouth of the cave thrums the earth.

'You know what miracle I am praying for?' Yasmin asks. 'Catey, can you guess?'

Cate's fingers coax music from her ukulele. She knows these strings the way I know an eggplant, my own belly, Frank's bald head.

'No idea, luv.'

'...if you would agree to meet your son.'

My ears tweak up, like Archie's at the squawk of pigeons. *Cate has a son.*

Cate continues to play as if no secrets have been spilled, no challenges posed.

'He made you a mother,' Kiri says.

'He made a fekking dog's breakfast of my perineum.'

'He's your family,' Kiri says.

'This,' Cate stops strumming and gestures at all of us, 'is family.'

'I don't think he's ever going to stop trying,' Fiona says. 'Especially now that he's a father himself. How old is she now, little Lilly?'

Cate shrugs. 'Few months.'

'You must be curious, Catey, to see what kind of a man he became,' Yasmin says. 'Maybe he's got your big eyebrows.'

'Not like he's asking for a kidney or bone marrow. He wants to look his natural mother in the eye,' Kiri tuts.

Cate shrugs. 'He's got parents. I made sure of that.'

'I reckon it's got to do with your wobbles,' Kiri says. 'What do you say, girls?'

'Yes,' Yasmin nods.

'Spot on,' Fiona says.

'What is everyone agreeing on?' Cate strums away.

'You the one throwing the word *burden* around,' Kiri says. 'Sorry for being such a drag, not carrying your own weight, all that claptrap. You had all kinds'a excuses before, and now, you waiting for results. You can't hold off everything while you waiting. One waiting just becomes another kinda waiting.'

'Children are not just parties and picnics,' Yasmin says. 'There is duty and responsibility also. Maybe he would like to take care of you.'

'Stop all this quacking. I did one fucking awesome thing in my life – I gave him up for adoption,' Cate says. 'Two parents are more than most people get. Samson doesn't need a third. That's just greedy. And you all know how I feel about greed.'

Something with teeny elbows lodges in my throat as a portrait of Cate starts to form. A son, conceived, born, given up, passed on. Now a man, tragic with adoration for his own daughter, looks at his face in the mirror and wonders if there was any want in the circumstances that brought him here. We all long to be more than a whoopsie, an accidental person. Who wouldn't want to own this enigmatic, wild, filthy-mouthed woman full of big life as your mother?

'I don't get the colour of your thinking,' Kiri says. 'He just needs to hear a little bit of your story so he can hold on to his own story, make a start, figure out the notes. You thinking about this arse-up, you gotta straighten yourself out. Here we got Emilie, who lost her mother young. But she at least knows her. She's carrying her. Samson just wants a little bit of you to carry with him. Help him to find his way. Maybe he's lost. And you're the map.'

Cate sighs. 'Put a frigging cork in it, you lot. Was this

whole yatra walk just a front for a meet-your-biological-son intervention then?'

'Children have a right to their parents. To have that love,' Yasmin says.

'They need food and shelter. The rest is bloody luxury.'

'Love is more important,' Yasmin says.

'You can't eat love, luv.'

'You *can*. See this – this cake, this is love,' Yasmin says. 'This is a cake baked for love, to chase away sadness. My mother baked it for me, when Banu…' She doesn't finish, but she is suddenly in a turmoil of grief and fury. Tears spring from her eyes.

'Ah, fuck, I'm sorry,' Cate says, putting her instrument down and leaning forward to lay a hand on Yasmin's shoulder. 'What did I say?'

Yasmin shakes her head and her hands in front of her face.

'Hey, Yas, don't take my decisions personally. I'm a stubborn old cactus. Don't let it upset you.'

Yasmin wipes her eyes. 'No, Catey, it's not you. It's not you. It's a long-ago story.'

'Tell us, darlin',' Cate says, putting her hand on Yasmin's. 'What is the story of this cake?'

'I remember the day. Still. My father came home, his eyes full of storms. *We are leaving Iran two days from now. Pack one small bag each. We will get new things when we arrive.*

'My heart was tumbling inside me. This was the first time he had spoken about us leaving. One bag only. My head was exploding with questions. *What about Banu?* I asked.

No dogs are allowed, he said.

'Banu was my dog. She was just a stray from the gutter who followed me home from school one day. She slept on the floor next to my bed. She was my best friend, even my protector from the school bully. My father took my shoulders with his hands and looked in my eyes and said, *Yasmin, we will get a new dog in Australia. I promise.*

'One thing I knew – my father always kept his promises. If he said, *I will bring you pomegranate or pistachios from the market*, he always brought them. If he warned, *I'll beat you if you don't help Maamaan*, you could be sure that he would take his strap to you.

'*But what will happen to Banu?* I asked him. *Who will look after her?*

'*Leave that to me*, Baba said. *I will take care of her. You go pack.*

'I went to my room to find a suitcase. I heard his footsteps in the courtyard and then his voice calling, *Banu, Banu*. And my stomach became a tight knot.

'I heard Banu barking. She was excited, thinking she had miscalculated the time, that it was going to be an early dinner or maybe she was getting some scraps from the lamb we had prepared for stewing. Then…'

Yasmin puts her hands to her ears. She shakes her head. Tears are pouring freely from her eyes. Dripping from her chin. Her nose runs. She wipes it with the back of her hand.

'Ears are for songs, like your voice, Catey. Not for some sounds. I heard Banu squeal from where he held her by the scruff of her neck so he could slit her throat. He slayed her. Like a goat or chicken. With a big hunting knife, like that one you are carrying, Catey. I looked down from my window to see blood gushing from her neck and her body still breathing. So he…placed his heel on her ribs and…' Yasmin shudders. 'The sound of cracking,' she sobs. 'Then he called my brother. *Elham, dig a hole*. My brother found a spade to bury Banu. He was sick, vomiting while doing this. Baba kept watching him. *Be a man*, he said. He was only nine.'

Fiona shuffles close to Yasmin and rests her head against her shoulder. They interlock hands.

It is Emilie who stands up and goes over to Yasmin and throws her arms around her. 'Sorry, sorry, sorry,' she whispers, and Yasmin loses her face in Emilie's hair.

When they separate, Yasmin's eyes are like small agates, glinting.

Emilie unwraps the scarf around her neck and hands it to her. 'It's okay, you can blow your nose, we can wash it tomorrow.'

'We got tissues, here,' Kiri says, passing a small wad to

Yasmin.

Yasmin takes her time blowing her nose.

'This is why I am lucky I got a quiet man, like Rajit, after Baba even though I did not choose him. Rajit is a gentle man – it is good for all my children. Leah and Fatimah have seen a mother who is stronger than a father. I will not be with a man who is violent. I did not love my father. I did not look him in the eye. Not from that day.'

I pinch my eyes shut as I absorb this wave of Yasmin's story into my blood. There is nothing sure about goodness and mercy following our daughters and sons all the days of their lives, not when we cannot shake the trail of blood and cries of our history. A dog, a knife, a cake fuse somewhere in the wet folds of the brain and forecast all the fear and longing we will carry into our marriages and parenting. Writers call this the backstory wound, and how we connive them so our characters will be richly conceived, exquisitely broken, wrought within an inch of irreparable wounding, but somehow capable of transformation when life hits them in the guts. Parents are nothing but terrified and terrorized people making tens of thousands of decisions about the lives of those we thrust forward, ahead of us, into a future we cannot control or safekeep. How can this be humanity's recipe for hope?

Cate's voice is strangled as she speaks. 'Samson, that's a good strong name. My boy, my son. I see you got my height, my bony arse, my better features. Those blue eyes? Not from me. Must be your dad's genes there. Studying law? How about that then? Following in your father's footsteps. He's a judge, been on the bench a good ten years, I'd say. Smart fella. My brother's friend. Top bloke, really. The devout Church-going type. Your average rapist.'

'What?' Fiona whispers. Her face looks slapped.

'Would you want to know? Over a cappuccino or a chardonnay or whatever the fuck he drinks?' Cate asks.

The air in the cave is sharp in my nostrils. Smoke and ice and biting wind.

'This is a very bad story,' Emilie says, holding her hand to her mouth.

'"I know why you think you're a lesbian,"' my mom told me once. "It's *understandable*." That was her word.' Cate snickers. 'Kenneth made sure I knew he was shoving his cock in me to "fuck me straight". Was a dyke long before he fouled me up from the inside.'

Fiona reaches for Cate's hand and Cate lets her have it.

It is Fiona who is crying. Cate's face is impassive.

'No need for tears, Fi. This story has a happy ending. I'm still gay,' she laughs.

'You couldn't terminate?' I ask. 'Might have made things easier for you.'

'Didn't have the dosh when I was sixteen. I made up a story about a stranger who pulled me under the pier. Mum knew Kenneth from church and wouldn't have believed it was him. She seemed more upset that I was knocked up.

Then she got wind of a couple at her church, who'd been trying for a kid and she figured we could cash in. I took six months off school. Mum gave me fifty quid for my efforts and bought herself a new telly.'

There is no kindness in any part of this tale, no mothering for a sixteen-year-old girl.

'Did it hurt…' Yasmin asks, 'to give up your baby?'

'Didn't see him. They whisked him off.'

'So he has no idea…?' Kiri asks.

'Nah, not a clue. Best thing for him. Least that kid deserves is freedom from the truth. How can knowing that be a bonus to anyone's self-esteem?'

'Couldn't you meet him and just not tell him?' Fiona asks.

'I'm shite at keeping secrets. Why ruin his perfectly good life with that bit of backstory bullshit?'

Emilie has been silent all this time from her corner in the cave. 'What about…the mice?'

'What mice?'

'The ones we were speaking about before. Your son is carrying this memory of violence from his father, if I am understanding epigenetics? Like the mice.'

Cate wants to argue, but she stops.

'You did not say yes to this child. And he did not ask for this story either. This is what you and he are sharing,' Emilie says. 'He is believing something is wrong with him. He is the only other person who was harmed in the same moment as you. You were in the same car together when it crashed, like

314

Kiri said.'

Cate purses her lips to speak but seems to have run out of words.

'Amen. Out of the mouths of babes,' Kiri says.

17

The Grandchildless Generation

Liz reaches for her boot.

'Where you goin' then?' Kiri asks.

'I believe my bladder finally needs emptying,' Liz says, 'if you're monitoring. Seems to have stopped raining.'

'Want some company?' I ask Liz. Safety in numbers surely rates as one of Kiri's first rules.

Liz hesitates. 'Sure.'

Outside, night's dark fingers stroke us, pressing up against our bodies, breathing down our necks. We displace it as we make our way down to the beach by the light of our head torches, clutching our toilet paper, funnels and a little spade.

'Do these things actually work?' Liz asks, examining her funnel.

'If you get the angle right.'

'Christ, if I got yanked any further out of my comfort zone, I'd snap. What about here?'

'Looks okay.'

I turn my back to her, pull my pants and underwear down, and brace the funnel against my pubic bone.

Our pees splash in spurts, first mine, then hers.

'Would you want to know?' I ask.

'What?'

'That your mother was raped? That's how you were conceived.'

'I don't know if all secrets need to come out. Maybe if we forgive ourselves, we don't need to lay the whole drama on others.'

I dig a little hole for our tissues, and we cover them with sand.

I zip up my trousers. I breathe in the salty dark air of this truth-studded night. 'You know, Liz, I didn't understand it then, but I get it now.'

'What's that?'

'Why you left it all behind.'

Liz jams her hands in her jacket pockets and kicks more sand over our tissues.

'It was gutsy. I couldn't have done it myself. I wanted to be a mother too much. I needed those key variables –

husband, children, house, pets, to hold me down and pin me like tent pegs. But I can see how that is also a prison, how sometimes you have to pull up those stumps and choose yourself before there is no self left to choose.'

My tribute has come out all mangled. It's almost certainly patronising and uncalled for, at best, inappropriate. All I wanted was to rain praise, in a place that has been praise-starved. To let her know that if I believe anything, it is that everything is ultimately forgivable, or it should be – that I don't know of any mother who ever set out to cause pain, and maybe everything heals if we stop trying so hard to fix things.

I hear the waves slapping the sand in the distance.

'Honestly, Jo, motherhood was just too damn hard. I had to excuse myself, like every father who ever walked out on his family because it didn't suit him. It looks a hell of a lot worse on a mother because we're all supposed to be so damn naturally maternal. I should have made different choices when I was Emilie's age,' Liz sighs. 'Her generation, our kids, they'll do things differently.'

'Imagine being so self-assured at twenty-one that you'd hike into the bush all on your own, without sanitary pads, enough food or a GPS,' I cackle.

'*That's* true autonomy. It makes you wonder whether we're better off dying young and throwing our kids to the wolves so they learn real survival skills.'

Sadness gropes at me. I don't want to believe my entire

life's efforts have done nothing but create obstacles for Jamie and Aaron, but perhaps if you strip it all away, that might be the most truthful and objective job description of motherhood.

We stand and listen to the wild night sounds.

'So are you going to leave Frank?'

'I don't...know.'

She waits. She clearly knows the power of the pause.

'I miss him and when I'm with him, I miss myself.' As I say this, something snares in my throat. 'He takes such good care of me, but that reliance, that dependence, it's distorted me. I wonder who I might have become without him steadying me all the time. I feel so...tame.'

'Ships in harbours are safe, right?'

'All I wanted when the kids were little was security. But we all know now, there's no such thing.'

Liz exhales a long and consenting, 'Mmmmm.'

'Sometimes I think the only reason I married Frank was because we immigrated. I wanted to settle, put new roots down, feel like I belonged somewhere. But now that the kids don't need me, I wonder...what other life is calling me. Without Frank, I'd probably be broke, living in a tiny rental somewhere out in the country, drowning in clutter. I'd have no private medical aid and god knows how many rescue cats.'

She turns so her head torch blinds me. 'I can see you all dreadlocked and sari-ed up with feathers in your hair.'

'Yep, that would be me, unedited.'

'But as a writer, you know the value of a great edit. Sometimes you have to sacrifice your little darlings.'

I turn off my head torch. She does the same. The darkness swallows us. Up above, a zillion tiny sequins flicker.

'Doesn't it seem improbable and almost a lie that we're made of stardust, every atom?' I ask.

'It certainly puts all our angst into perspective,' she laughs.

'Tiny, fretting flecks of DNA that we are.'

We stand still beneath the encrusted heavens, winking, glinting, stuttering like cosmic Morse code. My ribs billow into this familiar reach of eternity, and I am all at once near and far to my children, wherever they may be, my parents across oceans, my ancestors before me, my endless childhood, the invisible creatures around us, Helen in Santa Monica and CJ who has vanished inexplicably.

The silver studded sky pulls me closer, like a secret lover.

'You know, Jo, your book about Lot's wife…'

'*A Backward Glance*?'

'Yes, that one. It changed my life.'

'You read it?'

'I've read all your books. *A Backward Glance* is one of my top ten reads of all time.'

'I wouldn't have thought you'd have the time or interest…'

'…to what? Read an old friend's books?'

That phrase is like a caress, *an old friend*. I don't know why tears come and burn my eyes.

'It's why I left Carl.'

'No, why?'

'The right book, at the right time, can just speak to you.'

I know this is a compliment, rare and unexpected. I'm not proud at how my ego flares.

'She is such a powerful, tragic character, tied to her past, sacrificing her future, her entire life, with that one backward glance. That book may have saved me from a life that would have destroyed me.'

If this is 'success', I have misunderstood everything. My books, like my adult children, exist in the world detached from my plans and desires, creating knock-on causes and effects, and taking on lives of their own. I am partially responsible and blameless all at the same time. I hope Chloe and Brandon never find out.

'Do you know snow leopards live their lives as solitary creatures?'

'Snow leopards?'

'They meet up once or twice to mate, but then they part ways. Mothers raise their young til they can take care of themselves, then they turn and walk away. They never see each other again. They are Nature's true loners.'

'My spirit animal. Sort of thing Fiona would say.'

'Do you think they ever get lonely?'

'I couldn't speak for a snow leopard,' Liz says. 'But having the option of someone to grow old with is not something to lightly give up.'

'Would you ever consider Fiona's plan – a commune with

other women?'

'Could you honestly see me in a commune?' She shakes her head. 'Anything group-related is not for me.'

'But women know how to take care of each other. Look at all the trouble everyone went to for Fiona. Kiri carrying everything and the kitchen sink. Cate with her ukulele. Yasmin, and all the food, those fairy lights and rose petals.'

Liz laughs. 'I'll take credit for those blasted petals, thank you. Why do you think I was late this morning? Yellow roses aren't so easy to find.'

'You?'

'It's one of Fiona's less endearing traits — everything has to be yellow. You can call it butter, citrine, canary, amber, it's all the same. Didn't change how grotesque I looked as her maid of honour. Tell me, can I wear yellow? It is the worst colour for my complexion.'

The glittering fairy lights at the entrance to the cave twinkle in the distance as we stroll back up the beach towards them.

'It was like she knew from when she was a little girl... Chloe always loved the stars and outer space,' Liz muses. 'She was devastated when Pluto was demoted as a planet. That's when she declared she was going to be an astronomer, I mean, that's pretty specific for a nine-year-old. That's what she's studying now. I believe she's also become a vegan activist, so...she's living her best life, it seems.' There is no tone to conceal the longing in her words. 'How about Jamie?'

'She…had an abortion a few months ago. She just went ahead and did it without telling me.'

'Did you expect her to?'

I shrug. 'I am her mother. I only found out because of a short story competition she won. I read it in the supporting artist statement.'

'You raised a daughter who can manage the tricky parts of her life on her own. Congratulations, you passed parenting. You get the certificate.'

'I don't know. It feels like there's nothing more she wants from me.'

Liz stops and grabs my arm. 'Of course, there is. She wants you to let her go.'

'It had nothing to do with you, mum. It's my body.' Jamie was applying coconut oil to her upper arm. From the raw redness, a butterfly with a broken wing spanned her left shoulder in angry new ink.

I had leaned against the doorframe of her room, unable to fully enter.

'What happens to you also affects me. You are my child.'

'No, mum, you have no ownership over me or any of my choices.'

'Why didn't you tell me?'

I have known many types of pulling away. Friendships. Lovers. But none so painful as this one with my own child. My fantasies as a mother have never encompassed my daughter telling me she is pregnant and wants to terminate. And much as *that was my grandchild*, a delicious, forbidden longing, now I know, all a mother wants is to be present to ease, not complicate her children's paths. We don't want to berate them or judge them or make sure their choices match our own. Just to be in the room when it gets dark.

Jamie didn't meet my gaze. 'Because you'd have tried to take control. I needed it to be simple. Annabel and Felicia took me. And look what they arranged for Felicia's boyfriend to do – he's a tattoo artist. We went straight from the clinic.'

I would have held her hand. Been the one to tell her it was going to be okay. Stocked up on sanitary pads. Made her chicken soup. Filled a vase with peonies next to her bed.

'Don't get all sentimental about it. I just don't want children.'

This was the secret she had really been keeping from me, guarding to protect me from the heartbreak. That mine may be the first grandchildless generation.

'There's so much I still want to do with my life, places I want to travel, art I want to explore… I just can't see how children would be part of it. Never mind what a colossal fuck up the world is.'

There is so much she still wants to do with her life.

In this, she and I have so much in common.

In the corner of the cave, Emilie has passed out.

'She's exhausted, poor thing,' Fiona says. 'I think she'll sleep well tonight.'

'Extra bedding, extra warmth, she will have good dreams,' Yasmin croons.

'Does a grown woman need to be fussed over?' Liz asks.

'I just gave her my sleeping mat,' Fiona says. 'It's no big deal.'

'What just happened with the sleeping arrangements?' Liz asks. 'My stuff was right next to her.'

'You don't mind, do you?' Kiri asks. 'We rearranged the sleeping bags while you were out. I put your stuff over there,' she says, pointing to the other corner. 'Just gonna keep my eye on her.'

'The nurse is on duty tonight,' Cate chuckles.

'She's managed just fine without us for twenty-one years of her life,' Liz mutters.

The lantern casts its scattering of light as Cate begins to strum her ukulele.

'You never lay and watched a sleeping baby?' Kiri asks Liz.

'God, no. When my kids slept, I took that as my cue to do something I actually wanted to do.'

Kiri props herself up alongside Emilie.

'I used to watch my babies sleep,' Kiri says. 'Jackson was colicky. Oh man, was he ever a vomiter. Nothing went in that didn't come out again. Wasn't much sleep for the first two years of his life. Blake had allergies, eczema. He cried nonstop. I swear, I didn't want a third, but Tiffany sorta slipped through all the birth control, and there she was. A content little possum. Slept sound. Gave me respite. Ate whatever I fed her. I always said she was my prize for getting through the first two. And when she came, there it was. She completed our family, was the easiest of my babies.'

From where she has hunkered down in her sleeping bag, Liz's eyes are wearied. Cate's strumming warms the air around us.

'They say third children grow themselves up – they get the least attention. She was a quiet thing, undemanding. A late speaker. Compared to the other two, she took up so little space. Figured her way through school, a mediocre student, under the radar. No prizes, no failures. Even as a teenager, she dragged no trouble through the door. Unless you count five tattoos as trouble. Kept tellin' her she wasn't a damn car, fulla bumper stickers.'

I am starting to feel sleepy myself. The length of the day is deep in my bones, and with the night air chilling around us, I am dipping in and out, like a child falling asleep to a bedtime story.

'He was hard work, Jackson. The drugs and the drinking. And Blake, he kept skipping school. We had to be on his case all the time. Tiffany was the colour you don't see, like the sky, because it's there. She grew up from the corner of my eye. Thought it was just having a girl, you know. So different from the bloomin' boys. If I made a mistake, it was that I took my eye off her.'

I sense this story is about to take a hard turn.

'But I shoulda known. Mothers have a sixth sense, right?'

'There was nothing you could have done...' Fiona says softly.

Cate's strumming of her ukulele is a soft undernote.

The arms of the night close in around us.

'It was over an Easter weekend, gotta be more than ten years back. I remember the bunnies on the wall and the Easter eggs under the desk. I was on duty that night when a young mother brought her three-year-old in. *Something's not right*, she kept on saying. *Something's not right with Betsy.* Kid had reflux, a slight temperature. I can't forget the look in that mother's eyes. It was easy to mistake for madness. *I don't like how she sleeps. It's a terrible sleep, a too-deep sleep*, she kept saying. We did all the routine checks, couldn't find anything amiss, but she just kept saying, *Something's not right.* The doctor examined her, found nothing sinister. We sent that kid home with Panadol. I wasn't on duty the next day when she came back but I heard all about it – the mother apparently was proper hysterical. She pulled down the Easter bunny display, tore it to shreds. She demanded a brain scan. Said she wouldn't leave til they did one. Eventually, just to appease her, they did a scan.'

Kiri stops and holds up her hands, forefingers and thumbs touching to make a huge circle. 'There it was. A massive tumour on her temporal lobe. Left even a few more days and little Betsy would have died in her terrible sleep. They operated and got it out. You wanna know where Betsy is? She about to start high school. She's a black belt in karate too.'

'Tiffany was on her own sovereign path,' Fiona whispers.

'Massive tumour,' Kiri repeats. 'Massive.'

'Torturing yourself is not going to bring your girl back,' Cate almost sings to the tune trailing from her fingers.

'After Tiffany died, I stopped fostering kids. Couldn't count myself as safe hands.'

'I trust those hands,' Yasmin says.

'I took my eye off her. She hid her depression from me, like a professional spy. Honest to god, I did not know. We's all thought she was independent, living her life, working at the salon, keeping herself busy. When it was quiet from her, I thought it was a good sign.'

'But, Kiri, look what you made from such sadness,' Yasmin says. 'All the parents with hearts broken come to your group. You help them when they're grieving. You're their hero.'

'You don't wanna be this kinda hero. I didn't need to live long enough to lose a child. Especially not to suicide. Woulda happily died first. Like *Jesus Wants Me for a Sunbeam.*'

'We're not mind readers,' Fiona says.

I wish I had something to give to Kiri. It is my job, to find the right words – that's what authors do.

'Kiri,' I try, 'what if someone doesn't want to be here, in this world?'

'I wanted her here,' Kiri says. 'I wasn't finished being her mother.'

We are commissioned to losing our children. We don't choose whether we lose them to life or death.

'You are *still* her mother,' I say.

Everything widens in darkness, and in this night-trance, Cate starts to hum. From the first bars, I feel it, her power, the kind of self-knowledge a bird has of its own singing. Soon, Kiri slides in from the north with a harmony, and then Yasmin enters from the south. Fiona joins in softly from behind a note, and suddenly we are in a choir of hums, so deep and potent. I close my eyes and let the voices bathe me.

The humming thickens, like cream around us, and then we are inside, *Amazing Grace* carried on Cate's voice. My whole body tingles, aroused. Cate's voice soaks into us, a soaring fugue as Kiri and Yasmin glide in and out of the rising melody.

I gulp for air. I suddenly need to get out of this cave.

I pull down my sleeping back and get to my feet.

'Sorry,' I say, stumbling out into the darkness.

Outside, the night is velvet; the air is song; the earth, a drum; my body is water and no-one is watching; no eyes are pinching me into 'mother', 'wife', 'daughter'. I am an endless stranger, a spring of possibility. I spin like a whirling dervish.

My inhibitions fray.

And then I am being kissed with such ferocity. A memory so strong.

She had sex appeal. It was Helen who had said it.

And it was at 'sex appeal' that I said, 'I have to tell you something else about CJ. But you have to swear…'

'I swear, I swear.'

'If you ever tell anyone…'

'Who am I going to tell? Seriously?' With Helen, you just could never tell. Salacious details are her drugs.

'They were polyamorous – her and Kito.'

'What do you mean?'

'They were having sex with…other people.'

'Well, good for them.'

'…and…I'm just telling you this because I have to tell someone…' I closed my eyes as I said it. 'We hooked up. Me and CJ. The last time I saw her.'

'Hooked up how?'

'Don't you know what "hooked up" means? She... pashed me. We kissed. We...got dirty with each other.'

'You had *sex* with CJ?' Helen's voice was incredulous.

'More like a lot of kissing and some – petting. In a carpark. It was very teenage.'

Helen was silent. 'I can't believe you didn't call to tell me, like, immediately. Far out, call yourself a friend.'

It was a golden moment I hadn't wanted to share with anyone. A secret. A hidden treasure. Mine and CJ's. It wasn't for commentary, gossip or opinion.

'Yeah, well, you're impossible to get hold of.'

'What was it like?'

'It was...' I stopped and inhaled deeply, for this surely falls into full-blown thou-shalt-not adultery, '...spectacular. I mean, I was drunk, we were both drunk, but it was hot...'

'Who initiated?'

I remembered CJ looking at me with her head tilted. Biting her lip. Her hand on my knee. Shimmying up my thigh. And then...her mouth on my neck...her nipple in my mouth. Her fingers inside me. How I came. Twice.

'I can't remember... Why does it matter? She's...dead.' A small sob escaped me.

Helen was silent for a moment. 'That's a great way to remember her.'

I remember her wetness. The surprise of it. Her mouth

hot on my belly, her fingers deep inside me. My body a hive, filled with honey.

I'd blown my nose into a tissue.

'Frank can never know. We can never speak about this again.'

18

Back to Earth

My nose. I reach for it, but my hands are confined. I am all tied up. I manage to wrestle an arm free to touch the tip of it. It is a blob of ice in the centre of my face. My hair is in my mouth; I spit it out. Every bone in my body hurts. I have a crick in my neck. I scrunch my eyes open to the fragile light. My bladder screams for release. I cannot find the zip on this sleeping bag, so I shed it like a snakeskin. I fumble in my backpack for my funnel.

It feels like a hangover, but it's only the debt from startled increments of sleep, the sounds of the wild through the night, and a chorus of snoring from all sides. Fiona can have her bed-

on-the-floor. We all need our madnesses. This morning my
body is so pissed off with me. *Please don't do that again. Be kinder.*

As I scramble to make my way out the cave, I count one-
two-three-four-five bodies bundled in sleeping bags around
me. Emilie's hair is splayed, an explosion of copper curls, on
what looks like Liz's inflatable pillow. I count again – we should
be seven, right? One of us is missing.

I try not to wake the others but clatter against the enamel
plates from last night at my feet. 'Sorry, didn't mean to disturb,'
I whisper as I see Kiri's eyes jerk open.

I have caught her in time, the dawn. It is still dark and a bank
of clouds sits on the horizon. Soon emissary slivers of sunlight
will sneak out. The sand is taut from last night's rain. Our
firepit is a wet heap of charred wood and ash. I make my way
across the beach towards the boulders on the left that at one
time must have fallen from the mountainside and have come
to rest here.

I drop my pants and undies, fix the funnel as tightly as I
can to my girlbits and with my hips thrust forward. I sigh a wee
out of me, moving my butt so that I can piss the shape of my
name. J…O. I finally get what fun a penis can be. A small fart
escapes just as I smell cigarette smoke.

'Excellent pussy-penmanship.'

'Shit.' I pull up my pants and whip around.

'Well, that's not embarrassing at all,' I say. 'I didn't realise I had an audience.'

'What's a performance without an audience? Like a tree falling in a forest when no-one's around,' Cate chortles.

'With complimentary flatulence.'

'Frequent Farting Points – a menopausal perk.'

I make my way to the water's edge and dance away from the little wave slaps that chase my feet, until I catch the right moment to dip them in the water and rub my cold hands over my face. I make my way over to where Cate is seated on the rocks.

'How're you feeling about the trek back?'

'Uphill and me, we're not on such great terms anymore.'

'We'll take it really slow.'

The cigarette rattles in her trembling fingers.

'Maybe after some coffee and a good breakfast, that hill won't seem like such a bitch,' I offer.

She takes a long last puff of her cigarette and then suffocates it in the sand before putting the butt in her top pocket. She dusts sand off her boots. 'What shoe size are you?'

'A size 10, why?'

'Fiona's got tiny feet. Kiri's are too wide. You want these boots? Got these on a sale last summer. Five-hundred-dollar boots for $180. Damn fine hiking boots. Or you one of those squeamish don't-wear-other-folks'-shoes types?'

'Keep them for your next hike.'

She holds out her hands to me, as if she wants me to take them. But she is drawing my attention to their unsteadiness. We both look at her hands as they tremble.

'Got to admit, I'm a little disappointed. I'd have taken a shark. Faulty parachute. Helicopter. Shiv to the guts. After all the dangerous shit I've done in my life.' She shakes her head. 'If you're going down, you want a bang, not a whimper, don't you reckon?'

'I don't know. A friend of mine died in a motorbike accident last year,' I say, my voice cracking. 'It was a big shock. It's just as well we don't get to choose.'

'Sudden and spectacular is the only way. Here one moment, gone the next. Like a magic trick.'

'I'd rather have some dying time.'

'What the fuck for?'

'Goodbyes?'

'Like we're not saying them, every moment...?'

She offers me a cigarette from a pack. I shake my head.

'Yeah, motherfucker of a habit. Hey, look, here comes the sun. We really should wake the others, fancy missing this.' But neither of us moves.

It starts as a burn on the lip of the horizon. The morning pulls the sun from the horizon, like a teabag, and it is a pink and purple tea party of prisms as the light pierces through the clouds. It has all been worth it, the walk, the weariness, for this sunrise.

'I'm not especially waiting for test results.' She pauses. 'Matter of fact, I got them weeks ago.'

My belly tightens.

'Fiona and the others don't know. A degenerative disorder of the spinal cord and brain isn't anything to celebrate if you're infatuated with survival and long-term plans.'

Jesus. Fuck. I shake my head. 'Oh, Cate...'

'Apoptosis. Heard of it?'

'No.'

'It's when microbes spontaneously commit suicide. Self-destruction is part of nature. There's nothing personal about any of it. Take the emotion out of life and it's nothing but a series of farewells. We immigrants know how to do those, don't we?'

You don't forget your mother's vacant face. Your sisters' torrent of tears. Your own tremulous bicep as you hand over the pet basket to the friend who has promised to love Shadow-you-rescued-from-a-gutter as her own. You lose count of your goodbyes – the African sky, the bird sounds of the bush, the smell after a Highveld lightning storm. 'But it's different, to be...'

'...dying?'

A thrashing word, like a beached fish.

'Are you scared?'

'Only of overstaying my welcome, wearing down everyone's hospitality. Guess there's something in it for me, to give it all over to others, let myself be helped in all the ways I like to help myself. Never did get quite easy with that. Sally warned me I'd have to let my guard down some day and learn to just say "thank you."'

There is grit in her voice, a warrior grappling with the impending descent from competence that lies ahead, the final tearing away of the veneer of self.

'It's a hard ask when you're a tough old cunt,' I say.

She throws her head back and chuckles. 'You're an ace student of the old potty mouth. What do you reckon? Wouldn't take more than a day or two without food and water if I "twisted my ankle" by accident and you lot had to leave me behind.' She winks. Mischievous yet.

'Nice try. We'd never leave you alone. Someone would stay right by your side and the rest would bring back emergency crew to airlift you out of here.'

'You bloody pro-lifers,' she tuts. 'If I was a drag on the way down here, you'll need the patience of Job for the way back.' She shakes her head. 'Besides, I got me a granddaughter by the name of Lilly. Saved her up for a rainy day, didn't I?'

I reach out and place my hand on her forearm. *A granddaughter.*

'When are you going to tell the others?'

'Last possible moment. Let's keep the drama short and sweet, shall we?'

'Why did you tell me?'

She cocks her head. 'You look like the kind of woman who can keep a secret.'

When Cate and I wander back up the beach, we find Emilie cupped between Fiona's knees, and Fiona is braiding her hair into a French plait.

Yasmin tends to the billycan which is huffing with Turkish coffee on the gas stove. She hands me a small mug trailing a kite tail of steam. Kiri is tending to damper on the open fire, toasting them like elongated marshmallows on twigs, which we will eat hot with Fiona's honey, Yasmin's sour fig preserve, fresh walnuts, thinly sliced apple and radishes fanned out on a plate.

It's time for me to bring my Tupperware out. I salvage it from my backpack and offer it to Fiona.

'What is this then?' she pops the lid.

'I baked salted liquorice bread.'

'I love liquorice,' Fiona's face bursts into a smile. 'How did you know?'

'Lucky guess.' I mean, who doesn't love liquorice?

'How'd you make this?' Kiri asks, examining the slices of rich molasses-dark cake.

'Plenty of liquorice, some treacle, coconut sugar, molasses, almond meal. And salt, of course.'

'It is a love affair in your mouth. You don't know which way to turn, sweet or salty,' Yasmin croons. 'I must get the recipe from you. I will make it for my next Welcome Feast.'

'I wouldn't say no to a taste of that,' Liz says.

We all pretend not to watch Liz tuck in and then reach for seconds. Maybe love is too much of a commitment-word for her, but at least she got her Vitamin P today.

Kiri checks on Emilie's bite and Liz's blister. She reminds us all to take our medication. Out come the statins, iron, calcium, anti-depressants, hydroxychloroquine, insulin and heartburn pills as we slug back our tablets, comparing our deficiencies and infirmities.

And yes, I am the first one to pull off my shoes and socks, strip my top, bra, pants and underwear and skip shrieking into the icy water because if you're going to be a freak, you might as well go all the way.

It is ticklish, and for a moment icy as it swallows my feet, licks my calves and laps at my knees. I sink into this wet-joy, plant my knees in the sand, as the water rushes towards me and sweetmurmurs around my body. I sigh and let myself have a free wee as the air twitches with morning light and the ocean lets me be me, unedited.

Fiona follows, brandishing the scars beneath her implants, which are as pert and perfect as the day they were inserted.

Emilie yelps her high-pitched scream as she skips in.

Yasmin dances, high-stepping and whooping.

Kiri calls us crazy-as-batshit, but she wades into the water in her shorts.

Cate spills expletives as she makes her way in and it's 'a

340

fucking tit-freeze and cunt-clench' and then it is glorious and what a great idea.

We call her, 'Come on, Liz,' 'You're missing out,' 'It's gorgeous.' But she's not budging. We try to send splashes all the way up the sand but she's far away enough and safe from our raucous antics.

'I've exhausted my new experiences quotient for the year,' she says.

'Keep it,' Cate says.

'No, I cannot.'

'Be gracious and accept it,' Kiri says.

Emilie holds the ukulele uncertainly. 'But it is your instrument.'

'And I'm passing it on,' Cate says, holding up her hands. 'I'll get another one. I want you to have these strings.'

Emilie takes it gingerly and holds it to her chest. 'I will learn to play it and I will never forget that you gave it to me.'

'Use it to make people sing, is all,' Cate says.

'I will have a spare bedroom in Sydney from September when my daughter moves out if you need a place to stay for a while,' I offer.

'I already got a spare bed,' Yasmin says. 'Emilie, you will

come visit.'

'Two spare rooms in my place,' Cate says.

Emilie giggles as we jostle over her.

Hers is the only heavier backpack on the way out than on the way in, given all the fancy gear Liz offloads to her, including the inflatable pillow, down sleeping bag and a handheld GPS. I guess Liz didn't trust Spirit to get us here and back in one piece.

Kiri insists on checking us all for leeches. Fiona helps her douse the ashes of the fire with seawater in a billycan to make sure it's dead. Fiona strings the fairy lights around Emilie's bag. I strap Cate's backpack to my front like a pouched baby and she gives me a small appreciative salute. Yasmin offers us all her bright red lipstick and we all smear our lips like we're courtesans and divas. Yasmin's right, it does change your brainwaves.

All that is left is for Fiona to kiss the earth.

One by one, we close in around Cate, on either side, in front and behind, penguin-style. And we begin the long, slow, slippery walk up and out; a singing, heaving, cursing army of soul sisters and guardians moving as one.

The night before I left, I couldn't sleep.

I'd switched on the bedside light. Frank was snoring softly next to me. I'd turned on my side and studied his stubble. The shape of his nose. His shaved head. The hair on his arms. His tanned limbs from years of cycling and mismanagement of sunblock, evidence of the futility of nagging as an agent of change. His strong hands with the silver wedding band on his ring finger. A pre-emptive nostalgia rose in me, for each precious detail of him, as if they were about to be taken away.

Would I be able to describe him if he disappeared the way people are called upon to do when their loved ones go missing? What words would I fit to the pulsing compound of his smell, humour, quirky OCD-ness, the way he goes 'Ooohyeahbaby' when he tastes something good?

He must have sensed my scrutiny. He'd opened his eyes and squinted at me.

'Hey, you okay?'

'Yes, why do you ask?'

'You're looking at me funny.'

'This is just my ordinary face.'

He'd reached his hand out to touch my cheek before rolling over on his side, away from the light.

'Funny' and 'ordinary' are what Frank and I have.

Ours is a hardly-anything story of two people who joined forces to tumble precious human cargo into the world and shepherd them safely across the sand. Now we've come to the part where we release them into the wild. We're about to lose everything we worked so hard to create together.

I've been so muddled by my own unravelling, I haven't been able to see what is right in front of me.

'I'm fine,' he'd said. But I'd caught his face when Aaron declined his offer to drive him to Canberra for his soccer match with, 'Nah, I'd rather you didn't.'

'I get it. He's too old and cool to have his dad in the crowd,' Frank had said, disciplining his disappointment. 'He doesn't need me anymore.'

Frank had gotten his certification as a soccer coach to manage Aaron's team. Fifteen years of patience and instruction on how to pass and shoot a ball, perfect a header and imitate the Ronaldo chop, belittled to a dismissive 'nah,' not even a grammatically intact, courteous, 'no thanks.'

'I just miss watching him play.'

He is also grieving.

The rising seas have swallowed the kingdom we built together. Jamie and Aaron are not ours to take care of any longer. But there's no stronger bond than what two people lose at the same time.

Frank is the only earth I know. Our icecaps are melting and our ozone thinning, and godknows we are headed for vicissitudes we have no training to handle, not so far. We belong to the uncertain future which calls to us like the hunger to mate, to abide through the darkness.

It is said that this burnt island we chose as our adopted home is veined with invisible songlines from The Dreaming. Perhaps then there are ley lines that crisscross marriages, settle in the warp and weft between parent and child, even though they're not for seeing. If all kinship is infused with auric swirls, the kind of eddies Van Gogh painted, unseen, rhythmic patterns that hold us in place, nothing is ever truly vanished.

Maybe we get to choose someone, once when we're chasing marriage and motherhood, and a second time when neither marriage nor motherhood really matters much anymore. After a night in a cave at the edge of somewhere, with enough heartache passed around to make the heavens weep, the air is clearer. I know what I see in Frank – someone who can read me even when I am illiterate to myself.

So where but into his arms will I spill myself, bottlenecked with stories? Like how Yasmin can make an orange shimmy and Cate can tap into secret chords. I'm saving up Kiri's amputation comment; dark humour is his thing. I'll tell him about how Fiona found her way back to her childhood cove, mostly by instinct; and my book – can you believe – broke Liz's marriage, though it's not the sort of thing to flaunt, is it? I'll describe Emilie, that heroine, sailing without a fully developed prefrontal cortex but on track, *just like our Jamie*. 'You did what by yourself?' He'll smile because I made that fire with only a little help from Kiri. 'See, you're anything but Hopeless in The Wild,' he'll say, pulling me towards him. And when I'm emptied of all the telling, I'll challenge him to a pissing competition now that I know how to use that bloomin' funnel.

'You should write a book about it,' he'll suggest.

'Maybe I will.'

Cate stops and leans heavily on her pole. She pauses a moment into the mammalian music of her breathing before she points upwards with one of her trekking poles. 'See how the uppermost branches don't touch? Trees make space for each other; they don't crowd each other out.'

Above us, the clear blue of the sky forms an intricate web between the branches.

'It's called Crown Shyness.'

We all crane our necks to take it in, this majestic, courteous proximity.

'Oh wow,' Emilie squints at the light. 'Such a thing is real? They don't touch?'

'That's actually…pretty cool,' Liz says. 'I love a good boundary.'

'Maybe you'll change your mind about The Great Outdoors?' Kiri prods.

'You'd have to sedate me heavily to get me out here again,' Liz says. I turn to look in her direction to see if perhaps she is joking, but she isn't. She ventured out here for Fiona. And if that's not true love, if that isn't the essence of mothering, you tell me what is.

We pass our bottles freely from one to the other, down to our last sips of water. Thirst nags at me, but I can hold out. We are making our way back in increments to where we started. Warmth buzzes in my chest, nothing like a hot flush. It spills and streaks out of me to each one of these women like silken threads.

When Cate starts moving again, the others move on too. But not me. I linger in this spot to keep this wildness a little longer. I feel the sky in my skull, the fire in my feet and the wide beauty pulling from every side.

Up ahead, Fiona links arms with Liz, their backpacks bumping. Kiri whistles to lure a lyrebird. Yasmin sashays. Emilie's hand rests in the small of Cate's back, nudging her onwards. Cate plants one trembling foot in front of the other, not lagging or dragging or falling behind. She is saving nothing for a rainy day.

She is leading us home.

The Menu

Mango, cashew and ginger energy balls

Olives stuffed with preserved lemon peel

Coconut bark with pistachios,
raspberries and rose water

Corn on the fire with toasted Aleppo pepper,
sesame and coriander seeds

Persian jewelled farro with pistachios
and cranberries

Persian love cake

Turkish coffee

Salt and vinegar Kettle fried chips

Salted liquorice bread

Freshly made damper with fresh walnuts,
thinly sliced apple and radishes

Sour fig preserve

Cate and Fiona's honey

Water

Smuggled-in Japanese whiskey

Smuggled-in Tequila

Acknowledgments

Droemer Knaur, my German publisher commissioned the third in the *Secret Mothers' Business* trilogy despite how 'times and the market have changed, women's fiction has changed and even Jo has changed,' as Carolin Graehl, my commissioning editor put it. I am grateful for their ongoing belief in me and in a book for and about women who are mostly invisible from mainstream culture.

It's been the trickiest challenge of my writing career – to bring older women to life on the page who may be falling to pieces in places but who are wicked with wisdom, gracious with grief and storied with sorrow. You sure as hell wouldn't want to mess with them. I've had wonderful role models including:

- Barbara, Hilary, Drusilla, Tanya, Sandra, Louanne and Debbie who generously shared deep confidences with me over two virtual nights to help me shape the conversations women like us long to have;
- the women who volunteered to be part of the Secret Mothers' Business 3 Facebook group who didn't baulk at my nosy questions and who offered their stories and insights;

- the writers I've been blessed to mentor in my retreats and online courses including those in the Author Awakening Adventure and Write Your First Draft Masterclasses;
- my many beloved warm-hearted sisters and friends (Carolyn, Laura, Tracey, Ilze, Michelle, Faith, Lesley, Katrina, Gabriela, Bec, Deb, Sharon, Kaaren, Mmatshilo, Lorraine, Tanya, Yvonne, Natasha, Karen, Lana, Ruth, Lisa, Thanissara, Sherill, Rain and all the others I have inadvertently not mentioned due to a menopausal memory).

I was adamant about sleeping in the wild so I could speak truth from my bones in this story. My friend Kerry (a nurse and indigenous health expert) offered to meet me in Central Australia where we made a fire and slept in swags under the stars. I'm grateful the dingos that visited us in the night only took the milk. She also read a first draft of the book and helped guide the narrative in crucial places.

Leigh, Anna, Vicki, Christina, Marg, Tracey and Yaeli joined me for two nights in a cave in the Blue Mountains. It rained, we built fires, drank chai and Christina played guitar and sang. I carried these hours with me into the writing.

My friend Sharon has generously allowed me to include the inspiring story of how her mothering intuition saved her daughter's life.

I'm grateful to Dr Gary Aaron for checking some of my

facts about menopause.

My editor Kirsten Krauth brought her expertise to the narrative and guided me through two edits with her sharp insights and sensibilities.

Norie Libradilla did a fastidious job on the proof-read and cleared up my annoying grammatical tics.

Thanks to Ida Jansson from Amygdala Design for the beautiful layout.

Marg Rolla designed the original artwork for the cover of the trilogy, and Nailia Minnebaeva brought her artistry to the design.

The astonishingly talented Nada Backovic designed a cover that took my breath away.

I am a lucky soul to be surrounded by such brilliance and mastery, all of which weave themselves fluidly and silently into the final text you hold in your hands.

I'm hugely grateful to Greg Messina, my wonderful, patient mensch of an agent, for his support through the writing of this book.

Karen McDermott of Serenity Press has been a steadfast champion of my work for years, and I wanted her to publish the Australian version of this book. We came together to launch Lusaris, the literary imprint of Serenity with *Unbecoming* as its first title. I am so proud to be part of this venture.

Zed, how can I ever thank you for the decades of unconditional love, co-parenting and friendship? You've been believing in me since 2006, long before a single copy of *Secret*

Mothers' Business had been sold (never mind over half a million copies). Thank you for inspiring Frank though of course, you are much funnier.

Jess and Aidan, I'm relieved Jamie and Aaron are pure fiction. Whew.

To my mother Dorrine, what a human gem you are.

To all the women in their midlives who are caring for grandchildren, children, partners, ageing parents, pets, wildlife, gardens, forests and oceans whilst raging against the darkness, I hope I have done justice to your magnificence. You are my heroes.

About Joanne

Joanne Fedler is the internationally bestselling author of 12 books, which have been translated into many different languages and have sold over 750 000 copies worldwide. She is a Fulbright scholar, has a Master's degree in Law from Yale, set up and ran an advocacy centre to end violence against women in South Africa and has spent her life fighting for women's rights. She was selected as one of the women in *200 Women Who Will Change the Way You See The World* (Chronicle Books, 2017). Her book *Things Without A Name* has recently been optioned for the screen.

As a writing mentor, she offers writing retreats for women all over the world as well as online writing courses. Her courses include the 7 day free online writing challenge, 7 Tricks to Writing Your Story, The Author Awakening Adventure and Write Your First Draft Masterclass.

You can find out more or enrol here **www.joannefedler.com/courses**

CPSIA information can be obtained
at www.ICGtesting.com
Printed in the USA
BVHW070410160222
629080BV00004B/771